A Wall
of Light

ALSO BY EDEET RAVEL

Look for Me
Ten Thousand Lovers

A Wall of Light

A NOVEL

EDEET RAVEL

HARPER PERENNIAL

NEW YORK • LONDON • TORONTO • SYDNEY

HARPER ● PERENNIAL

First published in Canada in 2005 by Random House.

P.S. ™ is a trademark of HarperCollins Publishers.

HarperCollins books may be purchased for educational, business, or
sales promotional use. For information please write: Special Markets
Department, HarperCollins Publishers, 10 East 53rd Street, New York,
NY 10022.

FIRST U.S. EDITION

Designed by Laura Kaeppel

Library of Congress Cataloging-in-Publication Data
Ravel, Edeet.
    A wall of light : a novel / Edeet Ravel.—1st Harper Perennial ed.
       p.   cm.
    ISBN-10: 0-06-076147-4
    ISBN-13: 978-0-06-076147-9
    1. Mothers and daughters—Fiction. 2. Women—Israel—Fiction.
3. Grandmothers—Fiction. 4. Israel—Fiction. I. Title.
PR9199.4.R39W35 2005
813'.6—dc22   2004063417

06 07 08 09 10 ❖/QWF 10 9 8 7 6 5 4 3 2 1

for Fred Harrison
❧ *life artist*

and to Hope, Ken, José,
Rebecca, Alyssa, Adam, Garbriel,
and the entire California clan, with love

Acknowledgments

I am grateful for the assistance of the Canada Council for the Arts, which last year invested $20.3 million in writing and publishing throughout Canada. For their help and support in the writing and publication of the Tel Aviv trilogy, of which this is the final volume, I am deeply indebted to Meir Amor, Yudit Avi-dor, Yardena Avi-dor, Miki Bitton, Alison Brackenbury, Alison Callahan, Nada and Jihad Charif, Marwan Charif, Anne Collins, Pam Comeau, Richard Cooper, Jay Eidemiller, Rezeq Faraj, Rachel Goodman, Mary Harsany, Christopher Hazou, Eric Hamovitch, Michael Heyward, Malcolm Imrie, Matan Kaminer, Ruttie Kanner, Yitzhak Laor, Shimon Levy, Kfir Madjar, Mark Marshall, Michael MacKenzie, Rachella Mizrahi, Moshe, Adrienne Phillips, Ken Sparling, Gila Svirsky, Yafa Wax, Margaret Wolfson, Miriam Zehavi, the Headline crew, the staff of the Metropolitan Hotel in Tel Aviv, and the many fellow activists who have given me the strength to maintain hope in the midst of tragedy. A very special thanks to Joan Deitch for her brilliant editorial contributions, and to Claire Williams for her beautiful Web site design. Filling my life with fun and love, my daughter Larissa continues to inspire and enchant me.

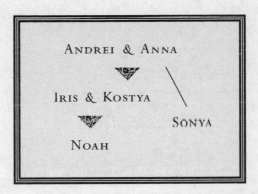

ANDREI & ANNA

IRIS & KOSTYA

SONYA

NOAH

All losses are restored,
and sorrows end.

—*Sonnet 30, Shakespeare*

A Wall
of Light

⁂ SONYA

I am Sonya Vronsky, professor of mathematics at Tel Aviv University, and this is the story of a day in late August. On this remarkable day I kissed a student, pursued a lover, found my father, and left my brother.

The morning began with a series of sneezes. The sneezes interrupted a dream I was having about a glass-walled elevator that had left its shaft and was shooting about wildly through immense futuristic building complexes. Like something out of Asimov, I thought. I was just starting to enjoy both the sensation and the spectacle when the sneezes woke me.

I like to sleep with the shutters open; I like to feel the sun on my body as soon as I wake. A warm, luminous world awaits me—or so I imagine. Ordinarily, I would have switched off the air-conditioning, opened the window and looked out at our garden; I would have turned my face toward the sky and breathed in the sweet, tyrannous August air. But today my sneezing distracted me. My late-summer allergies were kicking in.

I sat up in my queen-sized bed and reached for the box of rainbow-colored tissues on the night table. I set the box between my knees, which were protruding like two islands from under the sheets. A boxy ship, precariously balanced.

My mother, who slept next to me when I was little, always accompanied her good-night kiss with a quote—affectionate if she was sober ("Come, live with me, and be my love," for example), gloomier if she was inebriated ("Out, out, brief candle!"). Then she'd turn off the light and I'd snuggle up against her lace nightgown, breathe in her cinnamon perfume. My mother was a night bird; when she woke she was not in a quoting mood. But I am the opposite, more inclined toward poetry in the morning than at bedtime, and I suppose my choices are also somewhat less formal than hers. "You are old, Father William . . . ," I began, but didn't finish; a sneeze interrupted me.

Kostya, my darling brother, appeared in the doorway, dark and shadowy because the light was behind him. With his trimmed gray beard and his tall, still body he looked like a character in a French film from the 1960s, a film about alienation and ennui, with the male lead dark and brooding. In fact, he was there to offer me an antihistamine. My brother has very low tolerance for disruption, and the sneezes were annoying him.

But I'm being unfair: he was also trying to help. My poor brother lives with the guilt of my two catastrophes, neither of which he had anything to do with. Human error lay behind the first disaster: twenty years ago, when I was twelve, I was taken to the hospital with a kidney infection, and some nurse or doctor or hospital pharmacist gave me the wrong dose of the wrong drug. I moved into another dimension, spooky at first, frightening at first, then surreal, and finally exotic or ridiculous, depending on the day. I lost my hearing.

And human evil, which no one can entirely avoid, accounts for the artillery unleashed at me in an empty university classroom by stoned twin teenagers with shaven heads and dragon tattoos.

But guilt has a way of insinuating itself into the path of any series of events leading to a given outcome. Kostya believes, for example, that had he fixed our broken toilet, I would not have come down with a kidney infection in the first place. The toilet howled and groaned like a ghoul in chains and I was afraid to use it; my solution was to drink less in order to limit my visits to the bathroom. I didn't tell anyone about my aversion; had Kostya known, he would have attended to the problem. And then, had I not been deaf I might have heard the twins before seeing them (this is really stretching it) and escaped in time. These are tenuous links but well entrenched in our family mythology.

"Do you want an allergy pill?" my brother asked, speaking as he signed. "It's non-soporific." We'd developed so many signing shortcuts and private gestures over the years that by now we almost had our own language.

"Oh . . . kay!" I managed to say between sneezes. He vanished and returned with a small yellow pill, his heartbreaking offering of the morning, nestled in the palm of his large, intelligent hand. In his other hand he held a small bottle of Eden spring water.

I obediently swallowed the pill. "You're lucky I'm so nice to you," I said.

My brother smiled. It would be no exaggeration to say that he suffers from my misfortunes more than I ever did. He should take comfort in the fact that I have a good life, that I have fun—and maybe he does, to some degree. Maybe not. It's hard to know for sure.

"Tell me when you're ready for breakfast," he said.

I blew him a kiss and he left the room. My briefcase was next to the night table, and I emptied its contents in front of me. Exams, articles, receipts, notes and miscellaneous slips of paper floated out angelically and settled on the bed. I organized them all efficiently and quickly. Then I waddled to the bathroom like a goose headed for its mud pond, and had a shower. There is nothing quite as wonderful and endlessly surprising as a soft, heavy stream of hot water falling on one's shoulders and down one's body. I was filled with gratitude, as I always am during the first few moments of a shower, that something so lovely exists on this planet, and I was only sorry that it was not available to everyone. A few kilometers away, there was not even enough drinking water.

But, inexcusably, my sense of guilt soon faded, and as I ran the soapy sea sponge along my legs I succumbed completely to the pleasures of my morning shower.

NOAH'S DIARY, JUNE 20, 1980.

*In the news: the Yarden boy is still missing, day 11,
no leads, police asking people to check sheds. We
don't have a shed but I checked under the porch.*

This is me, Noah Vronsky. Only kids in yeshivas get called Noah—
just my luck. I got named after my grandfather, my mother promised
him when he was dying. But everyone at school calls me Noonie, or
Numi-Numi when they're joking around. I'm only Noah at home so
it's not too bad.

My family consists of five people: me, my gran (actress and wait
ress, tall with long blond hair, smells of cinnamon), Sonya (Gran's
daughter, which makes her my aunt but she's three years younger
than me if you can believe it!—chubby with curly black hair in cute
ringlets), my dad (bone doctor), and my mom (lawyer whose clients
never pay her, short with straight black pixie cut).

I also have a best friend, Oren, and I'm a pretty good soccer
player and artist. I like drawing things divided down the middle.
One side alien, one side human. One side Mom, one side Dad. One
side Mani our soccer coach in his uniform, one side Mani naked with
his funny thing hanging down (Oren and I caught a glimpse of it in

the locker room). For high school Dad wants me to go to a school with an art program, but I'd rather go where Oren goes.

Today was my birthday, I'm ten. Mom gave me a ten-speed bike, Oren gave me a cool poster of American basketball players, Sonya gave me logic problems she made up (the kind I like: "The man in the red sweater is sitting next to the wife of the cook's brother . . ."), Gran gave me songs of innocence and experience, and Dad gave me this diary.

He says he gave it to me because I have "interesting thoughts." This worries me. How much does he know???

❧ LETTER TO ANDREI, JANUARY 2, 1957

Dearest darling, I am so relieved that Heinrich managed to get all my letters to you during his last visit! What luck! Of course, by the time you get the letters they are out of date, and your reply with all its good advice is sometimes no longer relevant and it's frustrating as hell but no matter. Please, darling, promise promise to burn my letters at once, don't take any risks. It's a miracle as it is that you haven't been suspected of helping me escape. I can't even bear to think about the chance you took for me, and for our Kostya. And what could have happened . . . I promise to keep copies of all my letters for the day when we will be together again.

I am so happy, dearest, to hear that you are well. Needless to say, I worry about your health all the time. You must take care of yourself, my love. You write that the days are dark and empty without me, but we must think about the future, when you too find a way to leave our beautiful and terrible country. But it is no longer "our" country—only yours now. I must accustom myself to being a real Israeli, with a little identification booklet to prove it. How is that troublesome toe of yours, did the powder help? How is sweet Olga? I miss her as much as if she were mine. Don't work too hard, darling.

Kostya is fine, getting quite tall, and arguing with all his teachers—but most of them don't mind. Only one has taken a dislike to him, a young man whose skin is too delicate for his razor but who insists on being closely shaven and so is always covered with cuts. He came over to complain about Kostya, and sat here in our tiny one-room apartment, his knuckles white, his voice trembling, his leg so jittery it gave me vertigo. He was in the Sinai campaign last year.

He complained at length about Kostya talking back in class. I told him it's a free country (finally I can say that!!—the words roll off my tongue like pearls) with free speech, and my son can say whatever he wants in class, he's not harming anyone. But this poor man thinks his authority is being undermined. During the entire visit I was of two minds whether to offer him the last piece of cheesecake I brought home from the restaurant. So precious! I was really battling with myself. In the end for Kostya's sake I took it out of the icebox and gave it to him. He gobbled it up like a starved man and was much appeased, but he is still sending Kostya home with notes and punishments—for example, copying out long passages from the works of the Hebrew poet Bialik "with vocalization."

Our clever Kostya is fluent now in Hebrew, after only a year! I wish I could say the same for myself, but I am struggling with this language like Jacob with his angel. But now I come to my big news! A group of us are trying to start a theater. Our first production is going to be *As You Like It*—in Hebrew, of course. Now the only problem is to find a hall, a budget, actors and a translation—other than that we are all set! By "we" I mean really only four of us. First, the director, Feingold, who is very brilliant and brimming with enthusiasm and ideas which are constantly coming up against hopeless obstacles; it's a pitiful thing to see his face fall as each idea gets dashed against the rocky cliffs of reality. Please don't be jealous, dearest, because you know my heart belongs only to you and Feingold is overweight, has asthma, he wears the same shirt many days in a row and his fingernails are none too clean. He studied with all the greats before the war, however, and he really is a genius. It's a little sad to see him in these surroundings.

Then there's Tanya, who is seventeen—she says! I think she's younger and I believe she is a runaway. Tanya is full of life and maybe even possesses a hint of a trace of acting skill. The third in our little group is Carmela, who is forty or so and a second-generation Israeli. She's going to be our fund-raiser, trying to get grants and applying to all sorts of institutions here and abroad—and though she's shrill and bossy, we already depend on her entirely. The rest of us are just too impractical and we don't know the ins and outs the way that she does. The following exchange will give you an idea of how most of our meetings unfold:

> FEINGOLD: This is a play about disguise and identity and the instability of roles—the most important thing is costumes. I want the actors getting in and out of them onstage throughout.
>
> CARMELA: We won't have a budget for costumes.
>
> TANYA: I could have sex with the person in charge of grants if it helps.

Oh dearest, I miss you so much. If I didn't believe I'd be seeing you again, my life would lose all meaning.

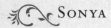 SONYA

I didn't stay in the shower for long because I knew my brother was waiting for me. Wrapped in a massive oyster white towel, I approached the closet. I'm very fond of beautiful clothes and I've collected quite a few skirts and tops over the years. That's what I like to wear: short skirts and matching tops—outfit of choice, I once read in a silly magazine, for shy but ambitious women. I deliberated for a minute or two and finally chose a silky flowered skirt and a white V-neck top with a strip of lace lining the V.

I dressed, inserted all my papers carefully into my briefcase, and made my way to the kitchen, where Kostya, the family chef, was preparing my breakfast.

Our household had now shrunk to two, but even in the old days, when there were five of us—Kostya and his wife Iris, their son Noah, my mother, and me—Kostya did the cooking. Iris was too busy with her law practice, and my mother was not the sort of person to take an interest in the culinary arts, to say the least; she lived mostly on pistachio nuts and orange juice mixed with vodka. My brother, on the other hand, was a fabulous cook right from the start. He consulted cookbooks with great dedication and used us as guinea pigs for his experimental creations.

As soon as I entered the kitchen Kostya began preparing two poached eggs with Hollandaise sauce for me. An elaborate salad and a plate of apple turnovers had already been set on the table, next to my empty plate. I made my own toast, feeling I should participate a little, even if only symbolically. When the eggs were ready, Kostya went to the bathroom to tidy up after me: spread and shake out the shower curtain, hang the towel properly, realign the bath mat. He used to make my bed, too, but I finally put my foot down and told him I'd like to decide for myself when my bed should be made. That was usually never, and I knew the disordered bedding was hard on Kostya, but he was stoic about it.

While he was tidying up I glanced at the newspaper. The usual mess; there was hardly any point reading the details. A Gaza air strike killing six, Qassam rockets killing no one, a soldier stabbed, settlements expanding, the Knesset in disarray, a pollution crisis looming. If you went only by the news, you'd think you were stuck in the same day forever. As an experiment, the newspapers should reprint an edition from four years ago and see whether anyone noticed. Or maybe even twenty years ago.

Kostya returned and we chatted about nothing in particular—the weather (unchanging), taking the car in for a tune-up (urgent), whether to rent a movie (yes)—and then he ran off to the hospital. He would not have had to put up with my sneezing for very long.

I stepped onto the back patio with my buttered toast and sat down on the first of three steps that led to the garden. I grew up in a comically malfunctioning house in north Tel Aviv, on Yahud Street; its only redeeming feature was a large and glorious garden. My brother methodically uprooted the garden on the day Iris was murdered but resurrected it when we moved to our new house. The new house was a big step up from the Charlie Chaplin bungalow on Yahud; this was thanks to an anonymous benefactor who read about the medical error that changed my life. The story made the front pages for a day or two, with my small, baffled face peering out at scandalized citizens from under a huge mass of black ringlets. Some rich person read about me and was horrified: a poor fatherless child (all my virtues were generously listed) who had gone deaf because of inexcusable negligence. Possibly his incentive was Zionist ardor, a desire to demonstrate that the country was not all bad and that wrongs could be balanced by good deeds; or maybe he simply felt sorry for me.

In any case, he sent a substantial sum of money our way, via a lawyer who was not at liberty to reveal his identity. My brother invested the benefactor's money successfully, doubled it, then reinvested his earnings and this time did even better. Luck has a life of its own. When my mother left for a nursing home and Iris died and Noah moved to Berlin, my brother and I decided to use the accumulated capital to buy a new home. For my brother the idea of family is sacred, like shrines or holy days for religious people, and I was the last of the Mohicans, now that everyone else was gone. So he bought this house for the two of us and we turned it into a mini Shangri-la. We were like children playing at make-believe, except that we had the means to make our fantasy come true. Our house was not particularly large; houses in this country are not usually extravagant in terms of size. Luxury takes other forms here: an oval swimming pool, original paintings on the walls, bathrooms with sunken baths and two sinks, a fireplace for the winter months, pine furniture, stained-glass windows and matching lamps, Persian tile murals. We went too far, in the end, and though I loved our cozy hideaway, I was sometimes embarrassed by it and more than a little ashamed that we had spent the money on ourselves and not on more needy people or causes. Iris would have disapproved, and even my mother would have preferred to see us help her destitute artist friends, but I believe Kostya wanted to compensate me somehow for my disasters, and like the storybook prince who builds a castle for the king's daughter, he was compelled by a sense of mission.

I was only slightly offended by Kostya's assumption that I would never marry and therefore didn't need a place of my own. His assumption was based, I must admit, on my own insistence that I had no intention of marrying, ever. I had told him many times over the years that I planned to stay single, but I may have expected a protest. "Nonsense, Sonya," he could have said. "You're beautiful, charming, and altogether irresistible to the opposite sex, and eventually you'll fall in love and decide to marry." But I'd never had a boyfriend of any kind and my brother doesn't like to intrude. I can't blame him for thinking that I meant what I said. Moreover, he assured me that I had only to say the word and he would move out; the house was in my name, and he continually reminded me that as far as he was concerned, he was a guest. Poor Kostya!

Noah's diary, September 15, 1980.

*In the news: a Skyhawk crashed right next to a
school! With 950 kids! 100 meters away! We are
freaked out!!!!*

Today I'll describe our crazy house and everyone in it. We live in
this pathetic tiny house in Hadar Yosef which is in the north part of
Tel Aviv, four kilometers east of the sea, on Yahud Street. The house
is totally falling apart and is only being held together by prayer and
electrical tape (that's what Gran says). It belongs to this Israeli couple
from the university who moved to Canada. They didn't sell the house
in case they ever get in the mood to come back, but so far they like
Toronto.

We don't have a living room. When you come in through the
front door there's a kind of corridor that's parallel to the front of the
house. It used to be a porch and it's dark and smells weird (Dad says
it's mold). This corridor leads to three rooms. In the middle, facing
the front door, there's a big open kitchen. Dad spends his life there.
Either he's cooking or cleaning up or reading or playing his horrid
screeching violin. On both sides of the kitchen, like a pair of ears,
are two bedrooms. Gran and Sonya (who's seven) have the bedroom

on the left, which is also where we have the TV because Dad never watches and Mom isn't home a lot. Mom and Dad have the smaller bedroom on the right. You get to the bedrooms from the corridor. We're always getting in each other's way and everyone needs the bathroom at the same time. Gran keeps joking that we're a very *close* family ha ha. The toilet is the scariest part of the house, all night it howls like some demented animal.

I'm the only lucky person in the house, as I get to live in the screened porch at the back. It's like sleeping outdoors—you can see the moon, the stars, everything. I have a sleeping bag made of down on my bed and I'm basically camping full-time. Oren is really jealous. Everyone in my class is jealous, in fact. Only in winter if it gets really cold I have to move to Oren's. But that's fun too. So all in all I'm the best off in this crazy house. From my bed I have a good view of my basketball posters.

Now for the people in my family, who are mostly quite strange. First, Sonya. Dad is her half brother, but she calls him Dad because I do, so people think she's my sister. Even I forget sometimes that she's my aunt, not my sister. Sonya's kind of an old-fashioned name, but Gran wanted that name. On Sonya's birth certificate they put Tziyona because Gran doesn't read Hebrew that well and couldn't tell the difference. But no one calls her Tziyona. Her kindergarten teacher, Mira, tried to call her Tziyona, but Sonya can be very stubborn, and whenever Mira said "Tziyona," Sonya pretended she didn't know who was being addressed. So Mira gave up and went back to "Sonya."

The big problem with Sonya is that she follows me everywhere. I can't get rid of her, she's stuck to me like glue. Super-glue. I have to take her with me to parties, soccer practice, biking, everything. When Oren and I want to be alone it's almost impossible to get rid of her. She's like a cat. You send her home, she shows up again. No matter where we hide she finds us. She still sucks her thumb and she's chubby and clumsy so everyone thinks she's a little retarded, but people like her. Actually she's sort of a genius but we don't tell anyone, as Dad doesn't want her to be a freak. Good luck, Dad!

As for Dad, he's the quiet type. He likes things to be at the same time every day. He pins our socks together so they don't get lost in the laundry. And that's all I have to say about him. I already mentioned the violin. Sonya plays too, by the way. What have I done, God?

Okay—now to Mom. She works nonstop, she's a lawyer. She's on the left which basically means that everything about the country makes her mad, and I mean everything. I don't tell people she's on the left because most people are on the right and they don't like people on the left. Even people who say they're on the left aren't really on the left a lot of the time so it's best not to take a chance. One time I used the word *occupation* in class and I almost got lynched—not one person was on my side. Even Oren was quiet, he only got involved when Shimi told me I should be hanged in the courtyard. And I heard Aida's mom, who's supposed to be totally on the left, tell Ariella's father that she no longer knows what to think.

Living with Mom means putting up with her moods. Last month she was in a bad mood because she lost a case. Her client got six months for demonstrating against closing the Abu Dis college, that's a college no one's heard of but it's near Jerusalem. Also he got a huge fine (Mom's raising the money). All he did was demonstrate but you have to apply for permission to demonstrate and they didn't. The judge said he was giving him six months because as an Israeli Arab he was supposed to be loyal. Mom was ready to hit the ceiling. But today she's in a good mood because she got two Arabs off a murder charge. She convinced the judge that they confessed "under duress." But of course Mom is never satisfied. She said the judge didn't care that much about the case because it was only a prostitute who was murdered. Sometimes I think Mom is just looking for things to complain about.

By the way, this house was Mom's idea because her parents came from Libya and they gave her this idea that you have to have a garden, you can't live without a garden, you might as well lie down and die if you can't have a garden and grow your own lettuce or pansies or whatever. I guess in Libya they have a different attitude to these things. Anyway we're poor so the only way we could have a house with a garden was renting this dump. We shouldn't be poor because Mom's a lawyer and Dad's a doctor. But Mom's clients never pay her and Dad's paying back all the loans they had to take out when he was in med school and Mom was studying to be a lawyer, plus he only works part-time so he can *be with his family* and make up for Mom being away a lot of the time.

That leaves Gran. Gran is a waitress, though I think lately she's been doing less waiting on tables and more just hanging out at the café with all her friends, who are always coming over for supper and reading us their horrible poems about dead horses, right when we're trying to eat. She's also an actress but she can't get good roles anymore because she can't act too well in Hebrew. In Moscow she was Juliet, but here all she can get are small parts. She was the housekeeper in *Uncle Vanya* (by A. Chekhov), the musician in *Twelfth Night* (by R. Shakespeare), and a neighbor and nurse in *An Electrician Named Desire* (by Tennessee Williams). She goes through a lot of vodka. Sometimes when she sends me to buy her a bottle of vodka at the supermarket the cashier says, "How's your gran?" I wish people would mind their own business.

That's it for my family. The only other important people in my life are Oren and my teacher Ruthie. She wears garters.

Letter to Andrei, February 13, 1957

Dearest, I have not heard from you in over a month and of course all my worries come to the fore and I imagine the worst. But maybe something has happened to our "postal service"—maybe Heinrich has been delayed in Vienna, or in Moscow. I wish he would write and let me know when he plans to see you, but it's very kind of him to act as our courier, and I don't want to impose on him further. Do you remember our "electrical service" when the fuses blew! Such memories fill my nights.

Kostya is thriving. He broke his wrist but it's healing well. He's involved in some very complicated war among the neighborhood boys (and two girls). I couldn't follow it if I tried. The intrigues, mixed loyalties, betrayals, and dramas could compete with anything that goes on you-know-where. Well, during one of their ambushes he fell and broke his wrist. He went to three libraries looking for an anatomy book so he could figure out exactly what happened to his bone, but he couldn't find anything that satisfied him, and the new university here isn't really on its feet yet and doesn't have a science library.

Now here is what happened, and it was quite wonderful. We have very good mail delivery here—everyone relies on it because it's so difficult to get a telephone. You can send plain white postcards in the

mail and they arrive quite quickly. Well, Carmela sent a postcard
to someone who knows someone else who works at the Hebrew
University in Jerusalem who has a daughter who comes to Tel Aviv
who is friends with someone else who works with Carmela . . . in
short, five different people coordinated the bringing of an anatomy
book from Jerusalem to Tel Aviv for Kostya! Everyone wanted our
Kostya to have that book, and they went to so much trouble for him.
I told you Carmela was invaluable.

Well, it was not a waste, because Kostya was glued to that book
all week (he was only allowed to keep it for a week), even neglect-
ing his playtime with his neighborhood friends. I thought this might
be a sign that he has a future in medicine. However, when I asked
him what he wanted to be, he said he wants to wait tables in a restaurant like me so he can get free cakes! I often bring home small cakes
and pastries that I've stolen from the restaurant. Of course, our dear
Kostya doesn't know that they are not exactly gifts . . . but don't
worry, dearest. Nothing at all would happen to me if I were caught—
they don't take such things very seriously here.

We now have seven actors of varying ages and ranges and a
translation of *As You Like It*! Still no stage and no budget, though, but
Carmela is hopeful about an American organization she dug up.
Tanya is not Slavic, by the way, in spite of her name. But I'm not sure
where she's from. She never mentions her family   I think I told you
she's a runaway. Not too clear where she's living, either.

Feingold and I had a bit of a fight. Not really a fight, you know
how I dislike any sort of conflict! However, he wants me to play
Rosalind or at least Celia, and he's quite stubborn. He doesn't understand that I simply cannot memorize such a long text in a language that is still so foreign to me. I will barely be able to manage
one of the smaller roles.

He feels betrayed. He says I am our only good actress and that if
I tried, I could learn the text—he would help me. I know my limits,
though! I would ruin the play, I'd forget my lines or get them all wrong.

Every third word is new to me. I am still searching constantly for ordinary words like *regret* or *flour*. Some Hebrew words are easy to remember (*bakbuk* is "bottle" and *galgal* is "wheel"!) but many are not.

In the end he gave in but he was sulking heavily. He's going to cast Tanya as Celia and start looking around for a Rosalind.

There was a performance of Stravinsky and I had no money at all. Guess what I did, dearest? Tanya showed me a place where you can climb into the auditorium through the window. Imagine it! The usher saw what I did but I sweet-talked him and he turned a blind eye. I was so hungry for some live music! I found an empty seat without difficulty, as some people buy tickets but don't show up. The players were very professional and enthusiastic and the first violinist was excellent. I enjoyed every minute and was only sorry that it ended so soon. It's so good to leave all one's problems behind for a small stretch of time and be transported to another world. I thought of you from start to finish and imagined that it was you sitting next to me and not a tiny Polish woman with blue-framed glasses.

My battle with the cockroaches never ends! Remember how we fought the bedbugs? But in the end we were triumphant. These creatures are indestructible. Darling, I saw one nearly the size of an infant's foot the other day, on the stairs of the building. I hit it with my shoe a dozen times at least. I hit it as hard as I could, over and over, but you know, this was the Rasputin of cockroaches! It just would not die. Finally I poured boiling water on the monstrous thing. I know I have to learn to live with this nuisance if I am to stay in this inexpensive neighborhood. Maybe I should move, but our rent is so low here and this way I can afford all sorts of other treats, like Kostya's favorite cheese, which costs a small fortune. At least in this country we don't have to wait in long lines for food!

Darling, I love you. I am enclosing a little embroidered doll's dress I made for Olga. I miss her terribly. Take care of yourself. If only I could send inside this letter some of the mild weather we are having. Dress warmly, darling.

ᶜ⧼ SONYA

I finished my toast, brushed the crumbs from my skirt, and looked out at the garden. We no longer had a vegetable patch which required daily weeding, a task we all shared when we lived in the house on Yahud Street—that is, apart from Noah, who found it tedious. When Kostya decided to revive the destroyed garden of Yahud, he and I were in our reckless post-Yahud phase, and we focused on comfort and pleasure. A winding trail led from the patio to a miniature fountain of Venus and next to it a white cedar garden swing dangled from its sturdy frame, waiting for customers. Sweet, healthy-looking flowers alternated with large stones or waved hi from handmade clay tubs.

The garden was slightly overgrown at the moment, and soft blue petals touched my knees as I sat on the steps. I was waiting for one of the neighborhood cats to come by for a treat. Until last year we'd always had a dog; King Kong lived to be very old, and so had King Kong II, but our most recent dog—a fragile, shaggy thing whom we called Zulu—had died unexpectedly in the winter. I'd suggested to Kostya that we take in a cat, but my brother said he preferred pets who could be trained not to scratch furniture or jump on tables. The minute your back was turned, he said, a cat did what it wanted to do. All the same, the cats on our street knew me. I liked giving them treats, and when I sat outside they generally found their way to me. But today they were either busy or asleep.

I was suddenly filled with desire. I longed to have a lover, for example, or to find an ancient coin buried in the earth, or watch a turtle moseying along. These waves of desire came over me regularly, in varying degrees of intensity. When they were at their most persistent, I felt that nothing short of a miracle would satisfy me: a goose laying golden eggs or angels hovering amid the yellow roses, which swelled against the blue sky like expensive gifts. I touched the silky petals brushing my knees and contemplated my virginity, a subject that was never far from my thoughts—especially in recent years, as I was getting ridiculously old for a virgin.

Technically I was not a virgin, of course. I was one of the few people in this country who, without being famous or dead, had made the front pages twice, and my sexual status was known to anyone who cared to remember the story. Stories never die here because people keep them alive. No one seems to have any secret tragedies and sorrows, except maybe my brother.

But since I'd never had a lover, I considered myself as chaste as a lily in May. I'd say as chaste as the driven snow, but we don't get much snow here and I've seen snow only twice in my life. My brother was constantly urging me to travel, visit other countries, broaden my horizons. He wanted me to see Venice and Paris and Buckingham Palace. But I didn't want to go alone, and if I had to travel with Kostya I'd end up strangling him within two days. My brother is fine when his life proceeds according to a fixed routine, but when he's away from his routine his obsession with order becomes extremely trying. How a person like my mother, who was vague and easygoing, managed to give birth to my brother was always a bit of a mystery. He most likely takes after his father, a married man whom my mother left behind in Russia when Kostya was eleven. Impossible to imagine, but my mother had once wanted to be a physicist; the mar-

ried man, Kostya's father, was her teacher. She was forced to abandon her studies after only one year because she'd slept through two
exams, and she ended up on the stage instead. It was mostly for
Kostya's sake that my mother decided to tear herself away from her
lover and attempt an escape from the Soviet Union. She was a well-
known actress by then, and she managed to get away while performing in Vienna. She decided to try her luck in Israel, where there
were subsidies for immigrants and which she pictured as a land filled
with palm trees and quaint sunny villages.

I contemplated my virginity as usual, came to no conclusion as
usual, and then noticed that I was running late. If I wanted to walk
to the university I would have to leave right away.

I took a bottle of ice water out of the fridge, strapped my briefcase to my back, put on a Lydia Bennett hat decorated with blue
ribbon and silk flowers, and set out. I may be the only person in this
country who willingly walks anywhere in the August heat. But I like
the heat because of its solid physical presence. It surrounds you and
presses against you; this makes me feel safe, as if I were in a womb.
And I like the blinding white light that turns the world into a vast
child's room, filled with sunlit toys: very bright light, like intense
cold, shrinks objects. Another reason I don't mind walking is that I
don't sweat much, and if I do it's only between my breasts, where
drops of sweat form and begin to trickle down slowly to my stomach. When that happens, I pour water inside my shirt; it cools me off
and dries instantly.

It generally took me between forty-five minutes and an hour to
reach Gate Seven: I walked west on Keren Kayemet Street and then
south on Ha'im Lebanon Street. Sometimes people who knew me
stopped their cars and offered me a lift, and I always accepted, to
be friendly, but I was perfectly happy walking. Keren Kayemet was
never the same, Ha'im Lebanon was never the same. The scene
changed, and of course the atmosphere varied wildly from day to
day, because it's always a matter of chance configurations, of who

shows up and what sort of mood they're in. Like a kaleidoscope. That's my field, by the way. Probability.

As I walked I tried to guess what sort of day it was going to be. Some days were peaceful and quiet, others were hectic and noisy. On the street, for example, if the cars were zooming happily along like tubby vehicles in a Dr. Seuss book, I felt like zooming, too, but if drivers were nervous and careless I found myself slowing down.

This morning I predicted a day of small unexpected events. I might see a land snail slithering along the sidewalk, and I'd have to move it to the grass to prevent it from getting squished. (If more people knew how complex and sensitive snails are, and how long they live, maybe they would hesitate to squish them.) Or else I might come across a photo I'd lost years ago and had been searching for ever since.

If it was going to be a particularly lucky day, I might even pick up a clue that would help me solve the mystery of my student Matar's eyes.

Noah's diary, March 16, 1981.

In the news: defective man shot at Berlin Wall.

I've been thinking a lot about bodies. What are bodies? Nothing. Just things we use, like a car. So why is there so much emotion attached to bodies? That's the question. Take for example Oren: why is the fact that he's taller than me important? Yet it is. Important to him and important to me and important to everyone around us. People notice it. He's tall, I'm not that tall yet. Everyone tells him he should play basketball. People like it that he's tall and they think we're a funny pair. Take Sonya: why does she like to snuggle up against me with that stupid smile on her face? And how come if I saw any girl in my class (especially Ariella) naked it would be a huge event, but I've seen Sonya naked a million times and so what. Actually lately I don't like it anymore. I really, really don't like it and I can't say why.

That's exactly what I mean. Why? That was my question: why are bodies a big deal? At the moment I have no answer.

Our teachers want more money so they're doing sanctions. As a result school started at 10:30. What bliss! I slept in and dreamed I was advising Ruthie on types of garter belts and she thanked me. I hope the teachers don't get what they want for a long time.

❧ Letter to Andrei, February 16, 1957

Dearest, our theater is on its feet! A grant arrived from Brooklyn Friends of the Arts in Israel—a charity run by an old woman, nearly ninety, but apparently very active and determined. We had champagne (or something like it) to celebrate, and rehearsals will begin immediately. Feingold gave us all a lecture on the play. Oh, dearest, he said such clever things, but I'm afraid hardly anyone was listening. Orlando had to leave to pick up his daughter, Oliver/William kept chatting nonstop with Audrey (Carmela) about cures for piles (!), Celia (poor Tanya) stared at Feingold with glazed eyes, and Touchstone was munching a raw onion in a very distracting way. Feingold himself will be Jacques, whom he calls a "protoparody of the existentialist." Only the Duke and Rosalind—a wonderful young actress who miraculously turned up from Haifa—were listening. I'm afraid he may be disappointed in us all!

Kostya is doing very well. An essay he wrote was published in the newspaper! Not in a children's paper, but in a major daily called *Ha'aretz*. Everyone was astonished that a child wrote it. It was about steps that must be taken if we are to have peace—he's become quite interested in politics. I wish you could see him now: he has grown so tall in the past year, and he's very independent. But then he was always such a capable child. Do you know, he has quite forgotten about the time he helped the girl whose coat was caught in the wheel! I've told him the story a few times, but he says he doesn't remember it at all. I think he likes hearing about it, though   he especially likes that he was the only one who noticed.

Today we had a little guest. A girl in Kostya's class had been away for a year in the United States and she came back last week with many treasures—a dozen colored markers and pens, such as you can't find here, and a special lunchbox with pictures of a handsome singer and actor (Elvis Pretzley), a wristwatch with a funny cartoon face, and other foreign toys. She brought them to school to show everyone, but their teacher is a devout socialist and he apparently gave the class a long tedious lecture during which he reprimanded her and her toys. The girl was in tears. Kostya brought her home with her bag of interesting items: she's a very nice girl with long braids and good manners. I told her about the time I came to school with a new blue coat and how I was tormented by the other children. She cheered up and gave Kostya one of her special pens before she left.

Lately Kostya no longer wants to be cuddled. I must say it's a little hard getting used to his new, older self. At bedtime he kisses me on the cheek, but I can see he's only being polite. When I try to hold him these days he squirms away and tells me he has to run. It's only natural—he's growing up. But I do miss hugging him and covering him with kisses, the way I used to do. At night, when he's fast asleep, I often peek into his little cubicle. Sometimes I kneel by the bed and stroke his hair, and my heart fills with such longing for the days when the three of us were together. Remember how you spun with him on your shoulders in our little room, and he reached up and tried to touch the ceiling? And he would tell you to go faster and faster— what a small, sweet thing he was! I will ask Carmela to take a photograph of our dear son to send you, so you can see how big he is now.

Dearest, take good care of yourself and follow doctor's orders. I worry so much. You are my heart and soul.

᷷᷈᷉ SONYA

Non-soporific," my brother had promised, but he was mistaken. During class I felt myself growing sleepy and I began to yawn. The lines, *"Oh, how do you like my feather bed, and how do you like my sheets?— And how do you like my fair young bride, who lies in your arms asleep?"* from a record of English folk songs we had at home, began tugging gently at me, along with the image of a very soft bed. My students also started yawning, because that sort of thing can be catching. Only my translator, a small wiry boy-girl, was as energetic and jumpy as always, oblivious to the spell that was falling upon the rest of us.

A room full of semi-comatose students might not be such a drawback in philosophy or literature, where proximity to an unconscious state could produce some inspiring notions pulled out of one's creative back drawer. But when students reach this state in ordinary differential equations, the situation is nothing short of hopeless; mathematical creativity requires a certain level of mental dexterity. And we were on a particularly difficult unit.

The math building was undergoing repairs, so the class had been moved to a small room on the second floor of the Gilman Building. It was a pleasant classroom, with tall windows all along the north wall, overlooking the campus. Students wear such lovely clothes, and I enjoy seeing speckles of purple and red and turquoise as I teach; it's as if everyone on campus has deliberately dressed to contribute to this marvelous collage. As if they've been cast in a children's play about birds and butterflies.

I had asked my seventeen students to arrange their desks in a circle; I wanted to see them all clearly. The lithe, overly slender girls never remembered to bring sweaters, and most of them would start rubbing their arms vigorously twenty minutes into the lesson. This was followed by lengthy negotiations which continued sporadically throughout the class: Should the two large air-conditioning apparatuses, which clung to the back wall like fossilized octopi, be turned on or off? One would be shut down, then turned on again, then both would be shut down, then one or both would be turned back on, and so on, back and forth, for three hours. I'd given up reminding the cold-sensitive students to bring sweaters.

My perky translator, Ma'ayan, tried to keep the class from yielding to the enchanted poppy field, but with little success: the students merely stared at her blankly, not absorbing anything. I didn't need Ma'ayan to translate both ways; I can speak, though I don't always choose to do so. My voice is my resident phantom, the ghost in the attic, or maybe the madwoman in the attic. Every Saturday afternoon I work with a speech therapist to prevent my voice from taking on a life of its own: like other natural skills, speech needs ongoing monitoring, a job our ears perform. In the absence of our own supervision, someone else must do the work.

The problem with speaking, however, is that your listener assumes you can hear. For that reason I prefer to sign in many situations. It would not kill people to learn some basic signing.

Ma'ayan was not only my classroom translator; I also relied on her to keep me up to date with all the gossip on campus. Luckily for me, Ma'ayan picked up gossip the way a positive ion traveling through the air attracts its negative counterparts. She knew things no one else knew, or before anyone else knew them, in the very early stages of their inception; clearly she had sources deep in the heart of the university.

I had worked with her for nearly ten years and we were very close. We often met outside of class to try out new restaurants or see Iranian movies that made us both weep profusely. But after all this time I was still confused by Ma'ayan's sexual identity. She was delighted when people took her for a male and addressed her in the masculine form, and sometimes she used the men's toilet. Shortly after she graduated from high school she fell in love with a fourteen-year-old girl she met at an ice-cream counter; Ma'ayan fooled the girl's parents into thinking she was a boy for two months, and she nearly went to prison when the girl's mother caught the two of them in bed. Ma'ayan was charged with seducing a minor, and the girl, to save herself from her parents' wrath, testified against her and claimed she'd been tricked into sex. But the judge was skeptical, and Ma'ayan was acquitted of misconduct.

I myself was a little unsure of her gender when we first met. I had placed an ad for a translator and Ma'ayan came to my office for an interview. We instantly took to each other. Ma'ayan's parents were deaf and she was fluent in Hebrew Sign; she also had a background in science, though she never managed to finish any course she began. When the interview was over, we both needed the toilet. She walked toward the men's room, was about to go in, changed her mind, and followed me to the women's. While I was peeing, I was tempted to peek under the door of the stall and see which way her feet were pointing, but it turned out that she'd only entered the stall to take a quick, furtive drag on a joint, the unmistakable smell of which filled the room a minute later. Before we parted I asked her, "Are you male or female?" She laughed and signed, "When I was born, the doctor said, 'It's a girl.' Was he ever wrong!" On the other hand, she disliked lesbian women and never had anything to do with them. More than once she'd been involved with a man, and sometimes when we saw a particularly good-looking boy on campus, a boy with delicate angelic features, she'd sign, "Ooh, I want him!"

"I apologize," I told my class. "My brother gave me an allergy pill this morning. He absolutely promised it was non-soporific, but he must have been misled. I can barely keep my eyes open. And now I see it's contagious. So we will have to rely on our devoted and wonderful translator to pull us out of this stupor."

My students grinned, grateful for any novelty that broke the monotony of our intensive summer course. They were good students. I always have remarkably clever students. This country is full of geniuses; every time young people get killed, we lose a few more brilliant souls. And it isn't just the university elite; I teach signing and math in a poverty-stricken community, and the children there are brilliant, too. Statistics show that academic skills are in decline among the youth, but I don't see it at all. On the other hand, I constantly come across stupid adults, adults whose stupidity is so overwhelming that one wants to give up hope on humanity. It seems there is a process of retardation that takes place in this country, which is capable of producing intelligent babies but manages to turn them into morons, gradually, bit by bit, until at fifty they are nearly brain dead.

With great effort we went over the homework I'd assigned; I answered questions and explained some tricky problems. I like to use colored markers on the dry-erase board: black, green, blue, pink. I say very little; I find that silence often helps students see procedures more clearly. The silence forces them to focus on my colorful arrows, exclamation marks, and signs. They squint and frown, and I see their faces suddenly change as they catch on. Not in any obvious way, because they're cool and tough and world-weary, but I can see the moment of illumination as clearly as if they had jumped out of their seats and shouted *Eureka.*

But today the students were so unfocused that I gave up and dismissed the class early. I watched as Matar, the student whose eyes had been haunting me from the first day of class, packed his things. Impulsively, despite my sleepiness, or maybe because of it, I decided to confront him right then and there. I asked him to stay behind for a minute.

NOAH'S DIARY, DECEMBER 2, 1982.

In the news: we are getting very unpopular.

Lots of people dying in Lebanon. Every day after the news you see the names on the screen one after the other, in black, and everyone wants it to be something else, not death, or not as bad as death. Like if you die for a reason it's not so bad. But it doesn't work, because in the end it's still the end, nothing. Earth and worms. You can't win over that, it's too strong. I tried to imagine dying but I can't, because if I imagine it that means I'm thinking and if I'm thinking I'm not dead.

Mom is furious, can't stop talking about the war. Dad probably feels the same way but he doesn't say much. Gran doesn't care at all. Sonya says she's a pacifist. She's nine but she skipped two grades so she's only one below me now. I don't mind having a genius for an aunt. She helps me with my homework actually. I don't mean that I need help understanding stuff. But sometimes I just don't feel like doing it and she adores anything to do with school, so I let her.

Despite her brains, she's very immature. She still sucks her thumb and has trouble falling asleep if Gran or someone else (when Gran comes home too late) doesn't sing her a lullaby or tell her a bedtime story. She follows me everywhere and whines if I don't take her with me when I go places. She makes soup out of her ice cream and then drinks it from the bowl, holding it up and pouring it down into her mouth—obviously it's a mess and I can't even watch. She drinks milkshakes with a straw so she can make bubbles. You'd think making bubbles was the most thrilling experience a human could have. Her friends are all around five years old and she plays house with them, or teacher. She collects lizards, bugs, snails, spiders, and even worms, and she has a tantrum and goes into heavy mourning if anyone by mistake flushes one of her creepy spiders down the toilet. She draws stupid faces on her hands so it's like a mouth opening and closing between her fingers, and I'm not going to describe the faces she draws on her stomach and chest, it's too disgusting. Sometimes when we're out walking in the park she crosses her eyes and pretends she's not quite right in the head. Everyone stares, it's very embarrassing.

So her pacifism is not something I can take too seriously, but about this war in Lebanon I have to admit I am torn. I think I agree with Mom. What exactly is the point? Also I don't like the way they lied about their plans. At least Sharon lied, and Mom keeps saying that's what Hitler did. She always goes too far! She says Hitler kept saying, only this, only this and no more, but he never meant it. It's disgusting, comparing Sharon to Hitler, and I told her so, but she said she was only pointing out this one similarity. I don't believe her, she only retracted to calm me down.

At school everyone is for the war—get rid of the PLO, smash them to bits, show them we won't give in, get rid of terrorism once and for all. But anyone can see (as Mom says) that this isn't going to solve the Palestinian problem. But what will solve it? I don't know. The PLO really do seem pretty evil. I don't like that Arafat, he really scares me. He never shaves. Oren has started shaving. Dad says he didn't shave till eighteen! But I don't think I take after him. He's into music and science and cooking and all that stuff. I think I might be a fashion designer but I haven't told anyone yet. I'm experimenting a bit with Sonya, I'm trying different outfits on her. She's a great model. Tall, broad shoulders, sort of chubby but symmetrical. And she's weird, so she doesn't mind if my designs are weird, too. She thinks they're great.

Dearest, I am writing late at night, after a long evening of rehearsing. I am afraid Feingold is going to have a nervous breakdown. He is thinking of abandoning the entire project, but we are bound to it now because of the grant from Brooklyn. Apart from Feingold and me, only four of the actors have studied acting: Rosalind, Orlando, Touchstone, and Oliver/William (at least so he claims, but is vague about details). I have been giving lessons to Tanya and Carmela, but there's only so much I can do in such a short time. At first I could not understand how Feingold could cast Carmela in the play. She's completely hopeless. But Feingold is using her inability to act to create a very comic Audrey. In any case she really does have very few lines, so even if she murders them it won't ruin the entire play. The fact is that we are short of actors as it is and can't give anyone up. We have had to make some adjustments to the text, but I am sure Shakespeare would understand and forgive us.

The real problem is that people are not showing up for rehearsals or they have to leave early—there is always some very good reason or emergency. Other problems: Touchstone's onion breath is bothering everyone, but he says he has to eat raw onions in order to "clear his nasal passages." People show up without their script. Oliver/William lost his. No one listens to Feingold or remembers his instructions. People come in from the wrong side. Twice our rehearsal space was locked up, and once it was double-booked and being used for a meeting of leftists. The hall we're supposed to be playing in has had a problem with the lights, and the place has to be rewired or it could burn down. No one knows whether the wiring will be ready on time; right now several walls have been taken apart. But I am encouraging Feingold not to give up. We will manage somehow. Kostya is helping, too. He's looking after getting the program and posters typeset and printed.

I am eating bread and cheese spread as I write to you. There are such excellent cheese products in this country. The bread, which I get with food stamps, is also delicious. The local *hummus* (a chickpea spread) is another inexpensive item, and it's quite tasty once you get used to it. In fact, it's addictive. Falafel is a wonderful local food that is affordable and tasty. It's made of ground chickpeas dipped in boiling oil, and you can buy it on the street. Kostya is very fond of cold borscht, which is made a little differently here. It's common to eat salad for breakfast in this country. The main meal is shortly after noon, when people come home to rest. Remember I told you about the siesta from two to four? Well, I always wondered why it was so quiet at that time. I found out the reason: it's against the law to make noise or play a musical instrument!

Even though people are supposed to go back to work at four, schedules are very lax here. Sometimes people desert their store at odd hours, and even official institutions are not always open according to schedule. So informal! What a difference from home, where everyone is obedient and afraid. I must say I do prefer it this way, even though there is a great deal of grumbling all the time about inefficiency. Yet the people who grumble are often the same ones who don't do their own jobs efficiently! It's quite funny at times.

I enclose a photo of Kostya that Carmela took on the city's main boulevard. You can also see, in the background, the lovely palm trees we have here. The palm trees are the only part of this country which I imagined correctly!

I am waiting for your precious letters.

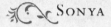 Sonya

Matar looked surprised when I asked him to stay, but only for a second. He assumed I needed a favor and that I was going to ask him to look up an article for me or move heavy boxes.

There was something shocking about Matar's eyes, which were far too intense for his age — or any age, for that matter. I couldn't get used to the discrepancy between those eyes and everything else about him. He seemed to be in his mid-twenties, and he was a good-looking guy, with dark hair and fine features. His build was slight, but one sensed that he was athletic, or at least very fit. He was, apart from his eyes, ordinary in every way, an ordinary student like a thousand others on campus.

His eyes didn't suggest to me that he'd been through anything horrifying, or even that he'd passed the stage of horror. We tend to recover from distressing events; I'm a perfect example. And if we don't, if we're still wandering the corridors of a psychiatric hospital, or walking stunned through life, then our eyes betray shock, or pain, or rage. Matar's eyes didn't express any of those things. The intensity of his eyes seemed to have more to do with a secret burden, as if he knew something no one else did but upon which our existence on this planet depended. Even when he laughed at one of my dumb jokes, or whispered slyly to his best friend—a fellow with a sun-bleached afro who was his exact opposite: loose, free, relaxed, crossing one hairy leg over the other, ankle over knee, arms clasped behind his head, leaning so far back in his chair that I was sure it would topple over one of these days—even then his eyes didn't relent. If I were his mother, I would feel I'd lost him, and I'd grieve.

I told Ma'ayan she could go. Before she left the room she winked at me and signed, secretively, "Remember the harassment regulations!"

Matar remained in his seat, looking at me and waiting patiently for his assignment. He always sat near the window, three seats from my desk.

I motioned him to come over to the board, and with my blue marker I wrote, *"How are you?"*

He grinned, picked up a green marker, and drew a happy face next to my question.

"Tell me a little about yourself."

He wrote: *"b. 1979. Dad: engineer. Mom: daycare worker. Two sisters, 14, 16. One brother, 9. 1983–1997: nursery, kindergarten, grade school, high school. 1997–2003, army. 2003–present: university. Favorite teacher: Sonya."*

I said, "You left out something."

He looked at me for a few seconds, weighing his answer.

"Secret," he wrote, and drew the opposite of a smiley face, a face with the mouth turned down. He added a semicircle of vertical rays for hair.

"Sorry. Didn't mean to intrude."

"Not that kind of secret. End-up-in-prison kind of secret." He picked up the black marker and drew bars over the sad face. He enclosed the bars in a square: the face was looking out of a prison window.

"It's okay. Sorry. I shouldn't have asked."

"You notice everything, Sonya."

"Hard not to notice in your case, Matar."

"I like it when you say my name."

Embarrassed, suddenly uneasy, I turned away and began organizing the papers on my desk.

He drew a square on the board to lure me back. I watched him. Inside the square he wrote *target*. Around the square he drew five Xs. Next to the Xs he wrote, *Unimportant people, aged 4, 7, 17, 19, 61.* Then he added a body to the sad face behind bars, and drew a medal on the figure's shirt. *Good boy in elite commando unit gets medal,* he wrote, and smiled. His smile was the kind one often sees in this country among the male population: half-cynical, half-challenging.

I wondered whether to let my paranoia get the better of me. Did he think it was safe to tell me military secrets because as a deaf person I didn't really count? On the other hand, this sort of thing wasn't a secret, it was reported in the papers all the time.

At least six different emotions, one of which was fear, collided in me. Meanwhile Matar had walked very deliberately to the door and shut it. He came back to where I was standing rather foolishly, unable to move, because I couldn't decide which of all the things I felt I ought to act upon. He placed his hands on my shoulders and I became aware of a sensation I couldn't quite place, something very pleasant. It took me a second to realize that what I was feeling was a tongue, and that it was moving gently in my mouth.

❧ NOAH'S DIARY, FEBRUARY 28, 1983.

> *In the news: 5 kids in Haifa stole 200 grenades and*
> *300 flares from an army base! No one noticed! They*
> *were 11 years old! The IDF spokesman has "declined*
> *to comment."*

I've pretty much moved out for the winter—I'm in Oren's room now. I've been here since January 2. Today is the twelfth consecutive day of snow in Jerusalem, which is a record. We saw on TV everyone getting their cars stuck in the snow. The previous record was in 1919, when they had seven snowy days in a row, and a total of nineteen for the winter. Tel Aviv is pretty cold, too, but it's nice and warm here—we have the kerosene heater on. I miss the porch, even though it's too cold to sleep there now. Oren's parents feel sorry for me that my bedroom is a porch. That's fine with me, it makes them really generous, so I don't tell them how great it is. Adults see things differently at all times.

Oren has a nice flat: huge with two bathrooms and a bidet (which he had to explain to me, and which I still don't really get) and you can see the whole neighborhood from the balcony. They also have these big art books which they let me borrow. They're not rich but they work like crazy and they have about seven mortgages and loans. Oren's dad is a contractor. I'm not sure what that is but everywhere I go someone seems to be a contractor. There must be more contractors in this country than any other profession. His mom is a nurse at a home for old people and she tells very gross stories from her job. Oren thinks they're hilarious but I find them disgusting.

I told Oren's mother about Gran. I don't know if it's the vodka or what, but she's becoming sort of mixed up. She's pretty old, around sixty. Oren's mother says sixty isn't old, but that's to make herself feel better, because she's probably close to sixty herself, or at least forty.

For example, when she reads—unless she's out late she reads to Sonya at night, and sometimes I sort of sit in the doorway because I like her voice. She leans back on her pillows with her hair in braids and she has a nice smell—vodka, but also perfume and something else, like cinnamon. Sometimes she reads about knights and witches—she does a good witch's voice—and sometimes she reads poetry in English or even a bit of *Romeo and Juliet*, that's her favorite play. I like the way she says, "'What, drawn and talk of peace?'" Sort of soft and sharp at the same time.

She also tells Sonya stories about her past, which interest me because I get to hear about my grandfather, Dad's father, who was a physicist but married—to someone else, I mean. Also about how she and Dad escaped, which is like from a movie. They hid money for bribes in Dad's teddy bear and they had to sneak past a guard who was asleep just by miracle, and then they almost got caught at the airport in Vienna, but Gran ducked into the bathroom and put on a different outfit. In the Soviet Union they had to learn Hebrew in a basement by candlelight—if they'd been caught they would have been in huge trouble, maybe even sent to the gulag or something to be a slave. Nobody liked Jews. NOW WE DON'T HAVE TO CARE HA HA.

But to return to Gran, lately she starts saying something and halfway through she forgets what it's about. Or she starts reading some poem about kids skating on a pond and in the middle she tells us we need to buy more rice. And yesterday Dad and Sonya were playing their screechy violins and suddenly she said, right out of the blue, "I'm against bird migration." That was creepy, I have to admit. I tried to joke around with her about it, figure out what she meant, but it turned out she barely realized she'd said anything.

The worst was when she forgot my age, and she wasn't just off by a year, like twelve instead of thirteen, or fourteen instead of thirteen. She thought I was going into the army!! Not yet, thank you. Actually I don't even know whether I'll go into the army at all. There's a new thing now—this group got started, these people are starting to say it's wrong to go in because of the occupation and the invasion into Lebanon, they say you should go to jail instead. Mom is really into all that. She put up a big banner in the corridor, TWO STATES FOR TWO PEOPLES. Now I can't invite anyone over, apart from Oren. I think I'd really hate the army, and that's the real reason I don't want to go. I could try to get a mental health exemption (I think I could act crazy if I had to, look at the house I'm growing up in!!!). It won't matter for my career if I'm a fashion designer.

Unless I design uniforms ha ha!

Maybe I should start doing crazy things now, so it gets into some sort of medical record. I could walk naked on the street singing "Hatikva" or something like that. It's good to plan ahead. Because the truth is, the army is really, really not for me, I can tell. No, I have to go, it's my duty. If I don't go that means I'm a coward and I don't deserve to be Israeli. It's the least I can do for my state. Maybe I can ask to be a jobnik—I don't have to go into combat. Dad says the most important thing in life, more important than brains or talent or any other assets, is to have courage, and everything else will follow from that. He says if you don't have courage you'll never have any kind of decent life. He doesn't mean the army specifically, he means just a general approach of facing things. But Mom says if I go into combat she'll consider me a war criminal. She always goes too far!! For the Vietnam War you could say you were gay—I saw that in a movie. I'm not gay but even pretending to be gay doesn't work here. No one cares. I know because someone told me that Mani's son is gay and he's a corporal. So I asked Mani about it one time after soccer practice when there was no one else around, and he told me his son decided on a military career because he wanted to be surrounded by men ha ha! People think fashion design means you're gay but they're ignorant. If I were gay I'd be in love with Oren and I'm not.

Dearest, not a word from you in so long, but I keep on writing in the hope that you will eventually get my letters and write back. I had a dreadful dream about you, dearest, that you were caught with my letters and they found out how you helped me in Vienna—and they shot you, and also poor Heinrich! In the snow, and you both fell. Olga was there, it was terrible. If only I had a word from you!

I am very homesick. I just came home from rehearsal, which followed a long day at the restaurant, and I felt so miserable I poured myself a drink and got straight into bed. Kostya makes his own meals now; he's so resourceful. He's borrowed a cookbook from Carmela, who also invited him over a few times to show him how to make kugel and vegetable stew and all sorts of inexpensive dishes. Oh, I don't know what I'm writing, I'm in such a swirl at the moment. I am not disappointed in this country, even if it isn't as I imagined it, and I don't regret leaving, as we had no choice, dearest. Kostya's future, ours, the risks involved . . . but I am lonely here. I've met many interesting people, and you know, everyone loves to read, there are bookstores at every corner, with boxes full of inexpensive books. There isn't a book that is too dog-eared or moldy to make it into a box. I've found some real treasures for only a few *grushim* (our lowest coin). Kostya is happy here. He has a future in this country, he can do something with his life.

Above all, we are free. There is much more nationalistic fervor than I expected, but it's not oppressive; on the contrary, there's something almost touching about it. I shouldn't be surprised—after all, my poor father was always so passionate about the idea of a homeland. I remember the hope in his eyes when he whispered news that leaked in. People here are the same, they want this project to work, and they're so excited about having a new country just for themselves, ourselves. I'm very tired, dearest. I will go to sleep now and hope that I won't wake up in the middle of the night with a cockroach making its way across my forehead: they are fearless, this breed. Good night, dearest. Wrap yourself up well. You and I are past our dancing days. . . .

SONYA

I had spent over a decade discouraging men who came up to me and asked whether I was free that evening and would I like to have coffee, see a movie, go down to Eilat. Some of the men were charming and nice, and I was tempted, but I never gave in. People thought my refusal had to do with the twins, but they were wrong. The twins had no bearing on my life; I refused to let them leave their mark on me, and it angered me when anyone thought they had. My refusal had to do with my particular world. I wanted to go out with a man who spoke my language, a man who would come up to me and sign, "Hey, Sonya, let's go hiking this weekend." And as luck would have it, the few eligible men who qualified were not my type. They knew how to sign but they didn't understand me or anything about me.

The closest I ever came to yielding was, remarkably, with Eli Yigal, philosophy professor and campus womanizer. The washrooms were filled with graffiti about him: *Eli will do it for free* or, more allusively, *Eli's coming and he thinks you are too.* At the gay and lesbian fair there were buttons for sale that said, *I didn't do it with Eli*; the money went to the AIDS Help Fund. I bought one just for the hell of it, but I never wore it, of course, though I could have.

There were many rumors about Eli; no one knew which were

true. Ma'ayan, who had told me various Eli stories over the years, admitted that most couldn't be verified. In the category of "definitely true" were stories from twenty years ago or more, when he taught at the Hebrew University: he would drive up from Tel Aviv to the dorms in Jerusalem to visit his students in their rooms, three per trip, in succession. He'd make the three dates in advance, an hour apart, and he'd move from room to room like a salesman offering a special deal on sex. He swore each student to secrecy—not because he was worried about his job, but in an attempt to keep them from finding out about one another and comparing notes.

In the category of "probably true" were stories about unstable sixteen-year-olds whom he'd driven over the edge; I myself had been present when his wife had jumped out the window of their second-story flat during a party. In the category of "unverifiable" were rumors about sado-masochism. He was famous in his field and he'd been married several times, though one of the things he was famous for was his philosophical position on the bearing of children, which he opposed for interesting reasons. He'd had a vasectomy at an early age and he kept a bowl of condoms on his desk for students; he described the features and advantages of each type and made sure his students knew how to use them properly.

I had been a student of Eli's as well, when I was doing my doctorate. I'd completed my master's degree in Beersheba; there was a teacher at the university there, Nava, whose work interested me, and I went down to the desert of Beersheba like a pilgrim following a prophet or sage. It had always seemed to me a stroke of extraordinary good fortune that thinkers of her caliber were to be found in our low-paying universities, for I was not ready to study abroad, in a foreign hearing environment.

Nava was well past retirement age. She wore baggy cotton shorts, leather moccasins with short white ankle socks that always bunched up, and shapeless sleeveless tops that allowed us to stare for hours at a time at her aging body: the loosening, spotted skin on her upper arms; the skeletal bones protruding through her upper chest as though impatient to take over. She wanted us to contemplate death. That was not the reason she wore sleeveless tops, of course; she wore them because she was hot. But she did want us to contemplate death—and life—and I felt that the exposure of her body was a reflection of her desire to probe our pitiful coordinates as relentlessly as possible.

But Nava left for a sabbatical in Holland before I began my doctoral dissertation, and she confided in me that she might not be back when the year was up. She'd had enough, she said, and yearned for some peace. There was no point in staying at Beersheba after she left, and I enrolled in Tel Aviv University.

I'd read one of Eli's books, *Presumption, Progeny and Power*, and I liked its elegant arguments and subtle humor. I signed up for a course with him and was not disappointed. Eli was a good teacher: organized, focused, generous. He had a pedagogical instinct; he really wanted to transmit the things he knew and thought, and he had a striking way of perceiving the world. He told funny stories, too, about famous people he'd known at Yale, stories full of sly slander and delicious tidbits: Hilton Morris inviting the *New Yorker* to photograph him slumming in a hick dive, Jacques Derrida buying a designer raincoat for his photo shoot. It was impossible not to be entertained, in spite of the way he looked at his female students.

I had no personal contact with him at the time, though I watched with amusement as beautiful young scholars entered the classroom decked in their sexiest clothes, expressed petulant doubts about Heidegger during the lesson, and went up to Eli after class with urgent questions about phenomenology.

It wasn't until I was faculty that Eli tried to seduce me. I was sitting at the outdoor cafeteria of the law building, correcting exams under the shade of a large striped umbrella that was secured to the center of the table. Out of the corner of my eye I saw someone coming toward me; it was Eli. He pulled out a chair, not opposite but next to me, and sank heavily onto it. Then he set down his coffee, took the pen from my hand, and wrote in the margin of one of the exams, *"You have your mother's eyes. How is she?"*

"Visit her and see for yourself," I answered, signing as I spoke. "My eyes aren't anything like my mother's," I added. "Are you sure you knew her?"

"Of course I knew her," he scribbled, in his barely legible handwriting. *"Everyone knew her. She was the life of the party. A golden-haired Russian princess."*

"She once studied physics," I said defensively.

"Yes, she was smart," he agreed. And without warning he slid his arm around my waist.

You can't acquire or attain through deliberate effort the sort of magnetism Eli had; it's something you're born with. I'd been aware of his charisma before, but only in the way one is aware of a bird's red wings or an ant's ability to carry a corpse twice its size on its back. I never came under his spell and I considered myself immune until he touched me. I was aroused, and suddenly I was also curious. When someone has that sort of reputation, you can't help wondering what it's all about. For a few seconds I was tempted, I felt I wanted to follow him to his car, bring him home and find out what made him special, if anything. But sanity prevailed. I got up and gathered my exam papers.

He wrote, *"I know what you went through. I'm sorry."*

"What do you know?" I replied defiantly. Even by Israeli standards, Eli operated on and elicited a level of directness that was unusual.

"The two men."

"Does that turn you on?"

"No, it makes me sad."

"Why?"

"I can't imagine anyone doing things like that to another person."

"People say you're into S&M."

He didn't answer; he merely stared at me with a pointed expression: partly amused, partly disappointed but forgiving.

"That event has nothing to do with how I feel about you," I wrote. *"I don't go to bed with men who don't speak my language."*

He looked surprised and a little confused. I spelled good-bye and left quickly, before I changed my mind. Eli made you feel he was inviting you to join a club, a very exclusive and wonderful club, and that was the problem, that was the lie. There wasn't any club, only Eli's insatiable hunger; and the fact that he had the ability to tempt women with this lie, tempt them by placing his arm around their waists, made his lie all the more inexcusable. In the end, I decided, he was nothing more than a wicked wizard who used his magic powers for his own benefit and, in so doing, created havoc and pain.

Matar, because he was more innocent than Eli, had managed to get farther: he'd taken me into his arms and kissed me. I moved away, taking a step back. What a strange thing kissing was—entirely instinctive and yet so unlikely. Why would two mammals want to slide their tongues into each other's mouths? No other species did that, as far as I knew. And yet it felt wonderful: generous and intimate, and somehow innocent, as if you were playing. Shall we have a round of checkers or would you like to kiss?

Not allowed, I wrote on the board, in small letters.

He wrote *Allowed* next to the Xs surrounding the square, and then he drew a heart and wrote under it, *Not allowed.*

I said, "Wait until the course is over. At least then we can talk." I sketched a cartoon version of Masaccio's *Expulsion of Adam and Eve*, with Tel Aviv University in the background, and *dean* written on the robe of the banishing angel.

Matar smiled, happily this time. *"I dream about you all the time,"* he wrote.

I picked up the eraser and erased everything on the board, wiped it clean. I felt him watching me. He had a crush on me, that was all. Maybe even less than a crush. Maybe just lust. That was the way things were in this country: people were promiscuous and sexually confident. No one had to talk about sex because everyone was doing it. I wondered what I would tell him when the course was over.

My drowsiness, which had vanished in the excitement of our exchange, returned with greater force than before. I suddenly wanted nothing more than to flop down on my bed and go to sleep. I said, smiling, "Take care of yourself," and left Matar alone in the classroom, looking at me with his intense and terrible eyes.

⁓❧⳩ NOAH'S DIARY, JULY 4, 1984.

In the news: nothing interesting.

I got into a huge mess today.

Since Passover, Oren's been going out with Ariella. It began when she had a fight with her family and she asked him whether she could go to his place for the seder instead. In the end she stayed with her family—they didn't actually make up but they convinced her to be at the family seder. Some crazy fight over a pair of boots she wanted that they said were too expensive or something. Her family's really rich, they even have a computer. They buy her lots of things, but there was some problem with the boots, I don't know exactly what.

Oren and Ariella started going out right after that and they also started doing it pretty fast, on the second date. Oren's given me quite a detailed description, which I'm storing in my brain for future reference. Anyway, for a few weeks he's been saying that Ilanit told Ariella, who told him, that she likes me. Actually I already knew—Ilanit made it pretty obvious, always coming up to me with questions about what I think about this or that and asking for help with English, touching my arm with her fingers but making it look like she didn't notice she was doing it.

Anyway, today was the opening of another part of the board-walk, from Trumpeldor to the Dolphinarium, and there was supposed to be a big celebration with all these performers and singers. I kind of wanted to go to that, because what if someone like Danny Sanderson or Matti Caspi showed up? But Ariella arranged for us all to go out to a movie followed by a picnic on a different part of the beach. The reason we had to do it today was that Ilanit's family won't let her go anywhere unchaperoned. But they agreed for her to come with Dad and me and Sonya and Ariella and Oren to the opening of the boardwalk. Luckily they themselves couldn't go because Ilanit's grandmother is in the hospital.

We told Dad we might "go off on our own" and he didn't care, of course. Things are a bit tense at home because Mom is in the worst mood ever and it effects Dad, who gets into a bad mood, too. Mom's in a bad mood because some Palestinian high school kids on a bus were tormented by a border guard, Cha'im, who made some of them get off the bus and stand up and sit down and stand up again and so forth, and when the other kids on the bus began to protest, Cha'im and the ten soldiers with him opened fire and five kids were wounded. Mom says the army invented a crazy story to cover up. Sometimes I think Mom is going to end up the most hated person in this country. Maybe she is already. Once Oren and I were at the pool and this furious woman came up to me and said, "Your mother is a Nazi whore." Oren said right back, "Even if you tried to be a whore you couldn't, you're too ugly."

So Dad, who's in a terrible mood but trying to pretend he's not, said no problem, we could go wherever we wanted, as long as we promised not to go into the water past our waists, because the life-guards are on strike and already a kid from Qalqilya and two old people from Tel Aviv almost drowned.

I have to admit Ilanit has a lot of guts, because if she'd been caught, her father and brothers would have killed her. Anyway, we went to see this movie, *Body Heat*, which was fantastic, with a really great ending—you couldn't guess it at all, it came as a total surprise. During the movie Ariella and Oren were making out like crazy. I guess Ilanit expected some move from me, too, but what's the point when your mind is on something else? You can't concentrate on two things at once. Kathleen Turner was fantastic. After the movie we took the bus to this beach farther off, which was completely deserted because everyone was at the celebrations. We sat on a blanket and ate pita and hummus and salad and stuff. We were starving.

It started getting dark, so Ariella and Oren took off their clothes and went in the water. I tried not to stare at Ariella but I couldn't help it. I mean, Oren I've seen naked a thousand times but Ariella it was my first time, so how can I be blamed? By this time Ilanit is in the worst mood ever and starts attacking me and crying and sulking like Sonya did when I accidentally killed her spider.

She said I was wrapped up in my own world, that was the gist of her attack. But she said it in several different ways, like that I don't notice anything around me, which is completely untrue but I guess she meant I don't notice *her*.

Then I did something really, really mean. It just came out of me, without warning. I didn't even know I could be so mean, but I was getting tired of listening to a list of all my faults and I said, "I notice things when they're interesting, not when they're boring, and if Kathleen Turner was here you'd see what I mean." Then I felt really bad, because I knew that what she really wanted was some move on my part, but you can't just make a move, just like that, with people around. You need to build up to it. It's like she had it all planned and I wasn't doing my part, but what about my plan? Maybe I have a different plan! I mean, I can't just do something because she decided that's what I'm supposed to do at that moment. I need the right mood and atmosphere.

And the worst part is that I like Ilanit. First of all, she's extremely cute, there's no question about it. She's a bit taller than me, but not so you'd notice. She has long brown hair, wavy, olive skin, nice eyes. I like her teeth, they're so small and perfect. Well, she walked off in a big huff. I knew I was supposed to run after her but I didn't. I don't know why. I wanted to, but something stopped me and then it was too late. Instead I watched Oren and Ariella making out on the sand. I figured I might pick up some pointers. It was like *Body Heat* part two.

Or should I say *Body Treat* ha ha.

I got quite a show, even though it was pretty dark, but I have good night vision thanks to all the carrots. I'm surprised they didn't mind. I guess they were too absorbed with what they were doing to care. It was a little strange seeing Oren doing something I never saw him do before. I mean, I've seen him in just about every walk of life but this was like he had another side I didn't know about and wasn't a part of. Actually, it was like it wasn't him from *his* point of view either. I mean, as if he was also just acting and he also knew it wasn't really him. But maybe that's the way it is with sex. Maybe sex is fake by nature. I mean, sex with another person. Sex with another person is pretty weird, when you think about it.

One thing was pretty obvious, though—Ariella was having a good time. She kept saying "More!" I think I'd get pretty nervous if a girl kept saying, "More, more!" as if you were a coffee machine or something, but Oren told me he likes it. To be perfectly honest, I was a bit jealous.

I feel terrible about Ilanit, though. I don't know what to do. I guess I blew it. I never realized how complicated these things were. My fights with Sonya are never complicated. But it's different when there's love involved.

Dearest, I feel I am sending this into the void, but I must continue writing to you, even if I don't know when these letters will ever reach you. If only I could mail them directly to you! But we are lucky to have Heinrich, so I must not complain.

We have had a small crisis. We were in the middle of rehearsal, Tanya was in a terrible muddle over her speech about Nature and Fortune but doing her best, and Feingold was doing his best to be patient and not burst into tears. Before anyone knew what was happening, a young man came into the room, or I should say stormed into the room, and began hitting her. . . . Oh, it's all very complicated, dearest. He didn't know Tanya was involved in a play, and he doesn't approve. We were all afraid of him but Touchstone (the onion-eater) was wonderful. He began yelling at him in such a voice! So at least the man left Tanya alone and he and Touchstone took it outside. We were all afraid to find out what happened, but when we finally went to look, there they were, sitting on two stones smoking together! But Tanya is out of the play. It's just as well. Feingold would have been forced to cut most of her remaining lines (he already cut more than half). We must find a replacement now.

I have been a little down, lately, my sweetheart. It is because I am so worried about you. If only Heinrich would write and give me some news!

I send you my love, I send you my whole self.

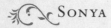 Sonya

I walked to Gate Four and pushed the tall revolving turnstile—four walls of horizontal bars designed to prevent terrorists from sneaking into the university. Then I looked around for a taxi. Walking home was out of the question today.

I made my way down Klausner, which is more of a mini–central station than a street; all day long cars drive in and out, dropping off and picking up students. A taxi sped past me and I waved, but I was too late; the driver didn't see me. Just before I reached Ha'im Lebanon Street I saw another taxi parked a few meters from the intersection. It was an odd place for a taxi to park, and it wasn't clear what the driver was doing there.

The windows of the taxi were rolled down and I poked my head inside inquisitively. The driver looked at me and nodded, so I got in and pulled out my map. I always carried a little map for taxi drivers, showing the route to our house, which was on a small dead-end street no one had heard of. The map was decorated with cartoon cats and Little Prince scientists with cotton wool hair on either side of their heads, pointing the way. Drivers tended to get quite chatty when they saw my map, and I had to explain that I was deaf. Often they didn't believe me.

This driver was different. He just looked at the map, seemed to be memorizing it, and then handed it back to me with another nod. He didn't speak; he was thinking about other things. *Maybe about how he needs to have the air-conditioning in his car fixed,* I thought, staring at the evil eye medallions dangling from his rearview mirror. The medallions were blue and silver: blue eyes on the palms of silver hands. I leaned my head back on the passenger seat, wondering about air-conditioners in cars, how much it cost to install them, whether they broke frequently—and, remarkably, I fell asleep.

I had not fallen asleep in a car since my student days, and even then I only drifted off during late-night rides from Beersheba to Tel Aviv, after a long week of classes and exams. When I was very little I nearly always fell asleep during car rides, and Kostya had to carry me back to the house. At that point I'd wake, but I didn't let on because I enjoyed being carried to bed. Now, for the first time since I was a child, I shut my eyes and fell asleep almost as soon as the car began to move.

It was the non-soporific antihistamine, of course.

I woke up with a start. The taxi was parked in front of our house and the ignition was turned off. I looked at the driver and was surprised to see that he had apparently not tried to wake me, but had instead been waiting patiently for me to wake up on my own. No, he was not really waiting; he was in a meditative trance, staring straight ahead, letting events unfold. Eventually the sleeping woman would stir; he wasn't in any hurry. Come to think of it, he had been in the same sort of trance when I'd first poked my head through the window.

I wondered briefly whether he was perhaps not all there; it also occurred to me that he might be stoned.

He turned to look at me then, and his eyes were friendly. He was not mad, definitely, but I couldn't yet rule out the possibility that he was slightly stoned. I paid him and quickly left the taxi. I didn't know that he was calling out after me; I had left my briefcase in the

car. It was full of important articles, important work; I'd never forgotten something like that in my life. An umbrella, yes, or a sweater—
but never my work. And even lost umbrellas are rare occurrences
for me; I am not usually forgetful or absentminded. But today I was
distracted. I walked down the front garden, took the house key out
of my shoulder bag, and slid it into the door, still unaware that anything was missing. I was about to step inside when I felt the driver's
body approaching me. I turned around and there he was, his arm extended, my briefcase in his hand. Seeing my briefcase in his tanned
hand was a little disorienting, but it was a pleasant, exciting sort of
disorientation—the kind people seek in amusement-park rides. A
little like my elevator dream that morning.

I was amazed at my carelessness. And then impulsively, because
I liked him, quite simply liked him, I invited him in. "Would you like
a cold drink?" I asked him. "Or a cup of coffee?" I opened the door,
and like a lady-in-waiting welcoming a guest to the castle, I waved him
in with a small curtsy. He seemed startled, and I saw him hesitating.
"Come," I said, and placing my hand on his shoulder, I ushered him in.

I walked straight to the kitchen but he tarried, looked around
inside. His eyes stopped at the large full-length mirror in the hallway
and he stared at himself, as if in surprise, as if he had not looked in
a mirror for a long time. Then he turned away, followed me to the
kitchen, and sat down at the table. When I looked at him he lowered
his eyes.

And there, in the kitchen, on this August day, after my short re-
freshing nap, I decided that finally I would lose my virginity, and that
it would be with this man, assuming that he was willing. I wondered
whether Matar's kiss had woken me from a hundred-year slumber,
whether he'd made me see what I'd been missing, and how ridiculous it was to go on missing it, because it was nice, it was splendid,
and I'd been a fool all these years to be so stubborn.

Or maybe it was something else, something about this man, his
silence, his appearance, the way he behaved with me. Maybe the

time had simply come. Maybe, maybe, maybe. In fact, I had no idea why I was suddenly attracted to the man sitting in my kitchen. It was the sort of charged, involuntary attraction I might have felt toward a movie star or popular singer in the past—but never toward someone I'd actually met.

Let me describe my taxi driver: three vertical laugh lines on either side of his mouth, a beautiful mouth, black hair, eyes full of life and intelligence. He was definitely handsome, but in this part of the world one sees handsome men every day. In the end, what draws you to one man and not another is apparently a mystery.

"Would you like cold juice, lemonade, coffee, tea . . . beer?" I asked, peering into the fridge and then at him.

"Coffee, thanks," he said.

"Coffee?" I repeated, just to be sure, and he nodded. I made coffee and arranged Kostya's apple turnovers on a plate. I poured milk into a porcelain creamer and set it down on the table along with a bowl of sugar cubes. Then I sat down facing him. I was too much on edge to eat, but he bit into a turnover with evident enjoyment. We drank our coffee in silence. He was waiting for me to speak but I had nothing to say, and in any case I didn't trust myself to understand his response. I had the sense that he welcomed the silence, that he found it peaceful. When he seemed ready to go, I touched his hand with mine.

He froze; he seemed astonished. He stared at my hand and didn't move. But he didn't protest, either—he didn't draw away or get up or give any indication that he didn't want me. I closed my hand on his and led him to my bedroom.

He stood in my bedroom with his arms hanging by his sides and watched me. He seemed very curious, as if I were an exotic animal in a zoo, as if he'd never seen anyone like me before. The bed wasn't made, as usual, and I straightened out the sheets a little. Then I closed the shutters; I didn't want him to see my scars. I returned to the bed and held out my arm, invited him to join me.

He didn't move: he was immobilized by indecision. I saw him standing there and deliberating. His body was in an odd state of suspension, pulled in opposite directions by two contradictory impulses. Caution was urging him to make an excuse and leave, but at the same time he was clearly turned on. I said, "It's all right if you don't want to."

This seemed to help him arrive at a decision. He approached the bed, removed my panties, licked his hand to wet me, discovered that it was unnecessary, unzipped his black jeans, and found his way inside.

I stroked his back through his thin ironed shirt, a sad white shirt with pale yellow stripes. I couldn't reach his face, which was turned away from me, but I kissed his shoulder and touched his hair, which sparkled as if it were made of black jewels. What a cute mating ritual, I thought. I wanted it to last a long time but it was over in a few minutes. He rose from the bed and pulled up his jeans.

I said, "You're my first lover ever."

He looked confused when I said that, and then suspicious. It was his turn to wonder whether he was in the company of a mad person.

"I'm deaf," I said. "Do you want to say something? You can write it if you like." I handed him a small notebook from my night table.

But this only made matters worse. He stared at the notebook, mumbled something about being in a rush, and fled from the bedroom, fled from the house.

I followed him outside and watched him hurry to his cab and drive away.

I sighed. What a disaster!

It was half-funny, half-depressing. I couldn't help seeing the man's quick escape as slightly comic; it was like something out of the Marx Brothers. And here I was, standing barefoot on the pathway, staring at the empty space where the taxi had been parked. I felt foolish, to say the least.

I returned to the house and poured myself a glass of lemonade.

I took the lemonade out to the back garden, sat on the white cedar swing, and rocked gently back and forth, the soles of my feet brushing the grass. I felt a great sense of relief, as if I'd removed a curse a jealous fairy had cast upon me at birth. Several things had surprised me: first, the intense physical pleasure of the moment he entered me. No wonder there were so many of us on the planet, millennium after millennium, despite plagues and earthquakes and every conceivable misery. I had felt the man's cock gently seeking a way in, finding its way like a little hedgehog burrowing in the earth, whispering to my body. Even though we were strangers, we were both aware of the intimacy of our coordinated movements, our coordinated pleasure.

Even more striking was what happened to his body when he came. Here was a moment of utter submission to the universe, to all the souls and ghosts and spirits of the universe. This was a man disappearing; replacing him was something elemental, like a crystal, for example, or a stone shaped by water. Here was a human body, gone, shivering, moaning, disintegrated by ecstasy. I felt a surge of power, as if all the control he'd given up had been transferred to me, and I was at that second the most powerful person who had ever lived. Male orgasms were evidently different from female orgasms, which I would compare to a delicious bowl of mashed potatoes dripping with butter and brie, delicately spiced, eaten when one is absolutely starving. Or maybe orgasms during sex were different from orgasms you had on your own; maybe one day I, too, would disappear through my orgasm, though I doubted it. I couldn't imagine vanishing like that, ever, even for a few seconds.

After he came, I felt his bafflement at the loss he'd experienced, I felt his need to reestablish himself in his own eyes. It took him a few seconds, and it was sweet and funny, watching him try to regain his dignity, his maleness.

Those things were interesting. I thought of the way he had licked the palm of his hand; it turned me on when he did that. Was he being considerate or pragmatic or selfish? Did he want to wet me so it would be more pleasant for me, or simply in order to make it easier for him to enter me, or did the licking of his palm mean that he didn't care whether I was aroused or not? Well, he could have assumed that I was; otherwise why was I lying on the bed waiting for him?

I rocked on the swing and sipped my lemonade. The heat surrounded me like an inflatable Humpty Dumpty toy, grinning mindlessly as it leaned against me. At the edge of the swing a ladybug was crawling precariously on a thin, drooping leaf. She, or he, decided the leaf was not steady enough to make the effort of looking for aphids worthwhile, and tried to exit via the stalk. For some reason ladybugs will always try to walk first; flying is a last resort. Do they have poor aeronautic skills? Or is it the hungry hunt for more aphids that makes them prefer a grounded stroll? There are fewer aphids in the air.

When I was little I interrupted these creatures' lives; I took them in and tried to establish relationships with them. But they were happier in their chosen setting and my attentions didn't appeal to them. There was one spider, however, who definitely became attached to me. She lived on the windowsill and knew when I was there, recognized my voice, looked forward to my treats. But Noah developed an odd antipathy toward her and she came to a sad end.

I watched the slow progress of the ladybug and thought about Matar—his eyes, his revelation, his kiss. He'd been responsible for carrying out an assassination; he'd received a medal for its success. He'd taken upon himself the role of God, handing out life and death. If God had eyes, they'd look like Matar's. That was what happened to you when you became God. You didn't look sad or guilty or pained because God doesn't feel those things, at least not our God. You looked the way Matar did. And you could never shake it off.

Noah's diary, October 3, 1984.

In the news: the Russian cosmonauts are back, they were in zero gravity for a record 237 days, including six space-walks. Also a 67 year old East German woman was arrested for spying! Guess she hid the secrets in her walker ha ha.

Today Dad got into a rage. This doesn't happen too often, he's not the type. Even when he and Mom fight, which is most of the time, he doesn't get angry, he stays calm, which I think drives Mom even more crazy. They always fight about the same thing. You'd think they'd either find a solution or give up.

Dad's side: She's away too much, we never see her, what about us, we're as important as her clients, she's running away from responsibilities, why did she bother getting married and starting a family, this house is just her hotel, she comes here to sleep and grab something from the fridge.

Mom's side: It's not her fault that she's doing the work of twenty people and it's not her fault that there aren't enough lawyers who care about what's going on, and she can't say no, people in desperate situations need her, and she's working on one case that might change the whole course of the country (she always exaggerates). She loves us and she's doing her best and she can't split herself into two and it's only temporary. (Dad says it's been temporary since they got married.)

I don't know whose side I'm on. I don't miss Mom, I'm too old now, so it's easier for me to see her point of view, but I can tell Dad misses her so I can see his point of view, too.

Anyway, the reason Dad got angry today was that Sonya's teacher let some scientists come to the school to do experiments on Sonya without getting Gran's permission (which means Dad's permission). It's the first time I've seen Dad lose his temper since the person putting a new string on his violin got a scratch on it, and that was around three years ago. I was with him in the store—it was pretty fearsome.

He phoned the teacher, Galit, and really let her have it. I felt sorry for her. But Sonya said she had a great time at the laboratory.

They were interested in her memory, which is very good. Or maybe they were interested in her whole brain. She can memorize any number she sees right away, and stuff she reads in books after just one time, and whole movies scene by scene. She says she sees things twice—first she sees it, and the second time there's a click and it gets locked in. I can't imagine keeping so much junk stored in your mind, but she says she has a lot of storage space, like a big gym, where each thing she remembers is just the size of a button. She can look at people in a room and tell you how many people are there without counting. Or matches on a table, up to about fifty. She can do math in her head and she understands university math books. She plays hard pieces on the violin and she's good at chess—she even beats Dad. Also she knows the time without checking a watch, but Shimi can do that, and he's probably the biggest moron in the class.

If they knew how stupid she was in other things maybe they wouldn't be so impressed, but they don't get to see her at home the way I do. They don't get to see her talking out loud to her dolls and spiders, nagging me, making stupid sounds outside the door while I'm peeing, and a million things I can't even begin to mention. And if they heard her playing violin they'd run from the house. They'd be lucky to have that option.

I have to go now, I'm meeting Ilanit at Ariella's. It's the only way we can meet, because of Ilanit's family. They're *very* regressive. We've already kissed and I saw and touched her boobs. The kissing was great. The boobs were a bit disappointing. They have a strange shape.

Dearest, what a wonderful week we have had! You know, I never really saw this country because I was so sick when we first arrived, and I couldn't go on any of those organized tours for *olim* (immigrants). Everyone I know told me it was a scandal that I had not set foot outside of Tel Aviv. When they heard that I had not even been to Jerusalem they were filled with horror and offered to accompany me that very day.

But really I have had no time, no energy, and no money. It's been all I can do to familiarize myself with this city and hold our lives together here.

However, I now understand all the expressions of dismay, because I joined Kostya and his school (as a class mother) on a five-day trip, and it was an unforgettable experience. There are such amazing sights here! You feel yourself transported to another world, a world of infinite time and of deep, buried emotions. We saw Jerusalem, Haifa, the Sea of Galilee, the desert, Caesarea, and many other places along the way. If only I had the talent to describe them, but I "pity the paper" if I tried, to rephrase Vanya. I missed you so terribly during every moment of this trip, wanting to share it all with you.

Jerusalem is pink and gold, the stones give off a pink glow, it's most unusual and mysterious. The Sea of Galilee, which is called Kinneret, is like a sheet of silk, so serene you want to be a water lily and float away on it. Now I understand the story about walking on water, as well as the haunting song, "My Kinneret," which asks whether the Kinneret is real or a dream. On the way to Haifa we saw fields covered with wildflowers—so delicate and passionate, so innocent and cruel! When I crouched down and touched the petals of a cyclamen (flowers with white, pink-tipped petals soaring up like the wings of a swan) with the tips of my fingers, I was nearly in tears. We saw some of Herod's ruins and coral reefs and ancient burial caves and the Dead Sea. This is a country full of soundless messages—everything in it is trying to tell us something we can't hear. It's painful not to be able to hear the messages, for one feels the landscape quivering and pulsing with the effort to express itself.

The children also climbed Masada, which you can read about in the writings of Josephus, my love. But I stayed behind, my feet weren't up to it. The landscape at Masada makes one feel small and important at the same time. Important because you have the ability to see and feel the red and orange and crimson hills, and small because no matter how much your heart swells at the sight, you can't embrace any of it.

Do you know, I believe I was asked to be class mother because word got around that I had not seen the country. I'm very glad they asked me, even if it was really not anyone's business. Throughout the trip I had to make an effort to cut myself off from the others so I could enjoy the magnificence around me. I paid no attention to the guides, and my poor Hebrew helped me do it.

Darling, I don't like to say this, but I simply can't stop feeling that there is something a little amiss with the school system here. It's the only part of living in this country that disturbs me at times. If only they knew where all these attempts to direct every aspect of the children's thinking can lead! They don't see the dangers, there is such naïveté in the air. The teachers are wonderful and the atmosphere in the school is not at all restrictive. On the contrary! It's very free and progressive, and the teachers take courses in all sorts of new theories of education. But all this enthusiasm—sometimes I get shivers. Maybe I am just reacting this way because of things we experienced. All those candies "Stalin" used to give us . . . but it's nothing like that here. The children are encouraged to form their own opinions, they are not intimidated the way we were. Oh, really I don't know what I'm saying. I'm all mixed up, maybe because I have just poured myself a little vodka.

I only missed three days of rehearsals, and I wasn't needed in those scenes. I am covered from head to toe with mosquito bites, by the way! Kostya fared better: his tent had a net.

My love, I am drifting off . . . good night, sweet prince.

❧ SONYA

My brain was quite empty, for a change. It was about five past one, but I wasn't in the least bit hungry. Kostya always tried to come home for lunch, but on most days he was too busy at the hospital and he phoned me instead. I wondered whether he'd show up today. "If he does," I said out loud, addressing the ladybug, "he'll have to eat alone."

I decided to shower, though a part of me didn't want to wash off the man's sperm, which had leaked out of me. There was no connection at all between what had happened today and the drugged assault in the classroom; a wall composed of several galaxies separated the two events. After the twins had left, all I could think of was washing. You'd think I'd be worried about other things, like whether my bones were broken, whether I'd ever walk again, whether I was about to die from a brain concussion. You'd think that what I would want most would be drugs for pain. But all I wanted was to wash. And when the janitor heard me moaning and found me, I said, "I need a shower." The ambulance arrived and I told the medics the same thing: "I need a shower." They tried to move me and I passed out. When I woke up in the hospital, the first thing I asked the nurse was: "Did you wash me?" "Of course," she spelled. I said, "Don't tell anyone what happened," because I didn't want people who knew me, especially my brother and Noah, to be upset, but it was too late by then. The whole country already knew; I was surrounded by flowers from well-wishers, and the police were waiting in the hallway to talk to me. An hour later the twins were arrested: how many identical twins are there in this country, with shaven heads and dragon tattoos on their arms? They were easy to track down.

What had taken place today was the exact opposite. I stepped into the shower a little wistfully; I was sorry to be removing all traces of my lover. Even though the episode had perhaps borne a closer resemblance to Bottom's version of *Pyramus and Thisbe* than to anything in Ovid, it was something I had wanted, something I had decided on. A man had never come inside me before; I had never felt a body shivering on top of me. The twins had come on my face.

When I stepped out of the shower I realized that I was no longer sleepy; instead, I was in the mood for a swim. Kostya and I both love to swim, and our biggest extravagance was the oval pool we had built on the east side of the house. I changed into my bathing suit and jumped into the pool with the imperiousness of an Olympic diver. I let my body fall down, down, to the bottom of the deep end. Then the water pushed me back up like seaweed or driftwood, unwaking, undrowning, impervious to human voices. I caught my breath, turned on my back, and propelled myself with my arms. I heard the rhythm of my body, the trickles and spurts and ripples of water caressing my body as it surged from one end of the pool to the other.

My brother appeared suddenly in my field of vision; he was standing by the edge of the pool. I smiled at him, or rather at his tanned feet, partly visible through brown leather sandal straps. I swam to the edge of the pool and lifted myself out. During the summer months my brother wears a navy baseball cap. With his short gray beard, blue jeans, and the baseball cap shading his eyes, he looks more like a fisherman or a bartender than a doctor. Fisherman by day, bartender by night.

He smiled at me.

"Am I getting too fat?" I asked, slightly self-conscious in my bathing suit.

"You're exactly the same, beautiful as always."

I went to my bedroom and put on a black skirt and burgundy top, which suited my slightly more sober mood. In the meantime my brother had poured himself a glass of wine, put on a CD, and settled himself on our living-room sofa, a rather outlandish but irresistible four-seater with a birds-of-paradise print, which I'd bought on impulse. Amidst these extravagant birds my brother looked wise and reliable, like a slender Buddha.

"I'm not at all hungry," I said. "I'll just keep you company."

"Unusual for you," Kostya said.

"Maybe because I had sex today," I told him, somewhat smugly.

He was taken aback, and immediately a wave of concern swept over his body. I said, "I met a man, a very nice man—polite, shy. I invited him in for coffee. He drank, he ate, he thanked me. I asked him to have sex with me and he agreed, but then he ran away in a panic."

"Who was he?"

"I don't know. A taxi driver."

"Someone you didn't know?"

"He drove me home from the university. He was nice, so I invited him in."

My brother looked exasperated. "Did you at least use a condom?" he asked.

I shook my head.

He was very upset by that. "That's extremely stupid."

"What are the odds?" I asked.

"What do odds matter when you're dead?" he said. "Now you need to get a test. Several tests. We had four new cases of hepatitis at the hospital just today."

"Don't be ridiculous," I said.

"You didn't use any contraceptive at all? What if you get pregnant?"

"Well, as it happens, just by luck, I'm two days away from my period."

He shook his head but didn't say anything.

"And by the way," I added, "that pill you gave me *was* soporific! I could hardly keep my eyes open during class and I fell asleep in the taxi."

"Sorry. It specifically says 'non-soporific' on the box."

"That's why I took a taxi. The driver didn't talk at all. He never said anything, so he didn't know I couldn't hear. I fell asleep in the taxi because of that crazy antihistamine, and I forgot my briefcase in the car. He ran after me and he was sweet, so I invited him in and after he ate I took him to my room."

"What made you decide, suddenly?"

"I don't know."

My brother could not conceal his dismay—not at my failure to protect myself from disease but at the cultural mores that had dictated my behavior. It was a subject that had often come up in our conversations. My brother found attitudes to sex in our country depressing. And it was getting worse all the time, he would say: male and female prostitutes invited to parties, sex in public bathrooms, meaningless mating between strangers. A carnality that bordered on pathology, he said, though in his more generous moments he attributed it to stress and constant contact with death: those things made people dispense with caution; it made them angry and their anger made them hungry and cynical. Monogamy used to mean something, he would say with a sigh. Some sort of . . . consideration, investment, respect. Now it had become an archaic concept. He found it astounding that not one of his friends or colleagues had a monogamous marriage. Either the husband was cheating and his wife knew but pretended she didn't, or the wife was cheating and the husband didn't know, or else they were both cheating. He was convinced this was a sign of a society in decline.

I didn't agree with Kostya; I teased him and told him, unfairly, that he was a prude. There was nothing wrong with sex, I said, nothing wrong with inviting a young attractive person to a party to satisfy the desires of the hostess. And if more people would learn to sign, I'd join in the fun. That's what I said, but my brother didn't believe me. He thought my situation was complicated, and he wanted me to see a therapist. I felt insulted by the suggestion. I was well adjusted, I told him, and far happier than almost everyone I knew.

"Maybe this was a sort of necessary first step," he said, supposedly to reassure me but really to reassure himself. "A first step to meeting someone, dating, getting to know them." The Valley of Death look I'd come to know so well crossed his face; he was thinking about the twins. I was reminded of the menacing shadow that falls dramatically on vulnerable protagonists in animated Disney cartoons, and the image of a cartoon Kostya peering up at the shadow made me laugh.

"What's so funny?"

"I just thought of you in a Disney movie. For heaven's sake, Kostya, stop dwelling on that. It's been fourteen years—I don't even remember what happened anymore. The only thing that bothers me at the moment is that my lover got scared and ran away."

"Do you know why?"

"He thought I was mad. I told him he was my first lover, and then I told him I was deaf. He mumbled something and ran off."

"I'm so sorry, Sonya."

"But I'm sure if I could just find him and explain, he would give me a second chance. I should have spoken to him first but I was too impatient."

"Oh, well, it doesn't matter now."

"It does to me. I think I love him."

"How can you possibly love someone you know absolutely nothing about?"

"You can know a lot about someone by spending some time with them."

"Not enough for love."

"Everyone knows there's such a thing as love at first sight."

"There's sexual attraction at first sight, that's all. Whether or not it develops into love, or whether we persuade ourselves that it's love, is a different matter. Besides, Sonya, he might be married."

"No, I don't think so. You know I'm good at sensing things like that."

"Yes, that's true. I'm really sorry," he repeated. "I was hoping your first experience would be more meaningful."

"It *was* meaningful. I love him. And I'm going to find him and explain."

"How will you find him?"

"His license number . . . It's odd, but I also kissed one of my students today."

My brother smiled. "Downpour after drought."

"It was just a coincidence. The student with the eyes—it turns out he has a crush on me. Maybe it wasn't a coincidence. Maybe that kiss brought me to my senses."

"Yes, very sensible to invite a stranger into your house and take him to bed."

"He probably lives in Jaffa."

"Jaffa?"

"That's my guess."

Kostya looked confused. "He's an Arab?"

"I'm not sure, but I think so."

He dropped his chin and folded his arms, the way he used to do when I was a child and didn't want to help with chores. In Kostya-language that meant, "Fine, do what you want, I'm not going to bother arguing with you when you yourself know what's right and what's wrong."

"What?" I insisted.

"Nothing."

"Why does it matter?"

"Think how he must have felt!" Kostya blurted out uncharacteristically.

"I have no idea what you're talking about. I'm sure I can get his address if I have his license number. Maybe I can go to the police, they'll be able to tell me who he is."

"That's the worst idea I've ever heard. They'll assume he's done something wrong and arrest him, after questioning you."

"I'll make up a story."

"What story?"

"I'll say he dropped something. And that I have to return it."

"Just how stupid do you think the police are?"

"Okay, I'll say I'm in love and I have to find him."

"An even better idea."

"You're not being a jealous brother, are you?"

"No, I'm a worried brother."

"Stop worrying about me. I'm thirty-two. I'm a university professor. I know what I'm doing."

My brother pondered for a few moments. Finally he said, "All right, I'll use my pull. I'll call the police and say he's a patient, I have his test results but we've lost his file—we only have his license number."

I jumped up happily and brought him the phone. "Do it now," I ordered him.

Kostya made several calls before he found the right department. He took his pen out of his shirt pocket and scribbled something down in the margin of a medical magazine that was lying on the side table.

"That was easy," he said when he was off the phone. "They believed me immediately. Doctors are holy in this country—a doctor couldn't possibly be making up a story in order to track down and harass some hapless stranger for his sister."

"What did they say?"

"His name is Nazim Sharif, and you're right, he lives in Jaffa. I have his address."

"Oh, what would I do without you, sweetheart!" I gave him a hug and kissed his cheek, or rather his beard.

Then I gathered my things, not forgetting to take my makeup. I wanted to look my best.

NOAH'S DIARY, NOVEMBER 12, 1984.

In the news: Spiegler got fired as coach because
Hapoel Tel Aviv lost again. A fan threw a rock
at his car window. Last season he got fired by
Maccabi Netanya after eight games. Soccer is
a heartless profession.

Sonya is extremely lucky I didn't strangle her today. Finally, finally, Ilanit and I organized a place and a time. We did it by skipping on the same morning, which took a lot of planning and ingenuity on both our parts. For two weeks that's all we've been thinking about and finally we managed it—we found a time when her whole family was away. She couldn't come here because of all the neighbors—everyone minds everyone else's business in this stupid place. Whereas in her building if anyone sees me they can't know which apartment I'm going to, and in any case no one's around during the day except the Fireman, who's about 100 years old. He's not really a fireman, people just call him that because he once set off the fire alarm when someone in the building burned their toast.

All I can say is, it's a good thing Oren gave me all that information, or I would have been a goner. It's so complicated. How come it's so simple for other mammals and so complicated for us? Well, everything's more complicated with us, obviously: we have *brains*. Without Oren's information I'm sure we wouldn't have managed to get anywhere. She wasn't wet at all, that still worries me, but Oren says it's nerves, on account of it being the first time. All I can say is, I can't wait for that next time. I will die waiting. It's impossible for there to be something this good that is also this hard to get. Probably like heroin. I came three times but the first two didn't count. The first time I wasn't even in yet, and frankly, I had no idea how to get in, but luckily the second time, after a lot of complications, I made it. But I was only in for one second. The third was normal, I guess.

And then we heard loud footsteps out in the hallway and someone turning the lock. We were on the floor, on a sheet I brought from home, and we froze. I have never been so scared in my life. Even if I'm in a war and I have to run through enemy fire I won't be this scared. If Ilanit's father or one of her brothers finds out, I can't begin to imagine what would happen. They're *extremely* regressive. I grabbed the sheet and my clothes and ran to her room and hid under the bed. I was sweating like crazy. Ilanit ran to the bathroom. I was trying to get dressed under the bed when I hear Sonya screeching at the top of her lungs, "Anyone home?" She had figured out what was going on and followed me, and she pretended to be unlocking the door in order to scare us. Ilanit wasn't at all amused. "You have to do something about your sister," she said after Sonya escaped. Everyone thinks Sonya's my sister, they keep forgetting she's my aunt.

I tortured her in the garden to find out if she'd told anyone but she swore she hadn't. Can I trust her? I'm so stressed out I can't even think, and there's a huge chemistry exam tomorrow. I keep expecting one of Ilanit's brothers to climb in through the window (or just give the damned porch door a kick, it's practically falling off its hinges, like everything else in this dump) and stick a knife in me. I can't sleep. Sonya thinks it's a big joke. She has no perspective at all.

I don't know exactly what she knows, actually. She's only eleven (twelve next week), and I don't think she knows anything about sex, though she does seem to be very interested in insect reproduction. She knows how all sorts of bugs and snails reproduce and keeps looking at eggs and things under her microscope. Once she forced me to look, there was just this yellow powder on the glass, but when I looked through the lens I saw a million little eggs. It was gross but I have to admit amazing.

Dearest, today was such a hard day! At the restaurant a man was very rude and I lost my temper with him. As you know, that almost never happens to me, but we've been having a bit of a heat wave, and perhaps this made me more irritable than usual. This man was rather distinguished looking, with gray hair and a scholarly air about him. First he complained about the flies—it certainly wasn't my fault that there were flies everywhere! Then he complained about the food, even though our food is not bad at all—but he seemed to be expecting a gourmet feast at Buckingham Palace.

Then he complained about the service, though I did my absolute best for him. And finally he complained about his heartburn! Even his heartburn was my fault! I had just about had enough, so I said, "Maybe you should eat at home next time, then you will be spared all these trials." I was quite angry by then. He left in a huff—I hope he will not be back.

The owners were very nice about it. They told me the man is a well-known journalist and that he's always acting superior to everyone. There isn't much tolerance in this country for people behaving as if they deserve more admiration than everyone else, and do you know, even really famous people wear sandals and are addressed by their first name. The owners told me not to worry about him, because in any case he lives in Jerusalem and only came to our restaurant by chance.

But I am not very happy with myself. I don't want to become the sort of person who fights with everyone. Many people here are continually arguing and having conflicts, and I can see how they are only making their own lives harder. I had no satisfaction at all, being so rude to that man. I must not let myself be affected by the atmosphere here!

I kiss you.

SONYA

I don't drive. When I turned eighteen, my brother wanted to buy me a special car with warning devices and flashing lights—maybe even (I imagined) a little clown popping out of the dashboard every time someone honked. I wasn't interested. Why throw yourself inside the tumult, when it's possible to lean back and allow God and the Devil to fight it out while you enjoy the scenery?

My brother locked the front door and I linked arms with him for the short walk to the driveway. He needs to be touched, and I also like feeling him beside me: his authoritative, capable body, tall and tough, trying to hold on to Ariadne's thread as he makes his way through the labyrinth. Dear Kostya.

The car, an antediluvian swamp green station wagon, was an airless furnace, and the first few seconds inside were unbearable, even for me. But soon enough we had the opposite problem: gusts of chilled air blew against our bodies, ready to freeze us to death. I lowered the air-conditioning and sang to myself. "Amazing air, amazing air, how sweet this lovely breeze; I once was cold but now I'm cool . . ." As I sang, I walked my fingers along the back of my brother's hand in imitation of a centipede. I enjoy watching people drive; their ease relaxes me.

My brother loves to hear me sing and his happiness filled the car. "Avant-garde atonal," I call my style, for I know I'm not even close to hitting the right notes. I prod songs from a vast, deep ocean; when you don't hear music, the whole concept of melody becomes slow and soggy. But singing was a part of my childhood: when we lived on Yahud Street we had a large, eclectic record collection and our entire family, including Noah and (when she was home) Iris, used to sing in unison after meals. The family favorite was "The Water is Wide," to which my brother would add a second voice in his deep baritone:

> Oh, the water is wide, I cannot cross o'er
> Neither have I the wings to fly
> Build me a ship that can carry two
> And we'll both sail, my love and I.

At a red light, Kostya said, "The car's making a strange noise, can you feel it?"

"No, feels okay to me," I answered.

"I have to take it to the garage."

"Good thing one of us can hear."

For reasons that may have been as obscure to him as they were to me, my brother refused to buy a new car. He said it was more ecologically sound to fix an old car, but neither of us believed this feeble excuse for holding on to our antique wreck. I switched songs: "You promised us brakes, and windshield wipers." I was parodying "The Children of '73," a song about the new generation of soldiers who'd been conceived after the losses of the October War, and had been promised peace by their parents: "You promised a dove, and olive branches." My brother smiled guiltily.

The streets were nearly empty; by August the heat and humidity have worn down most of the population, and the courage to venture out dissolves like sizzling water. "This is where Anna used to work," my brother said as we passed Café Cassit. I knew, of course. I had often sat in the cafés my mother frequented and tried to imagine what it was like for her, hanging out with the Dadaists and rebel writers. The artists and poets sat around being artistic and poetic, and my mother either waited on them or sat around with them, her wavy blond hair sweeping down her back, her shoulders bare above long Gypsy dresses. They all drank heavily: the bohemian patrons as an act of defiance against the pioneer ethic, and my mother because she was unhappy. Some of her friends had written poems about her, and the words of one had been set to music. The song became part of the popular repertoire and was often played on the radio.

These cafés were no longer the haunt of the bohemian crowd. Now ordinary citizens sat at the tables drinking beer or strong coffee while pinched-looking guards kept an eye out for bulky shirts that hid suicide belts.

My father, whoever he was, had also sat at these tables. My mother's pregnancy took her by surprise; she had thought she was too old to conceive, and only when she had a desperate craving one night for a horrid sardine sandwich did it come to her, in a flash, that she was expecting. She'd always longed for a daughter but had lost faith in her parenting skills. "I thought the only thing I was still good at was surviving," I'd often heard her say. "And remembering who ordered what," she sometimes added, with a slightly ironic but melodious laugh. Now that I was on the way, however, a new faith in life seized my mother. She switched from vodka to milk and went on a fanatic health diet. And so I arrived, not blond like my mother, or even brown haired like Noah and my brother, but with a mat of tiny black curls. Apparently I was playful and well behaved. It is proba-bly not a great feat to be well behaved in a family of doting adults who want nothing so much as to kiss your toes and sing you nursery rhymes all day long.

As I was growing up, I registered, on some level, that my mother was disappointed with life, but at the same time I was filled with admiration for her. She was exotic, placid, and surrounded by friends. She deferred to Kostya on the technicalities of child-rearing, but she was unstinting in her love, and sometimes skipped work to spend the day with me in the park. "The angels took pity on me and sent me you," she often said, as she pushed me on the swings.

I asked my mother on several occasions who my father was but she always replied, vaguely, that he could have been one of a number of people. When my face appeared on the front pages of our newspapers I hoped my father would notice that I looked like him, or like one of his other daughters, if he had any: my Medusa ringlets, the pouting curve under my bottom lip, the matching indentation above my upper lip, my crescent-shaped happy-clown eyes, eyes that make it impossible for me to look sad—none of these features came from my mother. I had her high Russian forehead and straight nose, but otherwise I didn't resemble her in the least. I thought at first that the anonymous benefactor who had sent us money when I lost my hearing might in fact be my father, but my mother assured me that she had never been so fortunate as to attract the attention of anyone with money.

It occurred to me, finally, to ask her for a list of all the men she'd slept with around the time of my conception, but her memory had already started fading by then, and she wrote down the names of people in the news, people she had never met and never known. Some of them were not even alive: Ben Gurion, as I remember, was one of the candidates. I always had it in the back of my mind to do some research of my own one day and try to find out who my father was. I would pay him a visit, surprise him in the middle of dinner. I'd bring a gift, and he'd say, "I'm so happy you found me, Sonya. I never knew."

In the news: who cares!

Two weeks now since Ilanit wrote me that letter. Every time I see her with Guy I feel like vomiting. If at least she'd dumped me for someone who is semi-human. But Guy is the sort of person who will go around his whole life cheating people. He'll sell them his broken car and he'll hire Arabs and not pay them and he'll bribe inspectors to overlook whatever crooked thing he's doing. He's been through three girls already—doesn't Ilanit see that she's just the next one in line until he gets bored? Why doesn't she talk to those girls? But he's a con artist and Ilanit is too naïve, that's her problem. I miss her, though. I really really miss her. I understand a lot of those songs now, I understand how you can feel like dying when someone leaves you and you're never going to touch her boobs again or kiss her or feel her all shivery under you.

Oren says just forget it. He says the new American girl likes me but I'm not interested. I don't like the way she corrects Caroline, our English teacher. It's mean, and she does it to show off. Sonya is a million times smarter than this girl and she would never correct a teacher; it wouldn't even occur to her. She tells us at home about all kinds of funny mistakes her teachers make but she'd never correct them in public or even tell anyone outside the family.

Oh, I forgot, we have a dog now, because apparently this house was just not quite crowded and insane enough for Sonya. She found this mutt half-dead on the road—someone ran him over—so she took him to the vet and saved his life, and now she wants to keep him. He's pretty shaggy and a very quiet dog, probably quite old, and he limps because of his accident. No one else wants him around. Dad says dogs are too much work, Mom says dogs are dirty, Gran says dogs belong on farms and as for me I think we have enough problems already but Sonya always gets her own way. She asked me to think of a name for him. I suggested Limpy but she said it would hurt his feelings and remind him of his handicap. So I said well why did you ask me then so she said how about Lumpy and I said it made no difference to me she could call him King Kong for all I care. She liked that, so that's what he's called now. King Kong. He sleeps on my bed at night and I guess he's okay.

It's midnight now in our crazy house. Gran's in the kitchen drinking hot chocolate. She's been trying to write her memoirs but it's not going very well. Poor Gran. Sonya's asleep. Sometimes she talks in her sleep but she's quiet tonight. Mom's making notes in bed. She looks really exhausted and stressed lately. She's got a million cases and they're wearing her down.

Letter to Heinrich, March 11, 1957

Dear Heinrich, I have not heard from Andrei for so long! I don't want to trouble you, and I am so very grateful to you for carrying our letters back and forth with you on your visits. But I am nearly losing my mind with worry. Please send me a note and let me know what is happening. When will you be seeing Andrei again? When were you there last? We will never forget your kindness. Hoping you are well,

Anna

SONYA

My brother, who had consulted his map, drove uncertainly down the narrow streets of Jaffa. In this landscape of frail, indestructible windows and ancient walls, a car seemed intrusive—even one as old and creaky as ours. Suddenly I saw the taxi. "That's it!" I exclaimed.

My brother asked, without signing, "Where?"

"There, parked next to that building." Even before I saw the license plate I had recognized the make of the car and the silver-and-blue-pendants dangling from the rearview mirror.

"Well, the driver could be anywhere. We're nowhere near his home, if my map's accurate."

"He's probably inside that building," I said. The taxi was stationed in front of a three-story house that appeared to be some sort of community center or hall. "I'll go look," I said.

"I'll circle meanwhile," my brother signed nervously. Someone was honking impatiently behind us—I could tell by the flashes of tense distraction that shot through Kostya's body as he looked in his rearview mirror.

I let myself out quickly, walked over to the parked taxi, and peeked inside, hoping for clues. There were none, of course. If anything, the interior of the cab looked somehow aloof, as though deliberately rejecting any connection to my lover.

I pushed open the gate of a wrought-iron fence and walked down a short path of uneven flagstones set among bits of pale grass. A bronze plaque next to the door informed visitors in three languages that they were entering an institution devoted to culture and social development. Carefully, I opened the door and stepped into a spacious lobby. The tiled floor of the lobby was a complex weave of intertwining ribbons and loops and diamonds, but the colors—black, ivory, copper red, indigo, and orange—were faded now, and the floor was as unassuming as the bare walls. On my left, a wide stone staircase rose invitingly to the upper floors. Each stair dipped slightly at the center, where years of use had indented the stone. A white-haired man with watery dark blue eyes passed me on his way out. "Excuse me," I said, wishing I could address him in Arabic, "I'm looking for Nazim Sharif—he drives the taxi that's parked outside. Do you know him?"

The man nodded and pointed to the staircase. I thanked him in phrase-book Arabic and climbed the stairs. I would call my lover aside, I would speak to him: this would be a second chance. One does not often get second chances in life, but this would be the exception. And who knew where things might lead? Maybe he'd ask me to come down to his car for a ride, maybe he'd take me to his home, or to a cove somewhere. . . .

There were five rooms upstairs. Two were deserted offices and the doors of the other three were shut. I knocked on one of the doors, and since I had no way of knowing whether anyone had replied, I cautiously opened it and peeked in. A man was sitting at a large desk, talking on the phone. He was surrounded by a jumble of office paraphernalia: computer, printer, fax, photocopier, paper cutter, overhead projector, coffeemaker—one on top of the other.

Between the machines, on every available surface, tall piles of file folders were precariously stacked. A potted plant wrapped in gold foil was perched so unevenly on one of the stacks that I marveled it had not yet crashed to the floor, spilling earth everywhere. The man at the desk was absorbed in his phone conversation and didn't take any notice of me.

I had more success on the next floor, where I found a lounge. Its double doors were drawn open like curtains pulled aside to reveal a stage set. The room was filled with smoke and male bodies. The men sat at tables or on worn easy chairs; some were playing backgammon while others socialized over plates of food and soft drinks, purchased at a minimalist snack bar in the corner of the room. Twenty-seven bodies, but not one of them belonged to my lover. I approached the table nearest to the door. Immediately all the men at the table gave me their attention.

"I'm looking for Nazim Sharif," I said, "but I see he's not here." They grinned, delighted at the novelty of this mysterious summons. Just like my students, I thought: eager for entertainment, eager for any little morsel of gossip that might break the monotony of their day. They raised their arms and called out, "Nazim, Nazim." A well-dressed young man rose from a sofa by the window and came over. He was wearing a fuchsia shirt and black trousers, both very fine and expensive, and looked as if he'd just walked out of a photo shoot for a fashion magazine, or was perhaps himself the photographer. "Yes, can I help you?" he asked. The men were watching us with anticipation.

"I'm looking for the person who drives the taxi down below on the street," I said. "The white Volkswagen with the medallions."

"That's me," he said.

"Was there someone else driving this morning?"

I couldn't make out his answer—I only gathered that it had something to do with Jerusalem, and possibly with someone's mother.

I said, signing, "I'm deaf, could you please write down what you said?" I handed him my notebook.

He wasn't sure of his Hebrew and passed the notebook to an older man at the table. As he dictated his reply I could see the deflation of interest, the turning away. The men were disappointed; the mystique of the situation had evaporated. A deaf woman: clearly there was no glamorous story here. I was hurt, of course. It's hard to be demoted, even if the position you were assigned was imaginary to begin with.

The well-dressed man handed me the notebook and I read in Hebrew cursive: *That's my cousin Khalid. He was here to fill a prescription for his mother. He lives in Jerusalem.* The spelling was Arabic, with extra vowel-letters generously inserted at every opportunity.

"Do you have his address?"

But now Nazim became suspicious. He couldn't give his brother's address to a stranger, and he was also worried suddenly, and afraid. He seemed to shrink inside his lovely fuschia shirt and designer trousers.

"He gave me a ride this morning," I said. "My brother is a doctor, maybe he can help his mother." And this was true: my brother would be more than happy to look at Khalid's mother. It was something I could offer Khalid, along with my explanation.

Nazim's face brightened immediately and all the men looked at me enthusiastically. I was back in their good books, deaf or not. "Yes, yes, a doctor," they were all saying, nodding. "Thank you, God bless you. She's very sick, poor woman."

Nazim wrote down the address for me; his Hebrew was fine after all. Probably a perfectionist, as one might guess from his clothes. He didn't want to make mistakes.

I thanked them and hurried downstairs. I saw my brother's sturdy body in the distance: his car was blocking an alley, and he was standing anxiously beside it, hoping no one would need to get through. I waved and he waved back. He kept his eyes on me as I walked toward him, as if worried I might otherwise vanish into thin air.

"His name is Khalid, he lives in Jerusalem," I said. "The taxi belongs to his cousin—he just borrowed it."

"So, what now?" my brother asked.

"Jerusalem," I said.

❧ Noah's diary, July 31, 1985.

In the news: mayhem in Afula.

This gay thing is hard to sort out. I saw this German movie at the Cinematheque that I couldn't get out of my mind and I was telling Oren about it and he said maybe I'm gay. I said what about Ilanit and he said maybe I'm part gay or maybe I'm hidden gay. I don't know who came up with the idea but finally we decided to do an experiment to see whether I'm gay or not. We'd pretend to be gay (except for kissing) and if I liked it I was gay, if I didn't I wasn't. I never thought in a million years that Oren would consider such a thing, but that's his personality—he'll try anything. He even snorted cocaine twice. The first time was just last Thursday at the Boy George concert and the second time was two days later at the Joan Armatrading concert—she did an amazing "I Am Not in Love"—though he didn't tell me until later. I thought he was acting a bit strange.

But the experiment didn't work, because the results are inconclusive and unclear. I've decided not to think about it too much. The strange thing is that Oren has been hinting that he wants another round. He's definitely not gay, but he said he kept his eyes shut and pretended I was Ariella (who won't let him do that sort of thing, she almost broke up with him when he suggested it) and that it was physically pleasurable like you wouldn't believe so he'd like to do it again. But I'm not sure. Maybe I shouldn't get into the habit. Girls turn me on. But, to be perfectly honest, so do certain guys. During that German movie, I have to admit, I had a hard-on a lot of the time. Maybe I should talk to Dad. He's open-minded. He might have some insights.

Things are really crazy in Afula. It all started when this little kid from Haifa got lost and this Palestinian teenager from Jenin found him and looked after him, and he got honored by the mayor of Afula. Then this teenager started getting tormented by all his friends that he was a collaborator. They have a lot of resentment.

I guess to get everyone off his back, he and two friends of his killed these two teachers from Afula who were driving home. Talk about peer pressure. Mom says no one would be surprised if they knew more about the lives of Palestinians, but no one cares. She *always* sticks up for them, she really has no balance at all.

Then all the Kahane people went crazy—it took 100 police officers to control them. Actually even before the bodies were found they were already standing outside the police station shouting, "Kahane! Kahane!" and attacking Arabs. I can't believe this Kahane guy is actually in our Knesset, even people on the right say he's a lunatic.

Anyway, the Arabs were afraid to leave their houses or go to work. They interviewed one guy who runs a falafel stand in Afula right opposite the police station. He said he'd be lynched if he went to work. Then the homes of those three boys from Jenin were demolished by the army, even though the mayor of Jenin risked his life to make statements against the murder and offer his help, etc. Then one of the Kahanist rioters who was arrested and released went to get some good deals in Nablus and he got shot in the back, and now the Kahanists are rioting again and attacking journalists because they say it's their fault for putting a picture of the rioter in the paper.

I'm glad I don't live in Afula.

Come to think of it, I don't actually know any Arabs. I *hear* about them all the time from Mom, but I never see them except once in a blue moon on TV. Oren does—his family goes shopping all the time in Palestinian towns and they've become friends with a few of the storekeepers and their families. Also, an Arab woman from Jaffa cleans their flat. But Dad cleans our place himself and he's not into scouting for better prices. He never checks the price of anything. "If I want it, I buy it," he says at the supermarket, loading our cart with all these expensive jams and cheeses and things. "This is why I work."

Dearest, the wait is becoming intolerable. I wrote to Heinrich last week, asking for news. I hope he will not think it rude of me to question him on his schedule. I am just so very impatient! But I know he is doing his best.

I have some news: I've switched restaurants! I was caught stealing. Actually they've known for months, but kept me all the same, I don't know why. I was very lucky: they didn't call the police—though I'm not afraid of the police here, darling! They all look like such nice boys and you feel they're on your side, not against you. The owners didn't even get angry. I think they realized these extra treats were all for Kostya, whom they've met several times and liked. I had sensed all along that I was not in any great danger, and that is why I took the chance. In fact, I have a feeling that I was fired for some other reason. Maybe a family relative needs the job.

But this was the best thing that could have happened to me, because I'm now working at a café that just opened up, the most interesting place to work in the entire city, I think. I got this job through Orlando. All sorts of talented artists and writers and musicians congregate here. This is a much better job for me, and though I only started last week, I have already been asked to sing once an evening. It started quite by accident, when I pointed out that a song someone was singing was originally Russian—at least the melody. And I sang the original. The owner was so pleased that he asked me to sing a Russian song each night. It turns out that many Hebrew songs have borrowed Russian melodies, and those are the ones everyone likes to hear. Thanks to my singing, which attracts customers, I received a small raise.

I bought a dress with the few extra pounds. I should have spent it on books for Kostya, but I have not had a new dress since I arrived, and it was very cheap. A long, flowered off-the-shoulders dress—I couldn't resist. How I yearn for you to see me in it, to run your hands down my body . . .

Kostya brought a friend for supper, which he cooked entirely himself! A red-haired boy, covered from head to toe with freckles. I've never seen such a freckled person. Maybe the sun brings out freckles here if one has a natural tendency to that sort of pigmentation. I suppose fair-haired people were never really meant to live so close to the equator. I find I need to hide constantly under wide-brimmed hats and sunglasses and light cotton shawls in order to avoid the sun, for even the tops of my feet burn between the straps of my sandals!

It was a lovely evening. Kostya made all sorts of dishes that Carmela has taught him to prepare, and with the most affordable ingredients. Everything was delicious. The two boys spoke about politics the entire time. Imagine knowing so much about that sort of thing at age twelve! Children here are quite astute. They worry a great deal about war. They are constantly afraid of war breaking out, they seem to think it's an ever-present danger, just waiting around the corner. Kostya is only slightly more optimistic than his friend. His friend is frightened every time his parents leave the house—what if war breaks out while they're away? Kostya assured him that there will be some warning signs and we'll know at least a few weeks in advance, but he agrees that it's quite likely there will be a major war sooner or later.

I can't form an opinion because I don't follow the news at all. I've just had all the news I can take, it seems! I am constantly counting our money and trying to figure out what we can afford, and that takes up all my concentration. I have to admit that even if I wanted to follow the news I wouldn't be able to, because I can't read most of the newspapers here— the Hebrew ones are all printed without vocalization and it makes me dizzy just trying to decipher the headlines. Kostya sometimes reads articles aloud to me, but I'm afraid my mind wanders. It's all so complicated! One minister says this, another says that, there are so many parties . . . I will only hope for the best.

I am very happy about one thing, however. I have heard that soldiers here can choose not to go into combat! And what's even better, in the case of only children, the parent must agree to let the son go into combat, I believe. That is a great relief, for I shall never give my permission, never. I know it's very selfish of me, for why should someone else lose her son and not me? Why should another young man die defending us in place of Kostya? But there you are, that's how I feel. I suppose I am very unpatriotic. If I told people, I'm sure they would be so disgusted they'd never speak to me again. One man here lost his three sons in a single week during the War of Independence and now he's alone and never speaks to anyone. There are many such sad stories, but I'm afraid they don't change my passionate feelings about Kostya. I tell myself he can contribute to this state in many other ways, with all his talents, but I know that is merely an excuse. The truth is that I am too selfish to give him up and too selfish on his behalf to let him give himself up.

Next week is Olga's birthday. I am enclosing a handkerchief I embroidered for her. Do you like the little chicks? I was pleased with the way they came out. Darling. Where are you?

❧ SONYA

I don't know about you, Sonya, but I'm famished," Kostya said. "I haven't had lunch. How about a bite before we head out for Jerusalem?"

"Sure," I said. My brother suggested an Italian restaurant near the American embassy, which he said had excellent food. I was very impatient and would have preferred grabbing falafel at a stand, but it made me happy to see my brother garnering some pleasure from life.

He drove to a gravel parking lot, paid the attendant, and parked the car. I had a sudden craving for a cigarette, though I had only ever smoked for six months when I was fourteen. Kostya had found out and made me stop. "I want a cigarette," I said.

"You'll regret it," Kostya said as we walked to the restaurant. "Besides, we'll be eating soon."

"I said I wanted a cigarette," I declared petulantly. "I didn't say I was going to smoke one. Bossy!"

"Sorry."

"I wonder whether Noah's lapsed." Noah had quit only recently. He'd phoned Kostya from Berlin and said, 'I'm in the bath, and I'm smoking my last cigarette.' Then, with Kostya as symbolic witness, he drowned the rest of the pack in the soapy water.

"Probably not. Decisiveness runs in the family."

Only one street separated us from the sea, and the air seemed lighter here, like faded batik. At the same time, this part of the city always looked a little lopsided to me, as if the buildings were tilting ever so slightly toward the road; the effect, as in a Cubist painting, was both claustrophobic and friendly.

It was dark and cool inside the Italian restaurant. The reassuring smell of firewood and garlic made me think of the large hardcover edition of *Pinocchio* my mother gave me on my fourth birthday. The detailed illustrations, with their warm, damp colors, looked as if they'd have exactly this smell.

My brother seemed disappointed that the table near the window was taken. He was suddenly very emotional; a huge cloak of sadness fell over his shoulders. We sat down in the corner of the room and I looked into his eyes. He looked away. He was thinking about other things.

The waitress knew my brother. She greeted him with enthusiasm and I saw her saying that she hadn't seen him in a long time. My brother answered politely, with feigned detachment. When she left I asked him what was going on.

"I used to come here every week to have dinner with a friend."

"You mean your famous Wednesday nights?"

"Yes. We used to eat here."

"Someone you were going out with?" He'd never wanted to talk about his weekly outings, and this had naturally aroused my curiosity—was he taking a course, doing volunteer work, playing chess with an opponent who offered him a chance of winning occasionally? I assumed it was something he was embarrassed about—but what could possibly embarrass Kostya? He was the most self-accepting person I knew. I would have nagged him to tell me, but he respected my privacy and I was forced, unfortunately, to respect his. One thing was certain: he was not secretly meeting a married woman, given his strong feelings on the subject.

"She was married. You know her, in fact. Or of her. She's the one whose husband was missing for many years, because he'd been burned in an army accident. Dana Hillman. Remember that story?"

"Yes, of course. We talked about it—and you didn't say a word, Kostya. You didn't say you knew her."

"It was clear from the start that she loved her husband, and that she'd never give up waiting for him. I was sure he'd killed himself but she was convinced he was alive."

"Were you lovers? If that's not too personal."

"No, just friends. I loved her, though. I think she knew that, but she didn't want to think about it. In any case, she was a lot younger than me."

"How sad, Kostya!" I reached across the table and touched his arm. "I wish you'd told me."

"There wasn't anything to tell."

"Such bad luck, sweetheart."

He nodded; we were both thinking not only of his love for Dana, but also of Iris. I was fifteen when Iris was murdered. It happened outside Elkanah, a settlement just east of the Green Line. She was on her way to see a client in Mas'ha, a small Palestinian town next to Elkanah, and she stopped at the Elkanah gas station to fill up. She decided to park her car there and walk to the town, which was just down the road. It was a warm autumn evening. She had meant to see her client during the day, but as usual she was overworked and had been delayed.

She didn't notice that she was being followed from her office in Tel Aviv. Or else she noticed, but with her usual fearlessness she shrugged it off. By the time she returned to her car, after the meeting with her client, it was already dark. She couldn't see the man crouching in the back of the car. She sat down in the driver's seat and the man shot her in the back of the head and vanished.

Iris took on dangerous, complicated cases, and the police told us that there were so many candidates for the murderer that it was hard to know where to start the investigation. Sometimes she defended her clients against fanatic Jewish settlers; but I knew it was unlikely that a settler would kill another Jew, in spite of their wild rhetoric. The police thought her murderer might have been someone who considered one of her clients a collaborator. That seemed even more far-fetched. My brother told us that he knew who had murdered Iris, or rather, had sent a hired killer to murder her; she'd received two explicit death threats just before she was shot. But he didn't bother informing the police. No one would believe him, he said, and even if evidence turned up, the judges would probably be bribed or threatened. Apart from her work on behalf of Arabs, Iris was involved in uncovering financial and political scandals among powerful Israelis; those cases were almost always linked, at some inevitable point, to the underworld. My brother didn't tell us who the culprit was. He was afraid Noah would spend the rest of his life looking for justice, and it would be a waste of time, he said, a waste of a life.

When the police came to our little ramshackle house to inform us that Iris had "gone to her world," as they put it, my brother thanked them, made himself a cup of coffee, then walked out to the garden Iris had loved and uprooted every single plant; the ones he couldn't pull out with his bare hands he dug out with a spade. The wilted flowers, dislodged bushes, and rotting vegetables lay there like a throbbing graveyard for several weeks. One afternoon, while my brother was at the hospital, Noah and I got rid of the mess. We borrowed a neighbor's pickup truck and made several trips to the dump until there was nothing left of my brother's anguished act. The two of us stood on the porch when it was over and looked silently at the barren strip of earth. Clearing the yard had been a spontaneous decision: we hadn't discussed it ahead of time. Noah said, "I'm going into the paratroopers brigade. Dad's already signed." We fought then; not just argued, but actually fought: I kicked him, he kicked me back, I picked up a dictionary and smacked his head, he twisted my arm behind my back, I bit him. For three years after that we weren't on speaking terms.

"It's funny," Kostya said, changing the unspoken subject. "Dana kept trying to persuade me to wear more casual clothes. She was always going on about it, but I refused to give in. The week after we parted I bought a pair of jeans. Maybe I thought it would bring her back. Or maybe it was a way of feeling close to her, or . . . do you think I was just being stubborn?"

"All three," I laughed. The waitress came to take our order. I wasn't hungry and asked only for tea. I signed my request and the waitress was pleased with herself for understanding me.

"Maybe you really are in love," my brother teased.

"Just be a good boy and eat your dinner."

Despite appearances, my brother did in fact have a sex life. It's impossible to live with someone and not know these things. He had a sexual relationship with Tali, a lively woman who worked with him at the hospital and was about his age. She was separated and had four children, one of whom was in the army. My brother slept with her every Saturday night and came home at four o'clock the following morning. I wondered whether it hurt Tali that he always left before sunrise or whether she was the one who asked him to go. Maybe it was a mutually convenient arrangement.

"How's your lasagna?" I asked him.

"It's okay, but it's been made by the replacement chef. He's not as good as their regular one."

"How can you tell?"

"He has a different style. The regular chef uses more spices, he balances them better."

"Listen," I said, "I think I need to write a letter to Khalid, in case he's not home. I don't want to go all the way to Jerusalem for nothing—I want to leave him a letter if he's not home. And the letter needs to be in Arabic. I'll phone Raya and see if she can do it for me."

"This whole project seems misguided to me," Kostya said.

I ignored him and texted Raya. *I need something in Arabic,* I sent.

"Come on over," she answered.

"It'll be easier to walk to her place than look for parking," Kostya said. "Or else I can drop you off and pick you up a bit later."

"Oh, come on, Kostya, be brave. Raya won't bite. Or at least, not hard."

In the news: I don't know.

I am ten minutes away from a complete and total mental break-down. These have been the worst three weeks of my life and proba-bly anyone's life. I came home from school and right away I thought someone was dead, I thought Sonya had died because Dad was sort of crying in the kitchen and Sonya was in the hospital and I swear my heart stopped beating. Dad said right away, "No one's died." Then I was relieved for about half a second before he breaks the news to me, Sonya's deaf and she's never going to hear again.

And it's the fault of the fucking damned idiot toilet, fuck it to hell, because now it turns out that Sonya got her kidney problems from not going when she had to go and not drinking enough and she did that because she was afraid of the noise and there was some sort of mistake in the hospital and her kidneys didn't flush out the drugs and that's why she went deaf. Once in August I remember I finished all the water when we went biking and she wanted some but I wasn't in the mood to go back, because I said to myself, who asked her to come along in the first place? But Dad says that it wasn't one time, he says she's had bad habits for years. He says it's no one's fault except the person who gave her the overdose of the drug. Still, I can tell he's feeling bad because he never got anyone to fix the toilet but nobody knew she was scared of it. She didn't say anything until the doctor at the hospital talked to her when she first got there and then it came out.

Meanwhile Sonya is a total mental case. First when she came home she was very calm, waiting for her hearing to come back. Then finally she wrote Dad a note. He was washing lettuce, I was there in the kitchen, he was washing dirt off this big lettuce from the garden and Sonya comes in with this note, *How soon until I can hear again?*

So Dad wipes his hands and sits down and he writes: *You were accidentally given a massive dose of gentamicin at the hospital— no one knows how it happened. The drug damaged the eighth nerve (organ of hearing). The damage is irreversible. We've all started learning sign language. We'll all help you.*

So she's still very calm and she says pathetically, shouting a bit, "But there's noise in my head. I'm not really deaf."

But Dad right away has to tell her the truth. I would never have had the guts. I would have lied and given her some hope. But he writes, *That's internal noise. It's not coming from outside. Your hearing is gone for good. There's promising work being done on technology to repair hearing through implants, but it's hard to say when that will be available, or how well it will work.*

Sonya went completely crazy. First she ran outside and stood on the road with her arms stretched out, and this poor guy almost ran her over but he swerved and went into a honeysuckle bush instead. Everyone came out, of course, huge commotion. Mom lost her temper completely, shook Sonya and yelled at her, but I came to her rescue. How could Mom be so insensitive? I don't understand her sometimes. Meanwhile Dad had to give that poor guy first aid. He was shaking and had his hand on his chest and Dad said it was lucky he didn't have a heart attack.

Then lots of tantrums, breaking dishes, kicking doors, for about three days nonstop. She almost broke her violin but Dad managed to save it just in time. Finally I think she just got exhausted. But instead of going back to normal she gave up. She won't do a thing, it's as if she's two years old. We have to feed her with a spoon and someone has to sleep with her, Gran can't do it all the time because Sonya thrashes and cries all night and clutches your clothes. So Gran and Mom and I take turns, though mostly it's me and King Kong because Mom is tired. I haven't had a decent night's sleep in three weeks. I try to imagine what it's like to go deaf suddenly and I can't. I tried shutting the sound on the TV to get an idea, and I admit it was scary and I can see why Sonya is scared. She even needs someone to go to the bathroom with her, she's totally regressed. I go with her, though it's incredibly embarrassing but I just turn away and she's so pathetic that who cares. I realized she can't hear herself going and so it's as if I can't hear her either. I'm worried that she'll stay crazy forever or maybe the pills also damaged her brain?? Maybe she's autistic now!! I have to ask Dad. If I believed in God I'd pray now. Please at least don't give her brain damage. But if God is so mean as to make her deaf in the first place, why would He listen to what I wanted or what anyone wanted? I'd do anything to hear her play the violin again—I feel so bad that I complained. Instead she just drools and rocks.

I think soon there will be two crazy people in the house because I am losing my mind slowly but surely. I started crying in class when the teacher read us a sad poem by Dan Pagis and I had to pretend I was sick so I could run out of class. Oren came out after me and found me in the washroom and put his arm around me and he kissed my ear. I don't know how much longer I can keep this up. By the way, Ilanit has been coming up to me quite a lot to say how sorry she is and can she help. I wonder whether Guy is starting to get tired of her or whether she just feels sorry for me. I would even say she was hinting she wants us to get back together. Maybe she figured out what a total jerk Guy is, and how he's just using her. But I can't think about that now. I dreamed Sonya was dead and I woke up and saw that she really was lying very still so I put my ear on her chest to see if her heart was still beating. But her boobs got in the way. They felt good under her flannel pajamas so I rested my head on them and drifted off. Oh, man, on top of everything else I'm turning into a pervert.

Letter to Andrei, March 22, 1957

My heart and soul, no word yet from you or Heinrich, but I shall go on writing to you under the assumption that there has been some holdup and eventually you will receive all my letters. I can only assume that Heinrich has stayed longer than planned in Moscow and is still with you. It is really too bad that we must wait so long! I know you are as anxious to hear from me as I am from you.

With only one day to opening night, Kostya and I were forced to move! The plumbing system here collapsed and the entire building was flooded. It happened while I was at work and when I came home I had to wade through ankle-high water to get to our room. Luckily I lost nothing, at least nothing that can't be dried out, like my winter shoes. Kostya's beloved teddy, the one we hid the money in during our daring escape, is soaked through, but a few days in the sun should fix him. This poor teddy has been through a lot. . . .

In any case, we have found a much better place, thanks as usual to Carmela. Really, it was about time we left that gloomy neighborhood. I am now in a very nice part of Tel Aviv, downtown, on a street with the lovely name Spinoza! I do like telling people that I live on Spinoza Street—it makes me feel very distinguished. In fact, we are now in Carmela's building—an old man who was living on the top floor died last week and his son is renting the place. I have mixed feelings about having Carmela as a close neighbor, but Kostya likes her and they can continue with their cooking projects much more easily. In this country it's the higher apartments that are cheaper instead of the other way around, because people don't like to climb the stairs to the top.

We still have only one room but it's much bigger, very cleverly designed, and there is also a much larger balcony, with a lovely garden below and a tall tree that touches the balcony, which makes it cool and pleasant. We are a ten-minute walk from the sea and much closer to Kostya's school. Best of all, the apartment came with a bed, a table, two chairs, and a gigantic bookcase—one of those old heavy pieces—which Kostya cleverly decided to use as a partition wall so that he has his own private corner now.

Luckily we have very few belongings and with Carmela's help we were able to carry everything in four trips. People were so kind and helpful on the bus! Everyone gave us a hand. It's a good thing, because I need all my energy for tomorrow. I am so afraid of not remembering my few lines. I am happy to be playing a comic character, however, for a change!

Guess what? There are no cockroaches in this apartment! That is, there are a few here and there, hiding under the sink or on the stairs—but not the infestation we had in our old place.

I await all your news, dearest.

SONYA

On the way to Raya's we stopped at a bakery and bought her a bag of almond cookies. Raya loves to eat; she's particularly obsessed with Kostya's lemon meringue pie, and he would always make it for her when she came over. I often told my brother that Raya was half in love with him and entirely in love with his food. She would invite herself for dinner and sit at the table like a child at a birthday party, stuffing herself in polite Arab fashion. She never gained weight, though, because she was so active.

Raya's apartment on the sixth floor was a cruel joke on hot days. You dragged yourself up the stairs, wondering whether you'd expire before you reached the summit. Clearly, this was another thing that kept Raya slim; my brother and I were both gasping for air by the time we reached the top floor. "I'm out of shape," my brother said, ringing the bell. "I need to get back to tennis, or jogging, or something."

"It's the heat," I assured him. "It makes it harder to breathe."

"I miss Noah," he said. He had played tennis with Noah, a long time ago.

Raya opened the door with an enthusiastic exclamation. She had just stepped out of the shower; she had a towel wrapped around her head, and her silk purple bathrobe clung to her skin in wet patches. She began doing an East Indian dance to match her turban, and singing "Ein Ani," a song by Fools of Prophecy that borrowed heavily from Indian music. It was from one of her favorite CDs and she had acquired the score for me so I could (in theory) share in her pleasure. *"Ein ani, ein ani, ein ani,"* she sang. There is no I, there is no I. Raya had a number of faults: she was impatient, she drove her several boyfriends crazy with jealousy, and she was easily vexed. A broken coffee machine drove her into a small frenzy; even a pen that didn't write properly could elicit an impressive supply of swear words—accompanied, if I was with her, by rather imaginative signing. But her capacity for love was astounding to me. I'd never known anyone to love, truly love, so many people. This included me.

Raya was the only person outside my family who had studied Sign for my sake. Even my poor mother had never managed to pick it up; her memory was already on the wane when I lost my hearing, and she had relied on Kostya and Noah, who were both proficient, to translate for her. And Iris was too overworked to learn, though she reproached herself for not finding the time and continually apologized. I think she felt particularly guilty because she always resented me a little. I had been imposed on her, and my appearance on the scene may have prevented her from having another child of her own.

Signing did not come easily to Raya, and she often supplemented signing with writing, but she tried hard. She said it was fun learning a new language that was so poetic and expressive, and not entirely unrelated to belly dancing, her preferred after-hours pastime. Raya had grown up in the suburbs of Cairo, where each house was a walled-in fortress and the favorite adult activity was hosting or attending lawn parties within those walls. Diplomats and artists, businessmen and professionals, married couples and single men accompanied by their beautiful girlfriends would spend the evening talking and eating eggplant caviar near the pool. The children chased fireflies and planned mischievous pranks which they never had the guts to carry out. Raya's cook was a favorite with her friends because she terrified them all with gruesome, vaguely prurient stories about white slavery.

When Raya was sixteen her father was offered a job in California, but Raya wanted to stay in the Middle East. Her secret dream had always been to live in Jerusalem, heart of the world's mysteries. Luckily, her mother was Jewish, though she'd converted to Islam when she married Raya's father; taking advantage of her convenient ancestry, Raya acquired Israeli citizenship and moved to East Jerusalem, where she lived with an adoptive family her parents had found for her. She finished high school at a private seminary and went on to study math at Hebrew University.

Though Raya loved Jerusalem, no one was surprised when she moved to Tel Aviv. Jerusalem was beautiful, she said, but too austere—like a choral mass: fine when you were in an austere sort of mood yourself, but not something you'd want to take on as a lifestyle. Raya wore showy, extravagant clothes; she had a mutinous sense of humor; and at parties she entertained everyone with her belly dancing. But her complicated identity was a continual source of distress to her. She once told me she was living evidence that the concept of the nation-state was unworkable and basically inhuman.

My brother said hello and Raya kissed him provocatively on the lips; she was not his type, however. She kissed me on the mouth, too; the concept of restraint was foreign to Raya. She was the only teacher in our department who got away with hugging and kissing students, or touching their arms and ruffling their hair. This was partly because women were less vulnerable to harassment charges, partly because she was so public about her demonstrative behavior, but mostly because her students loved it and had come to expect it, like cats waiting to be patted. And if she had a particularly untouchable student, someone who was religious, for example, or cold and angry, she kept a respectful distance, though not without teasing them a little.

"So, what's this translation you need?" she asked. Like Kostya, she spoke as she signed.

"I'll explain later. It's complicated."

Her flat consisted of three rooms: a tiny vestibule into which Raya had managed to squeeze a narrow bed and a television; a kitchenette to the right of the vestibule; and a main room up ahead that served as dining area, study, and bedroom. By downtown Tel Aviv standards it was a desirable flat: air-conditioning, solid plumbing, sunlight pouring in through the windows, and two large balconies with panoramic views of the city. From one balcony it was possible to see a startling patch of sea, naked and ethereal, hovering between two buildings.

We entered the main room. I was not surprised to see that Raya had another visitor: people continually streamed in and out of Raya's flat, at all times of day and night. This had led to some turbulent situations in which a lapse in visitor coordination had resulted in two lovers crossing paths.

Today a woman with shoulder-length blond hair and a sad mouth was sitting cross-legged on the bed looking at a newspaper spread out in front of her. Her age was difficult to determine: she looked young because she was slight and somewhat delicate, with narrow shoulders and thin wrists, but her blond hair was streaked with gray. There was something self-effacing about her, as if she didn't want to stand out, but she achieved the opposite effect. Her feet, peeking out from her jeans, were small and almost luminous, like polished stone. Though I was sure I had never met her before, she seemed vaguely familiar. I sifted through my memory and found her in a photograph at someone's house. Ibrahim's. A group photo with several other people.

As if to confirm my retrieval, Raya said, "This is Lily, a friend of Ibrahim's from London. She's the one who got shot in the leg by those lunatic settlers last year." The woman looked up and smiled hello.

"How horrible! I remember that story. Are you all right?" I asked her.

"Yes, I was lucky, the bullet just grazed me," Lily said. Raya translated, but it wasn't necessary; I had understood.

Raya said, signing only, "She's staying with Ibrahim. He says it's platonic. . . ." She looked doubtful.

I do not approve, really, of secret signing; people sense that you're talking about them and feel hurt or confused. But Lily didn't notice. She had returned to her newspaper, which seemed to absorb her completely.

My brother handed Raya the small bag of cookies. With elegant fingers, the fingers of a belly dancer, she fished out the little spiral discs. "Yummy, yummy. Okay, I'm ready for dictation."

Raya and I sat at the round all-purpose table. My brother approached Lily and asked her for a part of the newspaper. He sat down at the end of the bed and the two of them began to discuss something or other—probably one of the news stories.

I knew my brother found Raya a little overbearing, though of course he would never say anything; he was pleased that I had a close friend. When I was younger he used to drag me to all sorts of events for the deaf: dances, movie nights, discussion groups, courses, signed plays. At one point he even gave cooking classes in Sign, for one of the local organizations. I was his assistant, cracking eggs and bad jokes, and making sure everyone understood his instructions. I was never very enthusiastic about these forays into identity-by-functionality, as I called it. "I'm not deaf, I'm Sonya," I would announce, rather pompously. I did meet some very nice people, including extraordinarily courageous men who had not only lost their hearing in battle but were also paraplegic or blind or dependent on all sorts of medical devices. But friendship is a mysterious thing; it falls from the sky like the Snow Queen's shard, except that it warms you instead of freezing you. "Fusspot," my brother would reprimand me. "No one ever meets your standards." And I would defend myself: "Just because

I'm deaf, I'm supposed to be less particular?" He'd smile, because in fact he was exactly like me. He'd never had more than one or two close friends.

Then Raya was hired at the university, two years after I joined the department. I was on the hiring committee when she was interviewed, and as soon as she walked into the room I knew we'd get along. She wore jeans and a white T-shirt with a drawing of a coffin and the words COST OF OCCUPATION: DO THE MATH printed below the coffin, and she brought delicious butter cookies to the interview, which she handed out. "If you don't hire me, at least I'll know it wasn't because you were hungry," she said. No one minded. The math department is full of eccentrics.

When the semester began I invited her over for dinner. She arrived with tulips, chocolates, and a subtitled video of *Casablanca*. Over the course of the evening—or rather evening and night, for she stayed until three in the morning—she ate nonstop and talked nonstop. My brother translated and she picked up her first few signs that evening. I was surprised at the time to discover that she was twelve years older than me.

"'Dear Khalid,'" I dictated to Raya, "'My name is Sonya (Sophia). I'm thirty-two, I teach math at the university. I've been deaf since I was twelve. I took an allergy pill this morning and it made me sleepy, that's why I fell asleep in your cousin's car. I was in a very strange mood, I don't know what came over me.'"

Raya stopped me. *"What nuance do you want for 'mood'?"* she wrote on a separate sheet of paper. *"Emotional state? Or spiritual state?"*

"Emotional, I guess . . . 'I apologize for my behavior. I've never done anything like that before. A long time ago I had an unfortunate experience, which is why you thought you weren't my first partner, but I have never had a boyfriend—'"

Raya stopped writing and looked up at me, her eyes widening.

"'—and I came here to say I'm sorry. I hope we can be friends because I really like you, but if you don't want to, that's okay. I don't know more than a few words in Arabic, so my best friend Raya is writing this letter for me. With many wishes for your good health and happiness, Sonya, sonya@zera.net.il.'"

Raya grinned at me. *"So you finally did it!"* she wrote in huge letters beneath her question about the word for *mood.*

"I'm such a fool," I said. "I should have explained, talked to him, but I wasn't thinking. He got scared and ran away."

"He's the one who's a fool, if he was anything less than courteous and grateful."

"Don't say that. He was very nice. But he thought I was lying when I told him he was my first lover, and he also didn't know I was deaf."

"How could he not know?" she said.

"He wasn't talkative."

"How did you meet him?"

"He was driving his cousin's taxi and he drove me home from the university. I left my briefcase in the car, he ran after me, I invited him in. After sex he panicked and ran away."

She laughed. *"Probably afraid your brother or husband would come home and kill him."*

"No, he was afraid of me."

"Well, how was it, darling Sonya?"

"Too short," I signed emphatically, and we both burst out laughing. There are times when Sign is irreplaceable; words could never have conveyed so perfectly crude carnality, romantic longing and schoolgirl humor all at once.

"Well, too bad it was such an imperfect start, but all first times are like that. You've heard my stories . . . ," she wrote.

"I think I love him," I said.

"Oh, no," she said. *"Okay, I'm not saying anything more,"* she wrote. *"This should be interesting."*

"How's Rami?" Rami was her current favorite lover, a religious married man who wrote a column about impoverished people in the newspaper. Each week he focused on another family or person in dire circumstances: a woman and her baby living in a pigeon coop, an immigrant who had to rely on a blanket for a door, a foreign worker sleeping under a parked truck to escape the rain. At first readers had come forward to offer assistance, but the trend didn't last: there were too many cases and too few people with the means to help. Almost no one I knew still read Rami's columns.

Raya pulled the towel off her hair and gave her head a vehement shake, as if drawing pleasure from the release. She picked up the pen and replied, *"Yeah, he's okay. His wife just gave birth to triplets. Took a fertility pill so she wouldn't have to have sex too often. Apparently a lot of them do that, the religious women. Can you imagine? Can you imagine someone hating sex so much she'd rather give birth to three babies at once than have sex?"*

"Depends on the husband! I have to go, Raya. Thank you."

"You're going to give him the letter?"

"Yes."

"I still think you have nothing to apologize for."

"I just want to give myself a second chance."

Lily and my brother were still talking; they had not been listening to our exchange. I knew my brother had struck up a conversation with Lily in order to ensure my privacy, though I really didn't mind if this tranquil woman heard my story. But now I could see that whatever his initial motive had been, Kostya was enjoying Lily's company.

"Would you like some scrambled eggs?" Raya asked, using her own invented sign for "scrambled."

"Thanks, we just ate," I said. "And I'm impatient to go."

"How will you find him?"

"We did some detective work. He lives in East Jerusalem."

"Good luck, sweetheart."

I summoned my brother. For the first time ever, he seemed reluctant to leave Raya's flat.

*In the news: there was a nuclear accident in the
Soviet Union, they're saying only two people died
but everyone says it's hundreds and the clouds are
spreading all over the place. What if that sort of
thing happens here!? Everyone knows we've got
reactors in Dimona.*

Things are different now that Oren's moved to Herzliya. I'm bored
at school and I've stopped studying for exams. I know I should be
studying but I can't concentrate. Instead I just laze about doodling
and watching TV in Sonya's room. I don't really care much but I
need to pass high school to get into Bezalel. Dad thinks I should go
into costume design and not fashion design and he may be right. Not
for the reasons he says (art versus capitalism blah blah) but because
of last night. Last night Oren and I went to see Nina Hagen at the
Liquid Disco. We were really lucky because we couldn't get tickets
the first two nights, and last night she was supposed to be in
Jerusalem, but they couldn't sell any tickets there, so she did another
show in Tel Aviv instead.

People came all dressed up to impress each other and themselves, and she was wearing a shiny pink leotard with tiny light bulbs on the nipples, not the outfit I would have chosen for her. Punk has enormous possibilities but you have to know how to make predictability ironic, if that makes sense. Everyone was hoping she'd undress on stage and get off like she used to do, but she probably doesn't trust Israelis not to be obnoxious and she's right. Besides, she doesn't do that stuff so much since she moved to the States—her agent must have told her it wouldn't go over too well there. Anyway, the whole scene turned me off. People were just trying too hard. They thought they were being original and cool but they were just copying one another. As far as I'm concerned, it would have been more original to come dressed in a bar mitzvah suit. So I'm thinking Dad's right. I'd rather do theater where you have to fit the costume to the play and not the other way round.

Dad is calling me. I told him I'm busy at the moment. That will keep him quiet for at least half an hour. He wants to grill me on my "homework situation." He's enlisted Sonya to help me with physics and trig, not that I don't understand but I've fallen a bit behind. Luckily she already did these exams last year, so she knows what I have to cover. She's a good teacher, I have to say. She knows how to explain things and she's very patient.

She's coping amazingly well with being deaf now and no longer seems in the least bit unhappy. After all those dramatics, which scared us all half to death, she's decided that being deaf is no big deal. In her place I'd be depressed for the rest of my life, maybe I'd even kill myself or go live on some island somewhere with King Kong and a few other dogs and a horse, but she's in a good mood most of the time, just like before.

Actually, the strange thing is that she's a little more normal than she was before. You'd think she'd get weirder but the opposite has happened. She's actually acting like other people now. I guess she doesn't want to be left out more than necessary, so is making more of an effort. She stopped bringing lizards to school "to keep her company," finally got a haircut, has lost all the extra weight and started going to her own parties instead of tagging along on mine, no longer walks around the house in her underwear or draws goofy faces on her stomach and hands, doesn't announce at the dinner table that she got her period or clown around with her food. Our house is more normal too, because Dad hired someone to do repairs, even though we have to pay for it and it's not deducted from our rent. We have some interest now from the money Sonya got from the secret donor (probably the doctor who gave her the drug, that's my guess), and that's what she wants to spend it on. She still sleeps next to Gran but I think it's more for Gran's sake, not hers.

At first when she talked she shouted and sounded weird, but now she has speech therapy and she's back to sounding the same as before. You'd never know she was deaf. Funny to have to learn to talk all over again. She absolutely refused to go to a special school, so Dad found this old lady who looks like an apricot to teach her Sign and to accompany her to our regular school. Dad and I are still working on our signing. It's really hard but interesting, like a secret language.

Sonya also pretends she can't lipread but she can. I catch her lipreading all the time and she also knows if people are speaking Hebrew or English or some other language. Dad says it's important to talk as we sign, even though it's not always easy to do, it takes practice. But Dad says Sonya wants to know exactly what we're saying because she wasn't born deaf and spoken language will always be her first language.

They say if you lose one faculty the others get better. Well, it's true. Sonya can read people's minds—she knows what they're thinking and feeling just by looking at them. We were watching a newscaster on TV and she tells me, "He's holding in a sneeze." There was absolutely nothing about him to indicate that he was going to sneeze, but a few seconds later he did. Or at the supermarket this woman walked out with her kid and Sonya said, "She's stolen something."

She hadn't seen the woman stealing but she could tell by the way she was walking or the look on her face. Four days later the store detective caught this woman. She can read my mind too, a little. She knows when Dad's driving me crazy, even though I do my best not to show it and not even to feel it. "Don't plague Noah. He's very sensitive," she jokes around. She can even tell I'm hungry sometimes. If it was anyone else I'd get nervous, but Sonya doesn't use anything she sees or knows against people, she just notices and that's it, it ends there.

In the beginning she tried to get into fights with me and it really insulted her when I didn't fight back because that meant I was feeling sorry for her. But I *do* feel sorry for her, I can't help it! Well, I guess she finally figured out that I really, really don't want to fight with her and she gave up. I have to admit, now that she's acting more normal and got a haircut and lost weight and everything, she's quite good-looking. If anyone takes advantage of her I will kill them with my own bare hands.

I must tell you about our opening night, dearest! It was a resounding success, with standing ovations. There was such a flood of people coming to buy tickets when we opened the box office! We sold out immediately and we had to turn many disappointed people away. We couldn't sell any tickets for tomorrow's show because the tickets didn't arrive from the printer—not even today's tickets. We finally had to make them ourselves, by hand. Kostya and his friends helped because it was a frantic rush to get them done in time.

The credit all goes to Feingold. He used our low budget to great advantage, creating the entire set and costumes out of ribbons. We wore only white: white slips or white frocks for the women, white gatkes (long thermal underwear) and undershirts for the men. The colored ribbons were clothes, borders, water, walls, tug-of-war ropes, love letters on trees, and you see—we were all intertwined! All connected in one way or another. It had to be carefully choreographed, and our last rehearsal was such a disaster that we were quite worried. And yet, as often happens, under the pressure of a real audience we rose to the occasion.

I did forget one line. No one noticed but I was very disappointed in myself. It's just lucky for me that people are not familiar with this text.

Kostya enjoyed himself very much. He was an usher.

Being an usher is a very difficult job in this country, as everyone pushes in. Lines don't form in an orderly fashion: people just congregate in one place, such as a bus stop, in a chaotic, random way, and it's impossible to know who came first and who came last. Then when the line begins to move—let's say it's the line to the bus—everyone begins to shove, trying to get on. People press against each other with great intimacy; they are not afraid to feel a stranger's body close to their own. At the same time everyone keeps yelling, "Don't push! Stop pushing!" It's quite astonishing to watch this. As you know, I can't bear that sort of thing, and as a result I often walk instead of taking the bus, because so many buses pass by before someone takes pity on me and calls out, "Let her through, let her through," and I can finally get on.

Well, for the show we had marked seats. We went to a lot of trouble to tape numbers onto the folding chairs. But even so people were in a frantic state, acting as though their seats would be snatched away if they did not reach them in time. But Kostya was very calm and people respect him because he's tall and at the same time a child, and he has a strong presence, the kind all actors long to have.

Why are people so frantic here? They must have had many experiences of being left out, and are determined not to let it happen again.

Now we are waiting for the reviews. I am sure they will be excellent. I saw one reviewer everyone is a little afraid of; he came "backstage" to ask Feingold a few questions. He seemed to be glowing with pleasure, as if he had just eaten a wonderful meal for which he had waited a long time. Someone else told me they saw him applauding very heartily. But even without reviews, the response of the audience assures us that the play will continue to be a success.

I desperately wait to hear from you!

⚜ Sonya

My brother and I walked down the dark stairwell, encouraged at first by the recent memory of Raya's air-conditioned flat, but gradually defeated by the suffocating heat. I was fine once we were on the street and I could breathe in the sea air (mixed, however, with equal portions of exhaust) but Kostya looked as if he had shriveled on the way down.

"I can take a bus to Jerusalem," I offered.

"No, I'm happy to drive you," he said. "I just hope the car makes it."

My brother always delayed taking the car to the garage because he knew he'd get lectured on the futility of hanging on to it. Neither of us was surprised when it broke down halfway to Jerusalem. The police arrived first, then a tow truck, and then Tali in her sleek silver Peugeot. She parked at the side of the road and joined us. Her body looked compact and energetic in a green summer dress and she glittered with jewelry: rings, bangles, looped earrings, a beaded necklace. I felt myself childishly drawn to her jewelry, her red lipstick, her neatly styled auburn hair. Everything about Tali was deliberately cheerful.

In spite of her exuberance, or maybe because of it, I could not imagine involving Tali in my mission. "You go on home, I'll take a taxi the rest of the way," I insisted.

My brother was not happy with this plan. I could see him only reluctantly admitting to himself that I was in fact an adult and could do as I pleased. I don't know how he talked Tali out of taking me to Jerusalem.

We phoned for a taxi and waited in the shiny Peugeot. Twenty minutes later a slightly dented dark blue Mercedes pulled up behind us. My brother checked out the driver, an ancient toothless Yemenite. To my great annoyance he told the driver to take care of me. If anyone needed taking care of, it was the driver. He appeared to be about a hundred years old and was probably as deaf as I was.

"Call me when you get there," my brother said.

"Yes, Your Highness."

I sat in the back of the Mercedes. The letter Raya had written was in my shoulder bag; I took it out of its envelope and looked at the pretty Arabic script. Hard to believe the nearly identical-looking squiggles were distinct phonetic symbols. If it turned out that Khalid was interested in me, I'd take a course, learn Arabic. The idea excited me and I wondered why I hadn't thought of it before.

I slid the letter back in my bag and stared through the window at the silent hills and eternal patterns of stones that decorated them; it was easy to imagine a Roman soldier or some peasant prophet sitting on one of the stones and eating dates or ducking behind the brambly trees to hide from an enemy. You are dust and to dust you shall return. *This can't go on,* I thought. The words took me by surprise: I was referring not to the layers of bones that had fed these hills, but to my life.

I loved my brother, I loved the way he looked after me and worried about me and cooked for me. I loved his hands stirring batter or peeling potatoes for his famous mashed potato—chocolate cake. Who but my brother would discover a chocolate cake that called for mashed potatoes? Only Kostya.

And yet it seemed to me that the reason we still shared a house had to do, at least on my side, with inertia, though the inertia was fueled by solicitude. It seemed, after Noah moved away, that I was all Kostya had left: how could I do anything but stay? Possibly Kostya felt the same way—that he could not desert me.

I tried to imagine Kostya wandering like a lost soul through the nine rooms of our empty house if I left: it was an unbearable image. At the same time, I was seized with the conviction that often accompanies a sudden surge of annoyance: I could no longer share a home with him. Maybe I would stay and he could go live with Tali, I thought, conveniently rearranging his life to suit mine.

No, we would have to sell the house.

It was the first time I'd considered such a possibility. I had seen our home as indestructible—and as for our lives together, we'd achieved a self-sustaining state of mutual understanding. Now, in one easy move, I had destabilized the present by envisioning an alternate future. I was at the spinning wheel, trying to turn gold into straw.

And yet the house had never seemed entirely reliable; it was the sort of pleasure dome one expected to float away one day or simply vanish. I was deeply attached to the garden; I derived continual pleasure from our oval pool; and sitting by the fireplace in winter was almost a religious experience. But as I considered these things I realized that they already seemed weightless, and the unknown home that would replace them had, at the moment, a far more substantial presence.

What would Nava, my Beersheba teacher and unofficial guru, have said? She was the wisest person I'd ever known, and I missed her. She never did come back from Holland after her sabbatical, and a few years later I heard that she had died in her sleep. We'd exchanged occasional letters, and she invited me to visit; when she died I regretted that I hadn't taken her up on her offer. I must have imagined that she would live forever.

Her field was pure math, but she saw math as allegory. An allegory for human stubbornness, capriciousness, bewilderment, adaptability, sense of futility and fear. Phenomena in mathematics and physics inevitably revealed, in her view, the human impulse that created or discovered them. "Often," she said, peering at us through her deep ironic eyes, "we like to hold on to the ideas we have for as long as possible—and even beyond that." These phrases—and the wry smiles that accompanied them—came back to me when I needed to be harnessed. Or maybe it was just the opposite: maybe they came to me when I needed to run wild.

Nava was the only one who understood my high spirits when I was recovering from my encounter with the hoodlum twins. She visited me in the hospital and told me about her experiences during the war; she'd spent four years hiding in a cellar with her two sisters. "We passed the time by imagining and inventing our futures, the wonderful lives that awaited us. Imagination is the only thing that can save you in this life, Sonya. But to imagine alone is irresponsible, it hurts others. Imagination must be shared, it must be a collective enterprise."

Nava would have known that there was no going back. The idea of parting from Kostya had settled snugly inside me and was not going to budge. Maybe we'd find separate apartments in the same building, a building that was not far from a community swimming pool, and we could still meet at the pool and race one another. Or we could live in the same neighborhood; that would also be all right. But I needed my own place. A flat with a balcony and, if I was lucky, a view of the sea. Every morning I would step onto the balcony in my housecoat and look out at the Mediterranean, misty and powerful in the distance.

Predictably, the aged Yemenite got lost. He was a Tel Aviv driver; Jerusalem was alien to him. He drove bravely on, constantly talking into his intercom with a slightly desperate look on his face or calling out to other drivers at red lights, but their rushed instructions only confused him further. I had never realized Jerusalem was so large, though maybe it only seemed that way because we were going in circles; I was certain we'd been on Emek Refaim, Valley of Ghosts, at least twice. The street seemed appropriately named at the moment.

It finally became obvious that despite the many amulets hanging from his mirror—amulets nearly identical to the ones that had lulled me to sleep this morning—my driver's situation was hopeless. I told him to stop, gave him 150 shekels, and escaped.

I found myself on an unusual street, lined with renovated shops and trendy cafés: Jerusalem chic. The narrow trees and old stone walls seemed self-conscious in this setting; the contrast added to the street's charm. I wandered into the nearest store. Despite its polished exterior, the usual Middle Eastern chaos reigned inside: wooden crates, burlap bags, cardboard boxes, and the goods themselves all appeared to be eternally suspended in some mid-process of sorting and ordering. I bought a bag of pistachio nuts, an orange, and a bottle of water. For a moment I considered getting something for Khalid, in case he was home and invited me in, but I decided against it. I sat on a folding chair outside the store and peeled the orange. A warm feeling of satisfaction spread through my body. I was on my own, and I was going to see a man—a man I loved, a man who had been inside me.

When I finished my snack I entered the store again and approached the owner. He was a thin, middle-aged man with wild hair and restless eyes. I wrote in my notebook, *"Could you please order a taxi for me? I need to get to Mejwan: is it far from here?"*

I handed him the notebook and he squinted at what I'd written. He seemed confused and shook his head. He opened a drawer, took out a large sheet of paper, and wrote in large letters, *"Wait a minute,"* then vanished into a back room. I noticed that the sheet he'd written on had been torn out of a school notebook and there was writing on the other side. I turned the page over and saw, in a child's scrawl, a list of seven vocabulary words in Hebrew: *road map, elimi-*

nation, retaliation, ticking bomb, military solution, diplomatic solution, secure border. If I needed additional evidence that I lived in an insane country, here it was. This was the week's lesson for what appeared to be, from the handwriting, second or third grade. Look, Mom: today I learned how to spell *hisul*, elimination.

The owner came back and retrieved the sheet of paper. He wrote, *"If you wait ten minutes, my wife will take you a little closer."*

I thanked him and returned to my place on the folding chair. The heat was less intense here, on the hills of Jerusalem, and the gentler light of evening was moving in. It was nearly six.

A few minutes later the man's wife appeared. She was a striking woman and quite young; I would have taken her for the storekeeper's daughter rather than his wife. Her thick, copper-colored hair was wound in braids around her head, and I had the distinct feeling that she was a performer of some sort; this would explain her eccentric hairstyle and elegant posture. A small gold cross lay like a sleepy smile against her throat. I guessed that she was from Europe, and had fallen in love with her husband while on a visit. Maybe she had come to this very store, maybe she too had needed directions. But she held on to her faith; she had not converted for her husband.

The storekeeper and the young woman spread a map on the counter and ran their fingers along it, searching for Mejwan. They both looked puzzled, but eventually seemed to come to a conclusion.

The woman smiled and offered me her hand. I was slightly shocked; she thought I was backward. I scribbled in my notebook, *"I'm Sonya, math professor at TAU. Very pleased to meet you."*

She read the note, laughed at her mistake, and wrote, *"My husband never explains anything properly! Sorry. I'm Lorelei. I teach modern dance."*

We walked to Lorelei's car. She had some difficulty starting it but finally succeeded. She'd been driving for only a few minutes when we came upon a demonstration, and we slowed down to take a look. Six or seven protesters were trying to prevent a Palestinian house from being demolished. I remembered Iris fuming about the cat-and-mouse game: Arabs aren't allowed to build houses without permits, but the government refused to give them permits, so they went ahead without them; the homes were demolished; they rebuilt. The signs of the demonstrators read DEMOLITIONS VIOLATE HUMAN RIGHTS; SAVE THE MUBAREK HOME and, more poetically, IF YOU DEMOLISH OUR HOUSES, ARE WE NOT HOMELESS? Two police officers were dragging away a bearded rabbi who was lying flat on the sidewalk; he'd gone limp and refused to cooperate, so the officers were pulling him by his arms. On the roof of the house another officer tried to move a chubby old woman who, unlike the rabbi, was putting up rather fierce resistance. The officer found himself temperamentally unable to fight with an old woman and tried to be gentle, but she elbowed him sharply in the stomach.

Lorelei pulled over to the side of the road, and I watched with fascination as her body expressed a dramatic struggle, slightly reminiscent of my lover's moment of indecision when I invited him to join me on the bed. On the one hand she seemed about to spring out of her car; her body was tense with a kinetic impulse to run out and help the rabbi. But she was also weighing the consequences of possibly getting arrested and missing her class, and this held her back; it was a corporeal civil war, muscle against muscle. Maybe she could use this interesting dichotomy of movements in her next dance. Finally she shook her head, mumbled something to herself, and drove on.

The landscape changed; there was a ravine and small neighborhoods scattered in the distance, and then we were on a winding street with a chaotic assortment of multipurpose urban buildings, each with its unique character and inventive architecture. The street ended abruptly: a stone wall blocked our way. The wall stretched out on both sides as far as the eye could see.

"This wasn't on the map," Lorelei said, miming the words. She looked at the wall with curiosity; evidently she'd never seen it before.

"I'll get off here, thanks for the lift. You'd better go, you'll be late for your class," I told her. "I'll be fine."

She nodded with patronizing tact: she thought I wanted to assert my independence in spite of my deficiency, as she saw it. In fact, I just wanted to be alone.

"Thank you," I repeated, and I jumped out of the car, waved good-bye, and walked toward the wall.

❧ Noah's diary, July 5, 1986.

In the news: mayhem in the Shin Bet. Also, a
Palestinian was killed by a bomb he was handling.
I'm glad it was him and not me, but I must say,
these Palestinians have no luck in anything.

Just back from Eilat, four days with Ilanit and her mother. Ilanit was heavily chaperoned during the day but managed to sneak out of her room at night while her mother slept. I don't think her mother would have minded all that much. She's a tiny, jumpy woman who seems to be expecting lightning to hit her at any moment. I'm surprised Ilanit's father trusts his wife to keep an eye on us, but maybe it's me he trusts. They've decided I'm an okay boyfriend for Ilanit. Actually, Ilanit's father and brothers are not as old-fashioned as I thought. I think Ilanit exaggerated the danger. Her father is really nice, he just doesn't want her to get pregnant, and neither do I! In fact, if you compare him to Dad, he's probably *less* protective. Dad gave me about 600 safety rules to follow before we left.

I've thought about it long and hard, especially when we were down in Eilat, and I've come to the conclusion, even though I'm sad about it, that I don't love Ilanit—and what's worse, I know for sure that I never will. It's the way she eats *leben* in the morning, with a spoon, scooping it out bit by bit in this irritating way. Or the way she looks at herself after she puts lipstick on. Or how mad she got at the waiter—it's true he was hostile, but she just gets so mad. I mean, who cares? Why let things like that get to you? I never noticed her chin before she got mad at that waiter. Suddenly all I could think about was her chin, and the way it looked when she was telling him off. All day I couldn't stop obsessing about it and I realized I would never be able to get past her chin, it's just too pointy. Also I hate to say this, but she doesn't really have a sense of humor. It's not that she doesn't get jokes. I mean she's very sharp, she's always correcting people's Hebrew (a national pastime) and she writes really good poetry. She even corrected my Hebrew once or twice, and I'm good at stuff like that. But she just doesn't find things funny. Probably none of this would matter if I loved her. They're not the cause but the effect. Basically, I don't know why I don't love her. I tried to love her but I didn't succeed.

But the terrible thing is that she loves me and I think if I leave her she'll go crazy. She was a mess when Guy left her and she says she never really loved him—she says it's only now that she knows what real love is. She says things like she would die for me and so on. It creeps me out a bit. It got me thinking who would I die for. I don't mean like running through fire, which you might do even for strangers if they were trapped in a house or something. I mean, where you know for sure you'll die if you save someone else. But I couldn't think of any situation where I'd have to make that choice in real life. If someone started shooting, for example, I might cover Ilanit with my body, but not because I love her. It would just be instinct. In fact, even though I'd cover her with my body, I'm going to have to leave her sooner or later. It would only make her unhappy if I stayed with her out of pity, and I can't ruin my life just to avoid hurting her.

Maybe she means that she'd feel like dying if I died. The only people I feel that way about are Oren and Sonya and Mom and Dad. That's it. I'll be sad when Gran dies but not as much because she's old and also getting very confused. Lately she's been leaving the house and getting lost. Dad hopes she can go on living with us. He's put a loud bell on the door so we can hear her if she wanders out in the middle of the night. During the day the Fireman from Ilanit's building comes over and looks after her.

Another thing I've been wondering about lately is whether Dad and Mom are thinking about divorcing. They haven't said anything but it's really tense in the house. Dad wanted us to go on a family vacation to Italy and Greece, but Mom said she couldn't leave her work. He won't go without her and everyone's in a bad mood now, except for Sonya. She's aware of what's going on, of course, but it doesn't affect her mood. How does she do that? Maybe because they're not her parents.

It's really late, I should get to sleep.

❧ LETTER TO ANDREI, APRIL 5, 1957

Darling, what a joy it was to find your letter in the mail today! And do you know, I almost didn't get it! We have some mailbox thieves here and they opened your letter, looking I suppose for money, but luckily when they found nothing they dropped the letter on the ground. And there it was when I came home! My heart was pounding as I opened it.

But of course your news did not make me very happy. Please follow your doctor's orders, dear. You must look after yourself so that one day we can meet again. You say your life has lost all meaning since we parted. Please, please, darling, remember how we all depend on you. Darling Olga, and the two of us, and all your colleagues and friends who adore you and look up to you. As for the rest of your family, you must not let them upset you. Don't let those dark moods win you over, darling. I daydream constantly about how I will show you everything here, and how we will laugh together.

For example, when I buy butter, by the time I get home not only has it started to melt, but the blue print from the thin wrapping has seeped onto the butter! (It's a real extravagance to buy such a luxury item, but Kostya and I love Israeli butter—once the blue print has been scraped off, that is—and once a month we treat ourselves.) You would make one of your jokes about the blue print, as you always did when we had similar difficulties at home.

And when I walk down the streets I imagine you breathing in the glorious smells of this city—for no matter how dreary I feel upon waking, as soon as I step outside, the city's fragrances fill me with optimism and soften my heart. The scents come from certain plants that grow here in profusion, but I'm afraid I can't tell you their names.

Another thing that would interest you, dearest, is the number of somewhat insane people walking freely on the streets here and accepted by all. Of course, you and I are used to seeing drunk people at home singing and so forth, but these people don't drink. Some of them talk to themselves. Many of them have sudden outbursts of anger at storekeepers, or at customers if they are the ones running the store. They begin to shout and shout, a real tirade that makes very little sense and then ends suddenly, after ten or fifteen minutes. Often they begin to weep in a strange bellowing voice. Some have strange tics and movements, and act in very odd ways. Others are always certain that someone is following them and conspiring against them. We have one such woman in our building. They are everywhere, these mad people! No one would dream of locking them away. That is not to say that people don't often dislike them or yell back at them during their fits. Everyone avoids the woman in our building, who is really quite nasty and always accusing us of imaginary and impossible crimes. But at the same time, these people are allowed to live their lives in peace and some are even teachers and bank tellers and so on.

I think many of them are casualties of the war, and went through hard times in the Nazi camps. I don't know the details—no one likes to talk about these things here—but I'm sure those places were dreadful. Perhaps others came to Palestine because they were outcasts, and they were outcasts because they were unstable. I believe these mad people are tolerated because there is a sense here that we need every single body and soul, everyone is precious, and that anyone who chooses to live here is heroic to some degree. There is always a great deal of anxiety about having enough people, and if someone announces that they are leaving for the United States or some other place, they are despised and no one talks to them or sees them off. It is considered a great betrayal to leave, and a duty to stay.

I have myself fantasized about the three of us settling in Canada or the United States, simply because my English is so much better than my Hebrew. I feel I will never conquer this complicated language! I would be able to act in America, but here I may have to give up my career for good. But we know no one there and, besides, Kostya loves this country. He loves everything about it and is deeply attached to it. "Like a fish in water," as they say. And this is the only thing that matters to me.

I know we may have to wait a long time until you find a way to join us, but I also know that one day you will succeed. How I miss your tangled beard, your lined forehead, the way you peer at me through half-open eyes when you are nearly asleep—you, too, must keep these memories alive and not despair.

I'm so glad Olga liked her gifts! I am knitting her a white sweater with silver swans. I cannot write more as I must run off to perform. Our play is a great hit, my love! I have finally memorized my lines perfectly.

I will mail this at once. You can't imagine how much joy your long letter gave me, with all its detailed descriptions. Your story about the potato soup was so funny! And Olga having conversations with the radio . . . I have read the letter several times, tears spilling from my eyes. I was like a starving person, devouring every word, imagining your hands, your study, your fountain pen—how cruel, that we cannot even correspond freely! Even this last resort of separated lovers is denied us. But we are finding a way, and we will overcome all obstacles.

Your loving and devoted Annushka.

❧ SONYA

The wall was made of identical stone rectangles lined up side by side like giant discolored domino pieces, mute and clumsy and immovable. A game of dominos on some distant planet, where everything's gone wrong.

Two jeeps and three border guards were stationed in front of the wall. I went up to them and asked how I could get through to the other side. They came to life at once: for the third time that day a bored group of people was eagerly gleaning some diversion from my predicament. Hard to believe how many bored people there were in a country as volatile as ours, where not an hour went by without some dramatic event occurring either within our borders or in the territories we're occupying. But maybe that was exactly the problem: when the world around you was so jittery and unreliable, you had to make an extra effort to keep things in place, and that meant being impassive, cautious, aloof.

I saw myself through their masculine eyes: a tall woman in a black skirt. They wanted sex, and my presence reminded them that they wanted it. I responded defensively; I looked at them sternly and, I hoped, coldly. But they weren't deterred; they flirted with me and joked around—not in a blatant way, but subtly, through smiles and silly animated head movements.

"ID, please," the shortest of the three said.

He examined my ID carefully, trying to control laughter; his friend had said something that amused him. A bunch of teenagers were running this place, dominating an entire population, flaunting machine guns—it was just ridiculous.

"Where are you going?" he asked me. He was in fact curious, although he tried to maintain a military imperviousness; he tried to be indifferent. Like the Tin Woodman, except that the guard was hoping to lose his heart, not find it.

"I'm going to see a friend," I said. "He lives in Mejwan, I have his address here. His mother's sick," I added, hoping this would somehow add to my credibility.

His eyes narrowed playfully. "Your boyfriend?" he asked.

"I *hope* so," I said angrily.

I'd poured cold water on this party, that was clear. The three of them shut down, looked away. A minute ago I'd been fun, now I was a tedious job. The short guard moved toward a clipboard lying on the hood of the jeep. He flipped through lined loose-leaf pages, lifting one after the other, until he reached a blank page. No one was going to convince me that this was an organized or serious enterprise, these pages covered with barely legible handwritten notes, attached to a clipboard. He copied my name and details, then returned my ID as if it were a trivial item for which he had no further use.

He pointed absently at the road that ran along the wall and told me there was a gate further down.

"A gate?" I asked, to make sure I'd understood.

He nodded and waved me on. "I'm completely against this occupation!" I said. "You're tormenting ordinary people and getting killed in the process. What for?"

He ignored me and I walked away, my heart pounding.

I followed the route of the tall stone blocks. It was interesting seeing the wall up close, after reading so much about it. These heavy blocks were temporary, and would soon be replaced with a more solid construction, three times as high and topped with barbed wire. Unless a miracle happened, that is. A new, enlightened government; international pressure; Elijah descending in his chariot.

Most of the blocks were covered with graffiti. The graffiti was reassuring: a sign of life and commotion. Through the cracks between the blocks I could see slender figures darting here and there. A quarter of a mile further on, just before the wall began to climb upward along a hill, I came across a black metal gate. Unfortunately, it was locked with a padlock. Through the thin black bars I saw a crowd of people milling about, waiting to get through; they looked as if they'd been there a long time, but had nothing better to do than wait. About half were children, scrubbed and neat, their spotless navy school bags slung on their backs. "It's locked," they told me, rather redundantly.

Then they said something I couldn't make out, though it seemed to be advice.

"I don't understand," I said.

A child pointed up the hill. I thanked him and walked in the direction he'd indicated, not sure exactly what I was looking for. Maybe there was another gate farther on.

But what I found wasn't another gate. If one is so far gone as to put up meaningless ugly walls in the middle of neighborhoods, reasonable procedures are not to be expected. Halfway up the hill, people were climbing over the wall, partly hidden from view by a generous willow tree. Yes, the Israeli army was just the sort of army to be fooled by a willow tree! Peering down the hill at the tiny jeep in the distance, I saw that the border guards knew about this expedient crossing—just as they had known that the gate would be locked. I was not surprised.

The climb was not easy: one by one, people scrambled over the wall, I assumed from a ladder on the other side, and let themselves down by seeking with their foot a slight protrusion on this side. Young men and women in good shape jumped, but older people needed help.

This arrangement wasn't really useful for me, because there was no ladder at my end. "Can I borrow the ladder?" I asked one of the women who had just slipped down. She was elderly, but agile underneath her gray *hijab*. There was some discussion in response to my request on both sides of the wall, transmitted by a man in a suit who was crouching rather precariously on the narrow ledge at the top of the block. He reached over toward me and dropped his briefcase into my outstretched arms; I was the tallest person there. Then he propelled himself, with great difficulty, down the other side. "Is this fair?" he asked me in English. He brushed his suit and walked away with the serene disgust of someone who has decided to triumph by refusing to feel humiliated.

After a moment or two the ladder appeared from behind the wall like a prop in a puppet show. It was, I saw, not a real ladder, but rather an old window frame, and it looked very unreliable. Inch by inch it ascended above the stone block, then tilted forward and came crashing down to the ground. I lifted the frame and set it against the wall, wondering whether it would hold my weight—especially since it had become even more wobbly from the fall. Ladders would be confiscated by the army, I now realized, and a ladder was too expensive an item to risk losing; bits of discarded building materials were more dispensable.

I climbed on the frame, feeling self-conscious in my short skirt. I should have worn something sturdier and less revealing for this trip, I thought; I should have worn jeans. But when I dressed, it had not occurred to me that I'd be going farther than Jaffa, and I certainly didn't think I'd be climbing walls.

I pulled myself up to the top of the wall, and only then wondered how I'd get down the other side. I would have to let my body hang and drop down the remaining distance—there was no choice. I bent over the ridge at stomach level and lowered myself. Now I was afraid to let go, but it was too late to change my mind: I wouldn't be able to dangle for more than a second, and I couldn't pull myself up from this position. I was enormously relieved to feel firm hands on my waist, holding on to me and breaking my fall.

I turned around and saw an extremely fierce, masculine woman smiling at me from under her head covering. She was a little frightening: in a children's play she would definitely be cast as the witch. And yet her touch was gentle and warm; it didn't match her face. Two adorable little children were clutching at her gown. I wondered whether she was their mother or their grandmother.

"Thanks," I said. "I'm going to Mejwan. Do you know where I can find a taxi?"

She pointed downhill. I thanked her again and walked back the way I'd come, but on this side of the wall. A little further down, the street that ran along the wall met the continuation of the one Lorelei had been forced to abandon, creating an L-shaped intersection that served as an ad hoc city center. A small gathering of men, all standing around uselessly with their hands in their pockets, watched me as I approached. They were identical to their Jewish counterparts on the Israeli side: intelligent, cynical, stoic, sensitive. If ever we had peace we'd get along, I thought tautologically. But really, their whole demeanor was the same as ours. Proud, full of grievances, athletic. I walked toward them and asked whether anyone was going to Mejwan.

৯(৻ NOAH'S DIARY, OCTOBER 29, 1986.

> *In the news: U.N. resolution complaining about Israel, #1000001. Israel has to place all its nuclear facilities under international safeguards, now that Vanunu surprised THE WHOLE WORLD with his information. And we have to promise not to bomb other people's facilities again. Israel will quickly obey ha ha.*

They got rid of high-school army training. Mom is really happy. She's into demilitarization. I really liked some of that stuff, swinging from tree to tree, gliding, jumping from heights, all that. Anyhow, they decided to get rid of it but we had an option to sign up for a three-day endurance exercise in the woods, and Oren and I signed up. We had a blast, the girls were so funny. When seven of us were all alone in the woods, they said as soldiers-to-be we had to learn "rape impulse control." So they all stripped and tried to tempt us— in order to test our control. I won't go into details about how all that ended, except that everyone was pleased with the outcome. It's a miracle from God that we weren't caught. (It's the first time I cheated on Ilanit, but I don't think it really counts if you're forced into it.)

Dearest, what a funny day we had today! I was called into the principal's office at Kostya's school.

I say "office" but you must imagine a room crammed from end to end with piles of textbooks—on the floor, on a long folding table, under the table—so that it looks more like a storage room than an office. In the corner are the janitor's supplies (mop and pail and some cleansers) and a few chairs have been squeezed into the remaining space for meetings. Someone's tea glass and tea bags are on the windowsill next to a plant, and the lost-and-found box doubles as a container for the school's flute recorders. Things are so informal here! It's a relief, I must say, after our rigid lives at home, where, I realize now, everyone lives in a continual state of paranoia. It becomes second nature. Here it's the opposite! You never have to watch your back because everything is such a muddle; there is so much improvisation. And you feel that anyone could slip through any crack at all. It's a good thing there are no truly evil people here, because they could slip through the cracks, too.

But now to the meeting. Kostya was also invited, and I was sure we were going to be told again that he is too outspoken. But no, this was an entirely different issue. It seems that the children at school, and maybe the teachers as well, don't feel very comfortable with the name Kostya. As a result the children call him Vronsky. I had noticed that already, when they all play outdoors.

The principal feels this is inappropriate. First, because Vronsky in literature is not a very positive figure! Can you imagine? And secondly, because it makes a child feel less accepted if he is continually addressed by his last name. It isn't good for his "psychological and social development."

Therefore the principal, who is a very sweet and gentle person, put together a list of Hebrew first names for us to choose from, with some of the same consonants, so that Kostya may be renamed. People here change their names all the time, it's the easiest thing to do. The principal said I need only fill in a form, go to the minister of the interior, and *voilà!* we have a new name. It is considered a little unpatriotic not to want to change your name, and all the other children, I was told, have Hebrew names. Why should my son stand out? the principal asked rhetorically. He said it wasn't healthy for him or for anyone else.

Kostya didn't say anything. He looked out of the window at the courtyard and seemed quite impatient to be outdoors again. I don't think the subject interested him very much. I politely told the principal I would take the list home and consider the matter, as he'd clearly gone to a lot of trouble. Here are some of the names on the list, which he divided into categories to be helpful. *Biblical:* Yuval, Yoav, Ya'ir, Yona (Jonah), Yochanan, Yonatan (Jonathan)— as you see, it is now the fashion to name children after some of the minor or more troublesome characters in the Bible. *Modern:* Yaron, Yarden (Jordan). *Daring and original:* Dekel (palm tree), Narkis (narcissus!), Tal (dew) . . . and so on. It was a long list; he put a lot of effort into this and he's really a very nice man—sensitive, intelligent, cares about the children. Please don't think that he would ever impose anything on us! In fact, he sees himself as a friend, and seemed quite concerned about whether we had anywhere to go for the Passover feast, which is in two days. He invited us to join his family. I didn't tell him this, but do you know I have had eleven invitations? Neighbors, people at the restaurant, my fellow actors—and, of course, Carmela. Everyone seems worried that I don't have a seder (as it's called) to go to. How can I explain to them how little I care for rituals and ceremonies? I suppose I inherited these feelings from my father, who as you remember always got angry when he heard that some Jews were risking so much in order to follow an antiquated, superstitious tradition, as he used to put it. Or maybe it's my own rebellious personality, dear. In the end we decided that Kostya will join his freckled friend's family, while I will be very happy to have a quiet evening to myself at home.

But to get back to the names, in the end our Kostya said he does not want to change his name. I was very relieved. His name is one of my few remaining links to you, darling, here in this hot, odd place. Darling.

❧ SONYA

Several men began explaining something to me. I couldn't make out a word they were saying and there was no point telling them I was deaf, it would only confuse matters further. There are times when you can't ask people to start writing things down for you, and this was one of those times. If I were able to read Arabic, that would have been fine, but asking them to write in Hebrew or English was too embarrassing and too complicated. They were not Israeli, despite their blue ID cards, and although they'd learned English at school, it was an imposition to ask them to translate what they had to say into a second language. I forced myself not to feel frustrated; whatever they were communicating would be clarified soon enough. I nodded as if I understood, and when they seemed to be asking me a question I nodded as well.

Finally I was ushered into a transit van for which the word "basic" was invented. The main thing was that there was gas in the engine and the van moved when you pressed on the gas pedal and came to a stop, more or less, when you pressed on the brakes. As for seats that held you reliably and didn't seem about to come loose, or a smooth ride, these were merely details. I looked for a solid object to hold on to: there was nothing available other than the door, so I pressed the palm of my hand against the cold metal and somehow managed to stay put.

The other passengers were all male: three worn, persevering men wearing ageless suit jackets and in need of a shave, and in the seat next to me, a younger man in a very bad mood. The younger man had fine features and a short black beard, and for some reason he made me think of a medieval minstrel: I could imagine him, when in a better frame of mind, strumming a lute and singing, "Hey, nonny, nonny" (or the Arabic equivalent). I smiled at him, but he looked away; he didn't want to be distracted from his bad mood. That occasionally happened with some of my students: they entered class in an extravagant sulk and clung to it with stubborn determination. But in their case a falling-out with a boyfriend or girlfriend was usually the cause. The young man next to me more likely had had a falling-out with a checkpoint.

The transit stopped and all the passengers got off, but the driver didn't seem to expect me to disembark with the others. I remained in my seat and he drove on.

We continued for another fifteen bumpy minutes. Then the driver pulled over: clearly we'd reached the end of the journey. I gave him twenty shekels, which seemed to satisfy him; I had no way of knowing how much he'd asked for. He thanked me, wished me luck, and as soon as I was out of the van, turned and sped away.

I was alone in the middle of a town or neighborhood and I was facing another wall. But this one was the real thing, the final version, and it was impassable: it towered over me like a punishment from hell. In hell you'd be trying to reach your lover and you'd have to spend your life staring instead at this monstrosity. This was what the men had been trying to explain to me, and I'd not understood. *"It is your garden now, little children," said the Giant, and he took a great axe and knocked down the wall. And when the people were going to market at twelve o'clock they found the Giant playing with the children in the most beautiful garden they had ever seen.* Not here.

A heavy metal door had been installed at the center of the wall. I looked around me: there was not a soul in sight. White stone apartment buildings with wide, empty windows rose over a variety of small stores. Ornamental Arabic lettering identified the stores; in some cases there was an English translation, either correctly spelled or close to it: Jouabeh Bakery and Sweets; Jimoom Comunication Ltd. The predominant color, apart from the white of the stone, was blue in all its variations: turquoise curtains behind glass panes, blue billboards advertising the Taj Mahal Fitness Centre; a poster of a smiling driver in a blue shirt holding the wheel of a car. Small black water tanks dotted the roofs of the buildings; from a distance they looked like the shielded heads of medieval knights.

In the midst of this ordinary community, the wall rose like a bizarre mistake; someone's idea of a practical joke, which, like all practical jokes, would be evil only if it were real. One had merely to blink and the wall would be gone.

I peered more closely at the metal door. It didn't seem to have a handle and I wondered how its locking mechanism worked. My curiosity aroused, I began examining it with my hands, pressing my fists against the cold rough metal. To my amazement the door flew open. So the wall wasn't completed after all. This was my lucky day.

I passed through the opening. On this side the town was awake; people were up and about, walking along the sidewalks or congregating at storefronts. A knot of chatting schoolgirls passed briskly by. With their identical bell-bottom jeans, western knapsacks, white wimple-style head coverings, and striped tunics, they looked like a single moving entity, lively and impenetrable.

I was about to set off in search of yet another person who could direct me when I realized, quite suddenly, that I was utterly exhausted. I couldn't take another step without resting first. I sat down gratefully on a cement block by the side of the road.

I was not only exhausted: a profound pessimism, entirely out of character for me, was luring me into its dark cavern. How quickly the sad, oppressive atmosphere had penetrated my emotional state! Oppression, with its harsh instability, was physically draining: my shoulders ached with tension and I had to breathe deeply a few times. A spasm passed through my body as my muscles unclenched themselves. I saw that the skin on the palms of my hands had been scraped by the climb over the first wall; in normal circumstances I would have noticed something like that immediately. I was glad there was no one nearby: I didn't feel presentable and needed a few minutes to collect myself.

I had lost the thread of my journey, the certainty that what I was doing made sense. Instead I felt a surge of panic. What if Khalid was dismayed to see me? What if I found him surrounded by a brood of children, with a wife peering at me from behind his shoulder? What if he became furious with me for tracking him down—what if my presence here compromised or harmed him in some way? I felt stupidly conspicuous in my inappropriate clothes. Everyone would notice me: everyone would know where I was going. I was carelessly and clumsily invading Khalid's privacy. I knew nothing about his life, and the idea that I could coordinate this unknown life with the events of the morning now seemed absurd. From this setting, our encounter in my luxurious bedroom in Tel Aviv loomed as remote as a theater piece about another society in another universe.

Yet it was impossible for me to go home without seeing him, or at least trying to see him. I loved him. Love wasn't reasonable, and it wasn't altruistic. You couldn't afford to imagine that your needs were not identical to those of the person you loved: the idea was too painful to consider. I refused to leave before I knew, one way or the other, how he felt. That was another thing about love. No matter how pessimistic you were feeling, or how deep your fear, love meant that you were also hopeful.

From behind another stone block, a skinny orange cat peeked out at me with cautious eyes. I had a few cat treats in my bag and I took them out, set them on the ground. Purring loudly at this unexpected boon, the cat fearlessly came out of its hiding place and gobbled up the treats. I reached down to stroke its bony back and it brushed against my leg. If I moved out on my own I would be able to have a cat. At this thought my mood lifted and I began picturing my new flat with a kitten curled up on the bed.

Because I didn't hear it coming, I was startled to see a patrol car pulling up beside me. When you're deaf, things really do appear out of nowhere. A soldier called out to me from inside the vehicle. I went over and said, speaking softly, "I'm deaf, so there's no point shouting. I can speak but I can't hear. I'm here to visit someone but I've never been in this neighborhood before and I'm not sure how to get there."

The soldier tossed his head sideways in the Middle Eastern sign for *yallah*—that humbling term, applicable to both humans and live stock, which means "This way, let's go." I climbed into the military vehicle. It smelled of metal and stale rolls.

There were several questions I would have liked to ask but I didn't want to annoy him; I was lucky enough that he was helping me. He was probably being cooperative because I was deaf. On rare occasions it was advantageous to be considered handicapped.

"Where are you going?" the soldier asked, spreading his hands apart in the sign for "What do you want?" It always interested me to consider the signs used by hearing people in these parts: *yallah*, what do you want, come over here, wait, go, I don't know/care, don't you dare/you listen to me, *mea culpa*, are you insane/what the hell are you doing, yes, no (two signs), hello/good-bye, calm down, in two seconds I'm going to hit you, screw you, I love/want you (the one sign that relied on eyes only). Was it possible that all human discourse could be more or less reduced to these elemental transmissions?

I showed the soldier Khalid's address.

It was his turn to wish he could ask me questions: Why was I going to see this person? What was it all about? But he shrugged; he didn't really care. I could see that he was tired and cranky and

lonely. People in uniform didn't usually look lonely, but this particular soldier looked as if he'd just discovered that he was the last
human on the planet.

He turned down one street, then another, and stopped in front
of a two-story white stone building with arched windows on the
ground floor and small square windows higher up. He pointed to indicate that we'd arrived. I stepped down and he drove away quickly,
as if hoping to distance himself from what he'd just done, in case
something went wrong and he'd be blamed.

The white stone house had three doors; Khalid's was the middle
one. I went up to the door and knocked.

*In the news: someone offered a man at the Tel Aviv
dog show $150,000 for his poodle! Some people
have money to burn.*

I had a really long talk with Mom tonight. I don't know what brought
it on. She asked me whether I wanted to come with her for a drive
and I said sure. I have one last exam in two days but it's citizenship,
I don't have to study much for it. I'm already a perfect citizen ha ha.
Besides, you can't study every single minute of the day.

We ended up at this café and we ordered chocolate and cheese
crêpes and talked for a long time. She said she's involved in a very
important case that could change the political and historical direction of the country, but that once it's over she's going to take six
months off and we'll finally go on our vacation. That was good news!
She said she needs a vacation and she's earned it and the world won't
fall apart if she stops working for a few months, or at least not any
more than it's already falling apart.

She said she was sorry she hasn't been around for me but I told
her that was crazy, just Dad laying guilt trips on her, or projecting

his own feelings on me. She still feels bad that she missed my school play in grade *three!!* Mothers are crazy. I never even noticed and I barely remember, but she's still feeling guilty about that. Anyhow, I finally convinced her that I don't need her to feed me porridge with here-comes-the-airplane. I convinced her that she was just a plain, ordinary mom like all my friends' moms—that is, the lucky ones whose mothers work and don't have them breathing down their backs.

She asked about Ilanit and I explained about the cheating in the woods. She was a bit shocked when I told her, but she didn't say anything. She asked whether I was sorry that Ilanit left me and I explained. I didn't actually say "happiest day of my life," because women stick up for one another and I didn't want to sound like an asshole. But I did tell her I didn't really love Ilanit and Mom said maybe I cheated on purpose to get rid of her, that's what men do to get rid of women—they behave badly because they don't have the guts to leave, they'd rather be left, and she laughed. I haven't seen her laugh in so long I almost forgot she had teeth ha ha.

Then she asked me about my exams. I think Dad put her up to that. I told her I was going to pass everything and she seemed relieved. I don't think she worries too much about how I'm doing in school, but Dad made her mention it.

The last topic was my career, and how glad she is that I'm going into the arts but she hopes I won't have financial problems. Sonya's fine now because when she turns twenty-one she gets all the money from the secret donor, which Dad quadrupled about seven times. But Mom is worried about whether I'll manage, because she knows I'd refuse to take anything from Sonya. So I reassured her about that, too. Then she started talking about herself. She doesn't usually do that, but she was in a very revealing sort of mood. I almost felt she needed someone to talk to, because she doesn't have any really close friends, so things were kind of spilling out.

She told me that when she met Dad she had just broken up with a guy she really loved who was in law school with her. He left her and she said she almost dropped out of school because she couldn't even get out of bed. She just stayed at home eating chocolates and crying. That was a bit hard to imagine. Anyway, then Dad came along. She said she wonders whether she was fair to him, marrying him. "He was my second choice, was that fair to him?" she asked me, as if she really wanted an answer. She said she *still* thinks about that other guy all the time and once or twice she ran into him and it was as painful as when he first left her.

Poor Dad! That's what I was thinking, but I didn't say that, of course. I said, "It was Dad's decision too." She looked so impressed when I said that. She narrowed her eyes, drew back, and gave me that look she gives in court, that makes people listen to her. "You're really something, sweetheart," she said. She smiled again, but she was sad. "Maybe you should get out of here while there's still time," she said, back to her old self. "We're headed for darker times than people realize."

"I'll start working on that ark right away," I joked.

That's about it. We didn't talk about the army, there's nothing to say. I know how she feels. She left this book on my bed last year, this novel by Kenaz showing how army training is like being in a concentration camp—not literally, but how it's full of evil, and evil is the same no matter where you are. I didn't finish it, and anyway it's 1955 in that novel, things have changed since then. Conscripts don't get their heads kicked in the mud nowadays, they don't live in a state of terror. All the same, I haven't decided yet what to do. Probably I'll go in but I won't sign up for combat, I'll do some technical course or something. That's what Oren's doing. I personally think Oren will end up with a 21 profile. I think after three weeks (days!?) he'll just get bored, put on an act, and get himself a 21. He plans to go into business for himself, so it won't matter for his future. Or maybe he'll like the challenge of the army. Hard to know for sure.

I'm glad I had that talk with Mom. I wanted her to tell me more about this big case she's working on, but she says it's top secret for now. It's big, though. I think she's uncovered some huge scandal. She says I'll know soon enough.

LETTER TO ANDREI, MAY 8, 1957

Dearest, you know for a long time Kostya pretended not to remember you. I didn't want to tell you, even though I knew you would understand. When I mentioned you he would say, "I don't know what you're talking about," and he would pretend not to hear me. Well, guess what! Today he asked to write a letter to you! And you see, he remembers all his Russian. Here it is, dearest:

Dear Father,

I hope you are well. I have been having fun in school. We are doing electrical and magnetic currents, it's very interesting and we had a demonstration. We have had a lot of holidays in a row. We had Passover, a spring and liberation holiday. Then we had Holocaust Remembrance Day but no one wanted to remember so I'm not too sure what it was all about. Then we had Memorial Day for all the soldiers who fell for Independence. The next day, so it wouldn't be gloomy for too long, we had Independence Day with many celebrations. I have joined a secret group, I can't reveal our name. We are working on our

manifesto. I need some advice from you regarding this manifesto and I hope you can answer these questions for me:

- How would you define freedom?
- When does freedom become dangerous?
- How can you decide who decides?

Thank you.
When are you coming?
Your loving son,
Kostya

❧ SONYA

I waited and knocked again, harder this time. I didn't see a buzzer.

I was about to slide my letter under the door when it opened, and there he was: my lover. He was wearing the same black jeans he'd had on this morning but a different top, a short-sleeved navy blue T-shirt with a small, illegible logo on the upper left corner. We looked at each other and it was hard to tell who was more amazed—me, for having actually tracked down this total stranger, or Khalid, who surely had not expected to set eyes on me ever again.

Seeing him was completely different from imagining him. Two opposite things happened: on the one hand the exhilarating, quasi-transcendent, and practically beatified image I'd carried with me all day evaporated like mist, and was replaced by an ordinary person with ordinary characteristics. At the same time, this ordinary person was even more desirable and mysterious than any conjured man, because in my imaginings I was able to control all his attributes, while in real life I was unbearably disconnected from him: he was not known to me. O sweet pangs of love!

My anxiety about clumsily invading my lover's world also retreated. His world was familiar; it was not some extraterrestrial twilight zone whose parameters were unknowable. And he wasn't angry in the least; nor did it look as if he had a family. Maybe some neighbor or other had seen an army vehicle bring me to this building, but no one was interested in me or my visit.

He opened the door wider to let me in and I stepped into a small rectangular hallway. There was a closed door behind him and a living room on my left, its conspicuous carved furniture, patterned rugs and painted vases as solemn as museum exhibits. But Khalid didn't invite me in; he remained standing in the hallway with a puzzled expression on his face. Since I didn't know what else to do, I opened my bag, took out the letter, and handed it to him. What luck, I thought, that I'd written a letter! For now that I was standing here facing my lover, I was tongue-tied.

He took the envelope from my hand and stared at it as if trying to remember what an envelope was. Finally he pulled out my letter and read it.

He smiled at what I'd written and his body relaxed. When he smiled, the three laugh lines on both sides of his face deepened into sunny, delicate brackets. I had not seen him smile before, I realized. Casually he invited me in.

Bright outdoor light fell in thin, geometrical patterns on the rugs and furniture, but Khalid drew the heavy salmon-and-gold curtains across the arched window, erasing the elongated shapes. He didn't want anyone looking in; that was a good sign, I thought. He wasn't planning to get rid of me immediately. On the other hand, maybe the drawing of the curtain was merely a courteous or protective gesture.

Facing the windows, at the other end of the room, was an arched doorway leading to a kitchen. Khalid led me to the kitchen and invited me to sit at a table in the corner. Despite the miniature hallway, crammed living room, and tiny kitchen, the house seemed spacious, partly because the ceiling was high and partly because it was so carefully decorated.

I sat at the table and watched Khalid. Now our positions were reversed: I was in his kitchen and he was serving me. A mathematical idea came to me and I shut my eyes, gave it a few seconds to play itself out. Something to work on later, but I wanted to put the first inklings in place. When I opened my eyes Khalid was looking at me with concern. "Do you feel well?" he asked me in English, trying to think of a way to mime the question. But I had understood. "I'm fine," I said. "Just some idea I had. I'm happy to be here."

Khalid still looked worried. "Tea or coffee?" he asked, comically holding up a tea bag in one hand and a jar of ground coffee in another. I laughed. "Tea, thank you. Any kind at all."

He filled a whistling kettle with tap water and set it on the stove. Then he began opening drawers until he found a pen. He sat down across from me and wrote on the back of my letter, in English:

"Thank you for coming and for your letter. I respect you. I apologize for my bad behavior. I was very upset and worried about my mother. She died one hour ago and still I haven't told anyone. I have a brother and a sister in Jordan and one brother here, I must call. And I must call an ambulance and let her friends know. But I have not so far done so. She was sixty-two only."

"Where is she?" I asked with astonishment. It seemed inconceivable that somewhere in this sedate house, with all its complicated furniture and ornaments, there was an abandoned corpse, tucked away in some corner like secretly stowed contraband on a ship.

He motioned me to follow him to a long, narrow room adjacent to the living room. It was the only other room in the house as far as I could see, and I wondered where Khalid slept.

We entered cautiously, as if afraid to disturb any ghosts that might be lurking in the corners. Air from a small, high window was lured indoors by a ceiling fan with helicopter propellers, and the intimate glow of the overhead lightbulb reminded me of rainy winter nights on Yahud Street. There were two dressers covered with embroidered throws against the wall and a curved plastic lawn chair next to a single bed. The bed took up a quarter of the room. Lying under a white sheet was a gaunt woman with a navy blue kerchief tied neatly around her head. Her eyes were shut but her mouth was slightly open. She looked older than sixty-two.

The room smelled of death. The smell—dusty and slightly sour, like linoleum in a cellar—was new to me. I'd never been in the presence of a dead person, unless I counted Iris at her funeral, but she was already in a coffin and I was too preoccupied with Noah and my brother to pay her much attention. They had between them polished off an entire bottle of arak and were both extremely unsteady and slightly green.

I placed my hand on the woman's forehead as though checking her for fever; under my palm her skin felt like cold parchment. She was Khalid's mother. I would never know her.

"I'm sorry," I said.

The kettle whistled, judging by the urgency with which Khalid hurried back to the kitchen. I stayed with his mother—it seemed too horrible to drink tea in the kitchen while she lay alone on her narrow bed. I sat on the lawn chair and looked at her. Death was entirely incomprehensible. Was she here or not here? This was where mathematical paradoxes came from: from our world, which was incomprehensible. We tried to solve mathematical problems—each generation tried—and in the world of mathematical systems we made progress, we discovered and invented clever systems and concepts. In the human world, however, we had made no progress at all. *In the beginning God created the heaven and the earth.* That was our best guess, then and now—pitiful, really.

I wondered why Khalid had not pulled the sheet over her head. Maybe it wasn't a universal custom to do that when someone died; maybe it was just something you saw in movies.

Khalid came back to fetch me.

"I don't want to leave her alone," I said.

"Come," he said.

We returned to the kitchen. Khalid had set two glasses of mint tea and a plate of sesame cookies on the table. Like two obedient schoolchildren we took our seats. Khalid wrote, *"She isn't alone, her spirit is traveling in another dimension. She has been sick for a long time, and finally her suffering is over. I was able to look after her so she could stay at home. She didn't wish to go to any hospital. Today I was looking for a new drug, hard to find. I tried everywhere but I was unable to acquire it. She waited until I came home to die."*

"What were her last words?" I asked him.

"She wanted a glass of water. When I came back with the water she was already gone."

"Why haven't you called anyone?"

He shook his head. *"I'm too tired to start yet with everyone coming here, and all the melodrama. I need to rest first, then I'll do it."*

I took the pen and wrote beneath his messages, *"I love you. I wasn't sure until now, but now I'm sure."* I wondered how one said "I love you" in Arabic, and whether, as in Hebrew and French, the words for *like* and *love* overlapped.

Despite the somber circumstances, Khalid began to laugh. He wrote, *"I studied chemistry three years in Greece, two years in Denver. I came back to take care of my mother. I had a girlfriend in Denver and we were engaged, but in the end we broke apart. Don't take that antihistamine again! Who knows what will happen next time!"*

He was laughing, though his mother had died this afternoon. And I, who had dishonestly told myself that I'd come here without expectations, burst into tears.

It had been a long time since I'd cried on my own behalf. I often cried at sad movies or when I heard sad stories, but in general I had no reason to feel unhappy. My career was going well, my contribution was recognized, my students liked me. I had Kostya, Noah, Raya, a beautiful house in a city I loved. Noah had survived the army.

Now none of those things seemed important. I felt humiliated and heartbroken. I put my head down on my arms and sobbed.

In the news: a groom was arrested because he used
fake credit cards to buy things for the wedding. The
judge said he could get married but he'd have to be
handcuffed the whole time. That judge is a sadist.

The whole family plus Oren went to see *The Threepenny Opera*, a big production. It was pretty terrible. Oren fell asleep, Sonya was bored, Dad looked grim, Mom looked disgusted, and by common consent we all left at the intermission. Only Gran was happy. We were a little worried that she would be disruptive, but she sat quietly in her seat the whole time and seemed very absorbed in the production. When we were driving home she surprised us all by singing "Pirate Jenny" perfectly. She remembered the melody and all the words in English, with a bit of German mixed in. We applauded when she finished. The brain is a strange thing.

Mom is very depressed. Usually she's angry but lately she's been really down, not talking, not taking an interest in things, not even getting excited about her Big Case, the one that's a secret. I prefer it when she's angry. The only time she was her old self was when the pathologist at Abu Kabir said on the news, defending his erroneous report about how a Palestinian died, "Pathology is not an exact science." Mom gave a guffaw. She said, "Yes, you can tell whether someone died at six or ten in the morning, but not whether he died of pneumonia or because he was beaten to death."

Then she went back to her depression. She's been following Vanunu's trial. She hasn't been allowed in—no one is—but someone who knows what's going on keeps her informed. She said they're going to bury him alive and never let him see the light of day again, ever, and she's only surprised they didn't murder him.

On top of that, a guy she knew, someone called Awad (I'm not sure whether that's his first or last name), an American-Palestinian who came here to preach nonviolence, was deported. For weeks it's been Awad this, Awad that, I figured soon we'd find out what Awad had for breakfast. I wouldn't be surprised if Dad was starting to get jealous. But anyway, he had to leave. Yesterday I heard her tell Dad, "I don't know how much more I can take."

It took her a really long time to get a date for her Big Case, but it's finally coming up in two weeks. You'd think she'd be really excited and happy, but she isn't. She still thinks her case will create a big stir, but she's not sure anymore that it will really change anything. I've never seen her so gloomy! Maybe she's going through menopause.

Dearest, I do hope you are feeling better, and that you are not too gloomy. Please keep up your spirits, for my sake! Do you know, our play is still running! I must say it isn't easy working during the day and acting at night, even if one has a small role. It's very tiring, though luckily I've been able to shorten my hours at the café because the theater is actually making a bit of money now and we, the actors, are getting paid. This play is such a hit, some people are coming to see it again and again. It's been extended several times and might continue for a few months.

That is not to say that there have not been several problems. Oliver/William quit and it was hard finding a replacement. But Orlando's brother, who had seen the performance seven times, came to the rescue and is doing not too badly. With a good director, even amateurs can be fine.

Sometimes fights break out in the audience. It's disruptive. We used to try to go on, but now we have a new policy. There's a big sign that says: In the Event of Fights in the Audience, the Play Will Be Discontinued and There Will Be No Refunds. This way, when a fight breaks out, everyone puts pressure on the culprits to leave the hall.

There are other noise problems. Some of these audiences are not used to proper theater. They bring small children who suddenly announce in a loud voice that they have to go to the bathroom. People who don't want to admit that they are going deaf yell out that they can't hear, as if it's our fault and not the fault of their ears. But despite these setbacks, the audience has a great time. They are starving for entertainment.

I imagine you sitting in the audience every single time I perform. I'm so worried about those mailbox thieves! What if Heinrich sent a letter and it never reached me? But Carmela said (in a very affronted tone of voice) that mailbox theft is not a problem "in this part of the city." She thinks the last letter, which I found torn open and on the ground, was accidentally opened by another neighbor, who then realized his mistake and left it on the mailbox ledge for me, from where it must have simply fallen to the floor and drifted outside. She's sure no one was going through the mail looking for money. I don't share her certainty. She's quite snobby, and she says that sort of thing only happens in places like our old neighborhood, which she calls a haven for hoodlums.

I think of you.

SONYA

I felt my lover's hand on my arm and I lifted my head. Tears were streaming down my cheeks and my nose was starting to run. Khalid handed me a little packet of tissues wrapped in cellophane; the Hebrew letters on the packet, קומפקט, seemed out of place here. I pulled out a tissue, and as I blew my nose Khalid passed me my letter. In the last available space he'd written, *"I was not laughing at you, Sonya-Sophia. I laughed because you are such a funny person, nothing coming from you is predictable. You are always surprising me. I'm happy you're here. I like you very much."*

I am deaf, I thought. I am deaf, and no man will ever want me. No hearing man will ever want me. All those men who asked me on dates, they probably just wanted to have sex with a deaf person, to see what it was like. And that's the real reason I'd said no. I pretended it was a matter of principle, but it wasn't: I had said no because I was unwilling to give in to my vulnerability. I hated my life.

Khalid motioned me again to come with him—he would soon get fed up with having to mime and motion everything, I thought glumly. He led me to the little hallway, to the closed door facing the entrance. I had assumed the door led to a closet, but when Khalid opened it, I saw that the door concealed a steep flight of wooden stairs—like one of those secret passages you saw in war movies. We climbed the stairs single file. When Khalid reached the top, he took my hand to help me with the last step, which was twice as high as the others.

We were in a wide, low-ceilinged room with two windows, a double bed, a small night table, several bookcases, a computer desk, and two folding beds leaning upright against a corner wall. A fan whirred silently in the corner, intensifying the smell of lemon cleanser mixed with something else—a spice, possibly cardamom.

Khalid made the sign for "wait": thumb against index and middle finger. He disappeared and returned with a kitchen chair. He brought the chair over to the computer and we both sat in front of the screen. *"I'll show you something,"* he wrote on a blank page. He knew how to touch-type, and his fingers raced across the keyboard. I wanted to bend down and kiss them. Or lick them, like a cat.

What he wanted to show me was his Web site; it included an attractive table of elements and an essay he'd written on groundwater problems in the troposphere. He returned to the page and typed in, *"What do you teach?"*

Ordinarily I would have been interested in reading his essay and telling him about my own work. But I only felt insulted and depressed. This was all I was good for, apparently. I sulked and shook my head.

"Sonya-Sophia, what can I do to make you happy again?"

I wrote, beneath his question, *"It doesn't matter. I had better go, and you need to look after your mother. I'm sorry about her death. I came at a bad time."*

"I've been expecting this for many months. I don't want you to leave yet. You take my mind off this bad day."

"I'm feeling the pangs of unrequited love," I wrote dramatically.

Khalid tried not to laugh this time. He wrote, *"My girlfriend, the one I nearly married, she married someone else, but she still writes to me. I* never answer, but every few days I have a letter from her. Look." He entered his e-mail and opened one of the letters.

> Dear Khalid, I don't know whether you are deleting all my letters. Maybe you have blocked me. Today I was at the eye doctor, I need a new prescription. Remember you said you liked those glasses with the dark frames? I'll keep the frames, just get new lenses. Eddie is away for the weekend at a golf tournament. I think about where you are. I read all the news, everything I can, and I never know whether you are safe. You don't write to me, and I know I deserve it. If you said, "Debbie, come here," I would be there in twenty-four hours. But I know you will never forgive me. No, I would not be there in twenty-four hours, because first I would have to go on a diet. But as long as I don't hear from you I don't really care. But why am I writing about superficial things when you are dealing with such serious situations? What would you do if I showed up at your door? Debbie.

"She still loves you," I said. "What about you?"

He shook his head. "It's gone. I can't help it. We were engaged, we were planning our wedding, and just before the invitations went she let her parents talk her out of it. Now she is sorry, but my feelings have undergone change. She knows this."

"Poor Debbie! Can't you forgive her?"

"It isn't a matter of decision. I went through anguish and then I came out of it, and I can't go back. It's impossible. Nothing is left."

"Is her husband cheating on her? She sounds lonely."

"I'm sorry for her, but what can I do? I hope she doesn't show up, but I don't think she will. That was her problem, not seeking adventure, since in adventure comes knowledge. She didn't like to take a risk, even try new restaurants—always it was the same pizza pizza pizza. Or Chinese food. In the end she was afraid of me, she lost her trust. Her parents scared her, but she was scared too easily."

"Do you have a photo of her?"

He opened a drawer and took out an inlaid wooden box. The box was filled with photographs. He flipped through them and pulled one out.

Khalid and Debbie were standing under a tree on campus; there were other students in the background. Debbie was much shorter than Khalid, with round cheeks, glasses, and long brown hair. She looked smart and pretty. They were both smiling happily, and he had his arm around her shoulder.

"What was she studying?" I asked.

As if we were playing charades, he got up and began to mime the answer. People eating, fighting, loving, and an outsider looking at it all in a detached way, stroking his chin and making notes.

"Sociology!" I laughed.

He sat down and wrote on the screen, *"I'm happy to see you laugh, Sonya-Sophia."*

"Can I see the other photos?" I asked.

He seemed uneasy and I quickly said, "Never mind, it's okay."

"I don't have any secrets," he wrote. *"But it's boring for you. Relatives, people you don't know . . . You can look if you want."*

He handed me the box. I hesitated, but he extracted all the photographs and placed the pile on the palm of my hand.

I felt as if I'd been offered a treasure from some long sealed Egyptian tomb, and my heart began beating quickly. At the same time I knew that these glimpses into my lover's life, a life that had nothing to do with me, would only intensify my suffering.

I went through them one by one. I knew, when I came across a picture of a man wearing glasses, that this was his father, and I also recognized a young woman as his mother; a wedding photo confirmed my guess. And there was Khalid, six or seven years old, standing next to a bicycle and grinning. But most of the snapshots were indecipherable: faces staring into a camera, old and young, children and babies, entire families gathered on a lawn. An ancient, creased black-and-white photo of a white stone house. One of the lost houses, I assumed, in one of the lost villages. Once again tears began to roll down my cheeks.

"This is what I was afraid of! You see, I have already figured out some things about you," Khalid wrote on the screen.

"I don't know anything about you," I said. "I wish I did."

"I'll give you twenty questions, like in that American game," he answered.

"Don't make fun of me."

"We'll be friends, Sonya-Sophia, and you will find out all about me and you'll wonder why you ever thought I was something special. All my measles, mistakes, foolish dreams, and crimes."

"You never committed any crimes!"

"Yes, I did. At fifteen my friends and I stole a car and went to drive without any license for two hours. Lucky thing, we never were caught. My father would have let me have it."

"What did you father do?"

"Teacher, driver, food stand, politics, and finally import-export. He's still alive, he's in Qatar. But he has another woman there, and I haven't decided when to tell him about my mother's death. He paid for my university, I'm grateful for that."

"I've never had any relationships," I said, gazing at the photograph of Debbie and Khalid under the tree, which I'd left at the top of the pile. "I never dated anyone at all."

"I'm very sorry at how I behaved this morning. I had no idea."

"No, don't apologize. You must have thought I was very promiscuous—and who can blame you! And then you thought I was mad. You should have seen your face!"

"I admit I thought this was your hobby."

I wrote, *"All these years I thought I wouldn't fall in love with anyone who didn't know how to sign. But maybe I was afraid of this happening, of falling in love with a hearing man who wouldn't want me because I'm deaf. It was very unrealistic coming here, I can see that now. But it still hurts."*

"For most people it takes more than thirty seconds to fall in love, Sonya."

"Are you saying there's hope?"

"Falling in love and feeling you could fall in love both take time. They are almost the same thing."

"How long did you know Debbie for?"

"We were in the same comparative literature course. I knew her a few months, it was gradual. We went to see a movie and we didn't like it, so we walked out, and she came to my room, and it started. Even then I didn't love her right away. It took me a long time."

"But you would never love a deaf woman."

"Love doesn't have a prerequisite. Please don't think there is any reason besides that I don't know you."

"Are you just saying that to be kind? Be honest. I need you to be honest, and I promise not to cry again."

"I wouldn't lie to you."

"I'm sorry I didn't answer your question about what I teach. My field is probability. I'd like to make a really important contribution. I've made a small contribution, but I want to make an important one. I feel I'm coming close, I'm really at my height now. But it would be hard to explain to someone who isn't in the field. I live with my brother, he's a lot older than me. He was already married when I was born, and we all lived together. The house you saw, we bought that later, with money an anonymous person gave us when I lost my hearing."

"How did that happen?"

"I had a kidney infection because I was afraid of our toilet—it made scary noises. So I stopped drinking as much as I should have. And someone in the hospital, they never found out who, gave me a huge dose of something called gentamicin. My kidneys couldn't get rid of the toxins, and my hearing was damaged."

"They have implants now that can restore hearing."

"Not perfectly, not reliably. But it's true, there's been a lot of progress in that area."

"How do you teach?"

"I have a translator in the classroom and during appointments—Ma'ayan."

"Ma'ayan, a nice name. A water well. From the same root as our ayin, which means source *also in Arabic. Did you sue the hospital?"*

"No, we never thought of it. Then we got all that money just a few weeks later."

"Maybe the doctor responsible sent this compensation so you wouldn't investigate and sue."

"I don't think so. My brother worked at that hospital and he said the doctors looking after me weren't that wealthy."

"It's possible the doctor took a huge loan to prevent you suing and he is paying it back bit by bit, like in the story of de Maupassant, with the necklace."

"Maybe. I'm much more curious about who my father was. My mother never told me. My brother's father was a physicist in Russia, but my father was someone my mother met in Tel Aviv, where she was a waitress."

"I had a friend who didn't know who his father was, and it turned out it was the next-door neighbor, who was hanging in there all the time. Often it's someone you know and who knows you."

"We had lots of people visiting, but no one came regularly and no one showed any particular interest in me. I don't think my father knows about me."

"Do you resemble any of your mother's friends? Anyone with such curly black hair and charming eyes?"

"Well, one of her former friends does have curly black hair, or at least he used to—it's thinning a bit. He teaches philosophy at the university, I once took a course with him. But he's famous for not having any children. He had a vasectomy."

"When?"

"His wife got pregnant, and he made her have an abortion. And it was very traumatic for him, so he had a vasectomy. He wrote articles about it, and he's even written a book about why it's immoral to have children."

"Maybe he was with your mother before he had his operation."

"I'm sure it's not him."

"So you grew up with your mother and your married brother?"

"Yes, and his wife, Iris, and their son, Noah. But everyone's gone. My mother is in a nursing home, Noah's in Berlin and Iris was murdered. She was a lawyer, she was murdered in her car. My brother knows who was responsible but he won't tell."

"Not Iris Nissan?"

"Yes."

He shook his head in disbelief. *"You are fortunate to have relation to such a person. People here still commemorate her. She gave her life for us."*

"I don't think she did, Khalid. My brother says she was killed because she was going to expose something inside Israel. Some corruption, I guess. But it's true she died because she was seeking justice. Listen, Khalid, I should go. I feel bad about keeping you from your mother, you need to look after her. I've stayed long enough. I'm glad you're not angry with me for coming here." I felt depression slithering toward me—the tips of its tentacles were already touching me, and I wanted to leave before it clutched me in its entirety. I had not experienced depression for a long time and had forgotten how leaden and treacherous it was.

"Okay."

"You'll contact your family?"

"Yes. I guess I'm relieved that she died. It's funny, until she died I was crying. I had pain in my heart for seventeen months. But I think I was doing all my mourning prepaid. Now I'm just happy she isn't suffering. The end was really hard, she was on morphine, there was no point anymore. But my brothers and sister, they'll be much more upset, because for them it just happened now."

Neither of us moved for a few seconds; Khalid was politely waiting for me to take the lead. He had been kind, he had done his best, but he wasn't attracted to me. There was no point making him feel bad about it; it wasn't his fault.

Finally I stood up and he immediately got up as well. "Thank you for your kindness," I said.

We were approximately the same height, and taking inspiration from Raya, I kissed him good-bye on the mouth.

As soon as my lips touched his, he jumped back as if he'd received an electric shock. It was an involuntary reaction, instantaneous, complete.

We were both intensely embarrassed. Khalid began to say something but I didn't try to understand. All I wanted to do was disappear. Trembling with the effort to remain calm, I walked down the stairs, unlocked the front door, and left the house.

ꙮ Noah's diary, January 1, 1989.

*In the news: only a masochist would follow the
news these days.*

Dear Diary, Here I am in the North Pole, otherwise known as the
Golan Heights. Wrapped up from top to toe and still freezing my
arse off. All that training and where do they send me? To this god-
forsaken place to sit around all day and drink coffee from a Thermos.
Okay. Fine with me. Whatever you want.

Meanwhile Oren's in Brazil, lying in the sun on some beach, no
doubt, with a South American beauty he picked up in a nightclub. I
was wrong, he didn't get a mental health discharge. He suddenly got
diabetes, out of the blue. So he got a regular health discharge. I get
postcards from him, they make me sick with jealousy. By the way, I
started smoking. First it was just a cigarette here and there, now I'm
a total addict. It helps pass the time. Dad wouldn't be too happy, he
made Sonya watch a lung being removed when he caught her smoking in high school. Dad's a little crazy. But then so is Sonya—she said
it was "fascinating." I am truly the only normal person in the family.

I'm writing this because in the last package-from-home Dad sent
me some notebooks along with the sketchbooks I asked for, and I'm

bored, so what the hell, might as well write something or other. I'm a little out of practice, I may need help from Anne Frank ha ha.

I'm wearing a scarf some kid in Cincinnati knitted. Aaron and I had a fit of hysterics when we got that package of scarves and stuff and read the letters from the kids. It was a class project at some Hebrew school there. The things they teach them . . . We felt like writing back, and we even composed a letter that was really hysterical, but we'd get court-martialed if we sent it. Imagine if they got that letter. *Dear Sherry, Thank you for the lovely mitts. They will help us protect our tiny, struggling state and keep us warm next time we dance the hora. The photo where you're holding the flag was very nice, and we're glad you cried as you watched* Exodus. *But things get a bit slow up here in the Golan—all the action is in Gaza and Ramallah and all those places you've never heard of, where our friends are beating people up like it's going out of style. So if you and your friend Megan* . . . We got a little carried away.

Anyway, I'm stuck here for another two years. But I'm glad I'm not fighting the intifada—I wouldn't last one day. I've realized that basically I'm a saint ha ha. I'm doing some drawing, trying to get a portfolio ready. My best one is Aaron sitting on the can with that dopey look on his face, his rifle on his lap. That really came out good. Aaron wanted to buy it but I wouldn't sell. Dad sent me a list of schools in Europe that teach costume design. I think I need to get out of this country for a while.

Sonya's in university now, in Beersheba, combining her first two degrees. She wrote some important article, solved something, I'm not sure what, but she could have gone to Harvard or anywhere else she wanted. But for her, even Beersheba was a big step, and she comes in every weekend to be with Dad. He tried to encourage her to go to the Sorbonne but she said no. Dad wrote that Gran needs more and more looking after and I think he's going to put her in a home soon. Sonya's still mad at me and we're both too stubborn to make up. I did write her a letter one night when it was incredibly quiet here, but I didn't send it right away, and in the end Shmulik spilled coffee all over it.

The only break from the monotony is the soldier who drives the supply truck. She's nice. Her name's Marion, she's from Sweden. Cute little freckles on her nose, cute little nose, big gray eyes. I wouldn't mind getting to know her a bit better. Wonder where she lives. About the gay thing, when I finally told Dad he said I don't have to make any decision, he said people change all the time, moment to moment and hour to hour. He said I should just do whatever feels right and not care what anyone else thinks or says, but that I have to swear to him if I have sex with a guy again (I told him about that time with Oren) to use a condom.

I have leave in two weeks. It'll be nice seeing King Kong.

LETTER TO ANDREI, JUNE 15, 1957

I haven't told you, dearest, but I've been having problems with my feet. I suppose this comes from walking everywhere in my flat sandals, and then remaining on my feet all day at work—and again on stage. I finally couldn't bear the pain any longer and decided to see a doctor. But the doctor only recommended soaking my feet in water and baking soda, which has not helped at all. Now Carmela has told me of a special doctor, a "magician," she calls him, who does wonders for people with foot problems. He will give me a special insole, she said, and cushions for my sandals and all sorts of treatments. The only problem is that he lives in Safed, which is in the north, quite far from Tel Aviv. Carmela says it's an interesting city, one of the most ancient in the country. This expert on feet is a religious man and Carmela told me his family has been in Safed (*Tzfat*, as it is called in Hebrew) since the sixteenth century!

I've decided to set out tomorrow, Sunday, to see him—Sunday is Shakespeare's day off. Orlando, who seems to be quite wealthy, is lending me the money for the trip. It will be my first time traveling alone in this country! I hope it goes well. I will continue this letter when I return.

* * *

I am back, dearest, and what an adventure I had! The bus ride to Safed was endless, it took hours. But I sat the entire way. I took the Duke's cane (one of our few props) with me and this way no one expected me to stand for elderly people or children when the bus was very crowded. In fact, I had to take two buses, but in both cases I had a seat for the whole journey.

I found the house of this doctor quite easily; the bus driver was very helpful and let me off at exactly the right street, even though there wasn't a stop there. Safed is a lonely, fabulous, haunted city. The houses are made of very old rough stone, and many of the streets are also cobbled with uneven rectangular stones. Instead of inclining, the streets are built in levels, so that you suddenly have to step up a street stair as you walk. Or else you come across an actual set of stairs, which are however so irregular they look as if they've been made out of modeling clay rather than stone. Most front doors are set slightly above the ground, and one sees many little children sitting in doorways. They stare at you as you pass, as do the shaded windows.

The doctor's house was small and dark. His children were all indoors, a whole brood of them. The youngest was sitting on his lap, and I said, "What a sweet girl," but he corrected me and told me the child was a boy, even though he had long, wavy hair down to his shoulders! The children were very well behaved; I haven't seen such well-behaved children since arriving in this country. The boys had skullcaps on their heads and the girls wore long dresses. The older girls were also wearing stockings, in this heat! I felt sorry for them, but they didn't seem to be suffering. I was glad that Carmela had warned me to dress modestly. In any case I always cover my arms with a shawl so I won't burn, but I also wore my longest dress and cotton socks.

The doctor, who has black hair and a white beard, took me to his office, a small room at the side of the house. I sat facing him and he placed a pillow on his lap and massaged my feet for an hour (with my socks on). He was very stern and I understood that I wasn't allowed to speak to him or look at him. In any case, his eyes were closed for much of the time. Then he measured my feet and gave me orthopedic sandals. Luckily he had a pair that fit me. They cost a fortune, but I had no choice. He had several amulets in his office, but he didn't use any hocus-pocus on me! I think they were just there for decoration. He's a real doctor, and he explained the reason for my shooting pains in technical terms.

I felt so much better after his treatment, and the new sandals make such a difference! He also told me I have to take a week off altogether: no acting, no work, just resting in bed for a week. We do have an understudy, and she will have to replace me this coming week.

However, it was after this visit that the most extraordinary thing happened. I was quite hungry by then, so I asked a passerby where I could eat, and she directed me to a little family restaurant nearby. The restaurant consisted of five tables and they were all full, so I had to share a table with another woman. The woman had a congenital facial disorder that affected her nose and upper lip and made them look a little squashed. She was extremely friendly and, like most people in this country, began at once to tell me all about herself: she was thirty years old, from Haifa, and her mother had been a spy who was caught and executed. She told me this very casually and even a little resentfully, and I had the sense that her feelings about her heroic mother were very complicated.

She had come down to Safed to meet a friend of hers, a nurse who was about to get married. This was their last time together on their own, she said sadly, and she told me she didn't think she herself would ever find a husband. She knew she wasn't beautiful, she said, but that didn't make her any less particular. "People think that my brain is affected by my looks, but my brain is exactly the same as Elizabeth Taylor's," she said, laughing at herself. She had a very pleasant personality, and I was thinking that this really was a lucky day for me.

The food was delicious; the owners do all the cooking themselves and there's no menu; you just eat what they've prepared that day as if you were a child at your parents' home. The meal—bread and margarine, potato soup, fried fish, vegetable couscous, cookies, and weak tea (Israeli tea is not very different from our "white tea" at home)—was on the expensive side but I treated myself, for I still had a little money left over from Orlando's loan, and the portions were very generous. Toward the end of the meal my table companion and I both needed to go to the washroom. We were given a key and instructed to make our way outside to a narrow lane at the back of the house, where there was a green wooden door marked *sheyrutim*, which means "services," or washroom.

We found the lane and the sign, and I told my table companion she could go first. She unlocked the green door and gave a cry of surprise. I looked over her shoulder and there on the dusty, tiled floor was a tiny infant sleeping inside a tomato crate lined with blankets! He was unnaturally white, with thin white hair on his little head, and he had nothing on but a diaper fastened with two large safety pins. There were several large red moles or birthmarks on his back.

A handwritten note was tied to the crate. It said, *I can't look after him. He's albino, keep him out of the sun or he'll die. Please.* My table partner picked up the baby and there were tears of joy in her eyes: I could see that this was a case of love at first sight. The baby woke up but he didn't cry. He only stared at us with curiosity. He had such intelligent eyes! Very light blue, nearly transparent, and he looked as if he were contemplating the theory of relativity or his next sonata.

The woman looked at me with a worried expression on her face. "You don't want him, do you?" she asked anxiously, as if we'd found a diamond necklace rather than a strange white baby!

"Oh, no," I said. "I have a son."

"Thank you," she replied. What an odd person she was, but everyone in this country is a little odd, including me, I suppose. "You choose a name for him," she said kindly, as if to compensate me for my loss.

"Alexander," I said at once. That seemed an appropriate name for such a thoughtful child.

"I may never marry," the woman said, "but I've been given a baby. Hello, my sweet Alexander!" She was glowing with happiness.

I gave her my kerchief so she could cover him as we headed back to the restaurant. I was a little worried that she would not be allowed to keep the baby and that there would be some sort of official adoption process she'd have to go through, with a long waiting list. Babies are very precious in this country and everyone wants them, but she was sure it would work out.

She was right. We called the police and there was such a fuss at the restaurant, with many superstitious people making all sorts of comments about Divine Providence. One horrible man there began to say that the baby was abnormal and no wonder his mother wanted to get rid of him—he said the baby should be put away in an institution. But everyone jumped at him and he left under a cloud of disgrace. A journalist came and took a photograph. And guess what? My table companion was allowed to take the baby home with her. Apparently with babies there is a kind of "finders keepers" clause. I was so relieved for her sake. She will only have to sign a few papers.

That was my day, dearest. I traveled to Safed on my own, bought orthopedic footwear, and named a baby.

I slept all the way home. I can't tell you what a relief it is to have comfortable sandals. I also look forward to my week in bed, I must say. I have a tall pile of lovely books I can hardly wait to read, which I've found in bookstores all over the city: English and French poetry (including the complete works of Baudelaire!), a play I hear is quite wonderful by someone called Samuel Beckett, a book by Gertrude

Stein, short stories by James Joyce, a novel by Pearl S. Buck, two by
John Steinbeck—as you see, I will only have time for a few of these
treasures. How wonderful that there is no censorship, and I can read
whatever I want! If only I could mail you these books—or better
still, if only you were here to feast on them yourself!

ﹷᗱᑌᒄ SONYA

When I first lost my hearing I assumed it was a temporary problem. I thought that as soon as I came home this unpleasant side effect would vanish. I did notice a great deal of distress around me at the hospital, but I was sick and sleepy, and I assumed people were upset about something unrelated to me—a plane crash, for example, or a terrorist act. Someone came to take a photograph of me and in my confusion I thought they were belatedly celebrating my birthday. I had hallucinatory dreams and I wasn't always sure what I'd dreamed and what had really taken place. In one dream the nurses buried my body under a mountain of sand, the way Noah used to do at the beach, but my brother didn't understand that we were playing, and he sat with his face in his hands, sobbing. I wanted to tell him that I was fine, that the sand was just there to keep me warm, but the words were too slow and heavy to be intelligible.

Eventually I was well enough to go home. I seemed to have plugs in my ears; all I heard was a lot of rumbling inside my head. On my third day back I handed Kostya a note: *How soon until I can hear again?*

He was washing large leaves of lettuce from the garden. I watched the dirt splashing into the sink. He put down the lettuce, turned off the water, dried his hands, sat down at the table and wrote: *You were accidentally given a massive dose of gentamicin at the hospital—no one knows how it happened. The drug damaged the eighth nerve (organ of hearing). The damage is irreversible. We've all started learning sign language. We'll all help you.* Noah was sitting at the table, watching me; he looked like someone being led to the gallows. He reached out to take my hand but I shook him off, pushed him away violently.

A week of tantrums and histrionics followed. I ran out of the house and faced oncoming traffic. The unlucky driver who was speeding toward me nearly had a heart attack as he swerved and hit a honeysuckle hedge instead of my body. There was a huge commotion; everyone in the neighborhood came out to see what had happened. My mother cried, Iris was furious, and my brother apologized to the driver and also treated him for minor injuries. I didn't repeat the dramatic suicide attempt, but several times Noah had to restrain me physically or I would have broken every dish in the house, and possibly also my violin.

I finally collapsed from exhaustion; one can keep up that sort of thing for only so long. Instead, I panicked. The thought that I would never hear again terrified me and I began to cling to my family like an infant. I refused to leave my bed and someone had to be with me at all times. Noah, my mother and brother, and even Iris took turns. I laid my head on my mother's breasts and stroked them, I clutched Noah's shirt. I even needed someone to accompany me to the bathroom. I regressed from day to day and by the end of the week I was sucking my thumb and no longer feeding myself. My family spoonfed me, and when they went too fast I lost my temper and refused to eat altogether. *Slower!* I wrote. The word covered an entire sheet, and the pen ripped through the paper.

The social worker who came to see us disapproved of my family's collusion in what she saw as manipulative, self-indulgent behavior. Her view was that I should be treated kindly but firmly. She sat near my bed and began signing to me, but I shut my eyes against her and turned the other way. When she touched my shoulder I went limp, as if I were dead. She gave up.

The social worker also told my mother that our beds should be moved apart. My mother and I slept side by side, our single beds pushed together. The bedroom was so small it left us few options, but the arrangement suited us. My mother, leaning back on three fat pillows, her long blond hair braided for the night, liked reading to me or telling me stories at bedtime. And I loved having her nearby, smelling faintly of vodka and cinnamon, and warding off any monsters that might be lurking just outside the window. She spoke about her professor and lover, my brother's father, who was unable to leave his wife for her, and about her childhood in Russia; the stories were entertaining and also interesting, full of psychological twists and observations. "Listen to how people deceive themselves," she'd start. Or: "Stingy people think they're generous because it's so hard for them to give that when they do give they feel like Jesus, while generous people think they never give enough and see themselves as stingy. I knew a woman . . ." and she'd tell me an amusing anecdote about a neighbor's parsimony or an aunt's sly deceptions. My mother rarely spoke of hardship or oppression, though she must have experienced both to some degree. She learned Hebrew in a basement, by candlelight, at great risk to everyone involved, and it was a miracle that she'd survived her dramatic escape from the Soviet Union while performing in Vienna.

When she wasn't in a storytelling mood she read to me: Walt Whitman, Dylan Thomas, Shakespeare. Her favorite play was *Romeo and Juliet*, which reminded her of her moment of glory, as she put it, when she had played Juliet in Moscow. She would hold her glass of orange juice and vodka in one hand and turn the pages of her paperback Shakespeare with the other. "*It was the nightingale, and not the lark*," she would say softly, intensely. *Romeo and Juliet* was a play about hate, not love, she liked to say. Or rather about irrationality, and Romeo and Juliet were meant to be seen as fools from start to finish.

That was Shakespeare's point, she said, not hate versus love, but the insanity of both. She complained that she could no longer get good parts, for she had difficulty acting in Hebrew. Her biggest role in Israel had been Ruth in Pinter's *Homecoming*, long ago; she'd played alongside a brilliant actor, Ami Sarig, whom she had adored and who was later killed.

There were also days when she came home late, exhausted from waiting tables, and there were nights when she didn't come home at all. My mother was determined and resigned, lively and unhappy, charismatic and placid. She had many devoted friends, and I felt lucky that I had a special claim on her.

In the end it was my mother who pulled me out of the despairing panic I'd fallen into. The social worker visited several times, but she was ineffectual; the only thing she left behind her was the sharp smell of Castile soap. But one morning I woke up and found my mother's arm around my waist, holding me close to her. She was still asleep and I knew she was snoring because I felt the vibrations against my back. I had dreamed I was in a garden in Spain, and there were remarkable blue and yellow butterflies everywhere, but I was the only one who could see them.

I looked at my mother's hand lying on the sheet: the generous blue veins traveling like a map of rivers from fingers to wrist, the tiny scattered freckles, innocent and helpless, the stubborn shadows cast by her veins, the stubborn generosity of my mother's hand. I touched her pinkie, and in her sleep she intertwined her fingers with mine. It was true that I had become a lone traveler on a strange planet, but if my deafness was unalterable, so was my family's love for me. I was important to them, perhaps more than ever, or at least I felt it more than ever. I was like a moored ship, a ship everyone had waited for, laden with rubies and spices. The main thing, I decided, was that I could see and feel: I was sensitive to movement, vibrations, colors, shapes; these things sent out a million messages. I considered pi, the numbers stretching out in a long, solitary row like signposts in a meadow, and I felt an affinity to it. Math also existed in a world of utter silence; we were the same.

Looking at my mother's hand, I understood her vulnerability for the first time, or at least accepted it for the first time. The other members of my family were resilient, but my mother was treading water; and now even her memory was betraying her. If I continued in this way she would sink with me. "I'm sorry," I spelled on her hand. Then I slipped away from her, went to the kitchen, and made breakfast. When my brother heard me and came to see whether I was all right, I sliced an orange in two and handed him half.

Now it was Khalid's arm that held my waist, it was his hand that lay peacefully on the bed. His skin was nearly the same color as mine but his hand was of course much larger. I was moved by the black hairs on his arms—a thin, fuzzy coating designed to protect him from possible harm: wind, for example, or cold. He was asleep; I felt his cool breaths tickling my back. It was a deep sleep and no wonder: he'd spent the morning running around Tel Aviv looking for a rare drug for his mother, he had come home in time to see her off, and on top of all this he'd had to cope with me—not once, but twice. Seventeen months of caring for his dying mother must have also worn him out. I couldn't imagine what that was like, seeing someone you loved suffer day after day and watching helplessly as she got worse and cried out in pain. At least my mother was not suffering. Some of the other people in the nursing home wept or raged, but my mother was docile and apparently unaffected by her surroundings. It was a blissful forgetting, in her case.

Had Khalid relented out of pity? I had no way of knowing. When I left his house I was afraid he'd come looking for me; I'd have to hide until he gave up his search. I dashed to the back of his building and crouched behind an old gold car that appeared to be undergoing repairs. I was shivering, despite the heat, and I pressed my hands against the sun-baked pebbles in order to absorb their heat and also to distract myself with their hard, sharp edges. I was aware that I had to pee, but I couldn't remember what that sensation meant, exactly, or what I had to do about it; I seemed to have forgotten all the rules.

I'd either made a sound without realizing it, or else my hiding place was not very efficient. A shadow appeared on the ground, and I looked up: it was Khalid. When I saw him standing there in his black jeans and navy blue T-shirt, looking utterly miserable, I thought my heart would break—not for myself but for him—and I felt very contrite. None of this was his fault: he hadn't asked me to come into his life—not this morning and not now. I had imposed my desire on him and added to his unhappiness. I would do whatever he wanted, including allowing him to appease his guilt, if that's what it was. Was it? We had not exchanged a single word since he'd taken my hand and led me back inside.

I had not called my brother. He'd be very worried, but I had no intention of releasing myself from Khalid's embrace. Whether or not Khalid's surrender was an act of charity, these were the happiest moments of my life. Even if Khalid didn't love me and I never saw him again, I would remember this always as a small visit to paradise.

Whatever his feelings, he had enjoyed himself. No one could put on an act like that—for example, the way he'd buried his head between my legs like a thirsty person who's been wandering for days in the desert and has finally come upon an oasis. I felt sorry for Debbie; her mistake was my good luck. I imagined the American living room in which her parents had talked her out of the marriage: the neat white sofas, the magazine racks. They had destroyed her chance for happiness; they had found a golfer named Eddie to replace Khalid.

I supposed it was a sense of resignation that had enabled Khalid to move so easily from his mother's death to his own pleasure. He had done everything he could for her, and knowing this freed him. For the first time it occurred to me that my father might be dead, too. Or maybe he was dying, maybe he needed me: there was no way of knowing.

Khalid stirred and I turned toward him. He opened his eyes sleepily and smiled. He spelled on my arm, *"Okay?"*

"Yes. I have to call my brother, though. He's going to be frantic." I reached into my bag, took out my phone and dialed Kostya's number. *In Jerusalem, coming home soon,* I entered.

"See you then," my brother answered, generous as always.

I signed off and turned back to Khalid. He reached for my notebook. "I'm sorry," I said. "I'm sorry it's so hard to talk to me."

"I like this system," he wrote. *"It makes me think more about what I say. I want to say, I am worried about you. You don't protect yourself like other people."*

"I don't have to protect myself from you!" I said.

"Before, you startled me. I didn't want to kiss you because I didn't want to hurt you. It wasn't anything else."

"You need to get dressed and look after your mother," I said. "You can't put it off forever. I feel bad enough as it is, coming at such a time."

He lifted his jeans from the floor, but only to search the pockets for cigarettes. "Do you mind?" he mimed.

"No, I like the smell."

He lit a cigarette and stared at me with a slightly amused look as he smoked.

"What are you thinking?" I asked.

"You don't seem to notice that you're not dressed," he scrawled in my notebook, the cigarette between his fingers.

"You're naked, too. Why should it be different for men?" I asked.

"We're less evolved," he wrote.

I said, "Even if I never see you again, I'll always remember this as the happiest day of my life."

"Send me an e-mail when you get home. Do you remember the address?"

"Yes, I have a good memory. That's how I found you, I remembered the license-plate number of the car you were driving."

He finished his cigarette and pulled me toward him. I felt his fingers tracing the scars on my back. I lay very still, afraid to break the spell. Let this moment never end.

Then I realized that he was spelling a question mark on my back.

"What happened?" he asked.

"It was in Beersheba, I was studying there. I found a stray kitten in the morning and I brought her to class. She sat on my lap all day. When I was in elementary school I used to bring snails and lizards to class   I was very spoiled and the teachers let me do anything I wanted. I stopped eventually, it was too eccentric. But I guess old habits die hard, and that day I brought the kitten with me. It was a late-afternoon course, and she slept on my skirt and purred. But when classes ended and everyone began to gather their things and shout and so on, she got scared and dashed away. So I stayed behind to look for her. Everyone left the building and I was still going through all the rooms, looking under tables, trying to find her. Two hoodlums came in through a classroom window, they wanted to steal a computer. They were stoned—crack, probably, or some drug that makes you violent. But I survived. They didn't kill me, I was lucky, I recovered completely. The only thing left are those scars, and I don't even know what they look like—I refuse to look at them in the mirror. I didn't read the newspapers, either, and I didn't give the police anything. I just wrote 'This is accurate' on the medical report, without reading it. I never testified in court."

Khalid didn't say anything. His face was closed, his eyes were very still.

He took my notebook and wrote for a few minutes. Then he handed it to me. He'd written, *"I saw something like that when I was very young, eight years old. We had an outhouse then—you had to leave the house to use it. And once in the middle of the night I had to go use it, I had a stomach flu. I took the flashlight and went outside. I remember I had stomach pain and I thought I was moaning. Then I realized the moaning wasn't from me, it was someone else. So I shut the flashlight instinctively and quietly I crept out, and behind the outhouse I saw a gang rape in progress. It was horrible.*

*I will never forget it, ever. I was afraid of being caught, I was afraid that if I
ran back to the house to tell someone, they would hear me. So I hid behind a
fence where I could hear everything but I couldn't see, instead of trying to save
that person. I never told anyone. You're the first person I'm telling."*

"How awful!" I said. "You must have felt so helpless, and guilty
about feeling helpless. Like my brother, but worse, because you
were there. But what could you have done? You couldn't have
stopped it."

"I should have woken up my father and told him," he wrote, shaking
his head.

"It was too late by then, anyway. And they might have heard you
running. You have to trust the instincts that made you act as you did,
Khalid. They protected you from harm."

"That's cowardice."

"Not for an eight-year-old who sees something like that."

*"I was not the same person after that. I felt for years that I had a secret,
and that no one knew what I was really like, the weak side of me."*

"It's different for me—maybe because everyone knew, and felt
bad for me. People think I was affected by what happened, but I
wasn't," I said. It's like having a cold and then getting over it.
Nothing's changed. I'm exactly the same."

Khalid shook his head. "It's impossible," he said. Then he wrote it.
*"It's impossible. Everything changes us, everything. And especially something
like that. I'll tell you something else. I'm not sure it was a woman they had,
it may have been a boy. All that happens to us stays with us."*

I sighed. I'd heard it all before—trauma, defense reaction, avoid-
ance mechanism—but those things didn't apply to me. You could
control your responses to events, you could decide how to react. As
far as I was concerned, the entire episode had been relegated to the
realm of nonexistence; it had dissolved and vanished. Expressions of
melancholy or pity annoyed me. I wanted my experience to remain
flat and inert; pity inflated it.

Khalid wrote, *"If you were so not affected, you'd be able to talk about* it, you'd be able to testify and to tell me, too. I wasn't able to tell any person because I was deeply affected, and I knew if I talked I would feel it all again, go through the feelings again. I can't control that."

"But it's not interesting, it's not important. To repeat a story is to save it and honor it and keep it alive, give it relevance. Words give things life and some things don't deserve to live. Those two don't exist for me and that's my victory over them. I don't hate them because they're not worth it. They didn't even succeed in humiliating me. The only thing I'm sorry about is that they made my family suffer. I didn't want anyone to find out for that reason, but by the time I got to the hospital it was too late. If they had any victory, that was it."

Khalid wrote, "*It's not a question of victory. You say that by not remembering you're canceling them, but don't you see, you're canceling yourself. You were important for that story, just as I was important, hiding there behind the fence and vomiting*"

"It's funny that you say that. . . . You know, when the janitor found me, that's what happened to him, too—he was sick. It must be atavistic, some inherited instinct, that reaction to violence."

"*You are being so rational and distant, Sonya. I wouldn't want to be so distant from my own experience, no matter how bad. My mother in such pain and suffering, my helplessness watching her, my father leaving, Debbie breaking it off, a cousin tortured in prison, what my people are going through, it's all part of me.*"

"Yes, it's true, these things become part of us. Even your stories are already becoming part of me. You know, at the time, while it was happening, I was thinking about a photo I once saw. It's a famous photograph, I think, these resistance fighters caught by the Nazis and about to be shot—someone had a camera. And you see this young woman's face, held up high, facing death, refusing to be afraid, have you ever seen it?"

He shook his head. His eyes seemed darker.

"And I thought, I'm going to die but my death is useless, unlike hers. And I felt sorry for myself and begged, though I'd sworn to myself at first that I wouldn't. Then suddenly they were gone, because one of them was afraid of actual murder, and he made the one who nearly killed me stop. I thought, They're gone and I'm alive. I waited for someone to find me. In the end it's nothing but chance. The drugs, the window, the kitten. They never found that kitten, though I asked everyone to keep an eye out for her. She was a tiny gray ball of fur, with a tiny little tongue licking my hand."

My eyes filled with tears, thinking about the kitten. Khalid was sad, too, but in the lines of his mouth I saw the edges of anger. I looked into his eyes and I understood that even if he loved me and wanted me, there were parts of him I would never know, could never know. I longed to transform the moment into something else, something immutable and blessed, but I didn't know how. Humans were clumsy creatures. Clumsily, we consoled each other as best we could.

Noah's diary, January 10, 1989.

In the news: man, we are in the mire.

Dear Mom,

What would you say if you saw me now? You'd say, "Well, Noah, at least you've kept your own hands clean, even if you're part of the criminal military machine." You'd say, "Noah, you're a stupid fool, trying to punish me by signing up. I'm dead, you can't punish dead people." You'd say, "I didn't want to die. It's true I didn't hire a body-guard, but who in this country doesn't get death threats once they decide to fight the system?" You'd say, "Serves you right, the hard times you've had in the army."

Actually, Mom, it hasn't been so bad. It could have been a lot worse. The army isn't evil, Mom. Training isn't evil. It's just stupid. All these kids come full of eagerness and love for their country and a desire to serve and give everything they have, and before long they're nothing but deflated, bored, disgusted people in uniform, torn between wanting to do the right thing and saving their arse. The only exceptions are the good boys who will never stop trying to please whoever it is they think will one day approve of them, and the total jerks, who fall in love with it all and can't wait for more because

they've waited all their lives to bully people. Is that the idea, to separate the good boys and the jerks from the rest of us? So that they can
run the army while the rest of us drudge along after them? No, it's
not that logical. Anyone looking for logic in the army will be disappointed.

That's why you turn yourself off—so you won't be bothered by
the absence of logic, and you figure later you'll turn yourself back
on, but it turns out not to be so easy. A sort of emotional fatigue
takes over, because a person gets tired of caring, just tired, that's
what it is. But now I wonder whether it stays with you forever, that
tiredness—maybe you think it's going to be temporary but then you
realize it's who you are now. I don't know, I guess I'll have to wait
and find out. The real problem isn't the army, Mom. The army is just
a neutral thing. The real problem is that all we do in this country is
fight and die and fight some more. And along the way we're becoming brutes. The things that are going on in the intifada . . . if you
were alive, Mom, you'd have a nervous breakdown. A million lawyers wouldn't be enough for all the cases coming up now. I just try
to block it all out. You can't survive otherwise.

Mom, I'm sorry I took your chocolate crêpe and gave you the
cheese, I know you were just giving me yours to be nice. I'm sorry
I never told you what I thought about what you were doing. Most of
all, I'm sorry I didn't defend you to my friends and their parents. I'd
defend you now, but since you died no one's said anything against
you, at least not to me. I wish they would, but they just get embarrassed if I bring the subject up.

You should have agreed to that trip, even though I'm not sure it
was such a great idea. Can you imagine the four of us in a hotel in
Venice? Dad would be planning our day second by second, you'd
fight with him because you'd want to wander aimlessly down the
streets, Sonya would want to spend about six hours staring at one
fresco, and I'd just want to sit in a café and soak up the sun and
maybe strike up a conversation with someone interesting.

Still, Dad wanted it a lot and you should have made the effort.

I'm forgetting what you looked like, it's weird. Sometimes I had the feeling you didn't like Sonya, that you resented the way she came into our family. You once told Dad she was spoiled, I overheard you. But you were always so careful to hide what you felt, you were so careful with what you said. You were like Dad that way, but for different reasons. He's careful because he doesn't want to hurt anyone and he wants what he says to be the right thing. You were just secretive, Mom. Did you become secretive because you were a lawyer, or did you choose to become a lawyer because you were secretive? Is that why you worked alone, because you didn't trust anyone? If you hadn't worked alone, maybe you'd be alive now. I remember once you had a fit of laughter, I don't even remember why. You laughed so hard your jaws hurt and you were clutching your stomach.

That's all I have to say. I miss you and I'm also sorry you had to miss out on the rest of your life. I think you'd want me to get justice done and find your killer, but Dad refuses to tell me what he knows. I begged and begged but you know how stubborn he is. He says you wouldn't want me to get involved. I think he's wrong but we can't ask you, can we? I'm still a bit mad at you, Mom.

Darling, I am now more worried than I have been in a very long time, for it's been three months without a word! I've made many friends here, because you know everyone is friendly. Even when you go on the bus, within seconds perfect strangers strike up conversations with one another, revealing their life stories or complaining about a hundred things. I cannot imagine a more plaintive people! Complaining is a national sport. So different from what I'm used to, and I must say it's very amusing.

But even though I meet so many people all the time, no one truly understands me, and only you are in my heart. Sometimes I laugh and everyone thinks I'm happy. They don't know that my heart is breaking. When I sing, though, at the café, all my longing comes out and it infects the entire room. Oh, our Russian songs are so sentimental!

Our play is now in repertory. We take a month off, then go on for a month, and so on. It's not always uniform. It depends on so many things, too silly and complicated to get into. There is always squabbling in the arts. I suppose there is squabbling everywhere. Rivalry, jealousy, gossip, petty resentments. Feingold now has several enemies, for he is not always diplomatic. I stay away from it all.

My greatest joy is our Kostya. He is so responsible and kind-hearted. I think I forgot to tell you in my last letter: he won three top prizes at school. In this small country, where there is such a need for people to fill all sorts of roles, he could do anything he wanted with his life. He could go into politics or law or medicine or the humanities—every day he reminds me more of you. No matter what happens, I will always have you with me, in this way. That is the great gift you and fate gave me. My love. I am filled with dread. Where are you, my Andrusha?

❧ SONYA

We dressed with the sobriety of adults returning to the serious business of life after a temporary suspension of everyday rules—or at least of ordinary experience.

Khalid phoned someone he knew and asked him to drive me to Central Station. A stocky, healthy-looking man showed up in a taxi. His rather dour wife was sitting beside him in the passenger seat, and they had brought their two little boys as well. The boys sat quietly side by side on the backseat. The family was secular or possibly Christian: the man's wife was not wearing a head covering and her long black hair was gathered into a purple clasp. Khalid had told them I was related to Iris Nissan, and as a result the driver was very well disposed toward me—or maybe he was just being effusive because I was Khalid's friend, or because he was an Arab and I was a guest.

Our parting was necessarily formal. Khalid spoke to his friends through the car window, then shook my hand. I got into the car and shut the door. Khalid waved good-bye as we drove off.

Khalid's friend took a roundabout route in order to circumvent the walls. Instead, we had to pass two checkpoints, but we had no difficulties at either one; the soldiers or border guards peeked into the car, checked our papers, and waved us through. No doubt God had sent the checkpoint angels to help us. The little boys beside me were very still and solemn; it seems that a protective passivity almost instinctively descends upon children when they know their parents are themselves vulnerable. I had to suppress a strong desire to lift one of them onto my lap and hold him close.

Because of the detour, it took us over an hour to reach Central Station, and I was distressed at having put these people to so much trouble. I insisted on paying "*lil-uwlaad,*" I mumbled in embarrassment, hoping I was saying it correctly. The man wasn't keen on taking payment but his wife firmly said, "*Shukran*" before he had a chance to refuse.

The bus for Tel Aviv was just about to leave. It was only half-full, and I was grateful to have two seats to myself, for I desperately needed anonymity and privacy at the moment. There were several things I had to sort out.

If Khalid wanted me, if he loved me, I would take a sabbatical and rent a room in Mejwan. I'd start learning Arabic immediately; it wouldn't take me long. Kostya could stay in the house or sell it, it would be up to him. If Khalid didn't want me, I'd know at once. I'd know it from his first e-mail, if there was one—I'd know late tonight or tomorrow morning. I didn't want to think about what it would be like if he didn't want me. But I'd need to be on my own, I'd need to mope in a cheap rented room downtown, where my surroundings matched my unhappiness. I would need the freedom to feel wretched, without Kostya hovering over me and suffering on my behalf.

Khalid had insisted on using a condom this time. Even when I thought I'd never marry I hoped to have a child one day: possibly by finding a sperm donor and hiring a hearing person to help—maybe even Ma'ayan. She was reliable and she'd be good with children. Now I wanted Khalid's child, but it was possible that even if he loved me he would not want to have a family with me. For one thing, we'd have to move—for if one were to be honest with oneself, peace was not going to descend upon us anytime soon, and a child with mixed parents would encounter endless difficulties. I could apply for a job in Britain and Khalid could study there, do his doctorate.

But even if Khalid wanted to see me again, it would probably take him a long time to decide how far he was willing to go with the relationship; he wasn't like me. Maybe in general men took longer in these matters.

I shut my eyes and drifted into a bizarre, chaotic dream. Nava was in Khalid's room, looking down at the two of us as we lay naked on the bed. She was wearing her usual moccasins and ankle socks, but a beautiful African gown had replaced her shorts, and she was young and healthy in the dream. Khalid and I were feeling a little conceited because we were so content, and we weren't paying proper attention to her. She was talking about the numeral two, and in the dream I could hear her, but Khalid couldn't. "Two will often take you by surprise," she said. "But in fact there are exactly eight integer solutions of $x^2+4=y^3$." I was glad Khalid couldn't hear her. There were mourners downstairs who had come to mourn Khalid's mother, and they'd accidentally let in several stray cats. I had to go down and feed the cats, make sure they were safe, but then it seemed that they weren't cats at all but miniature lions, and I'd have to put them in cages and return them to the wild. Then Khalid turned to me and said, "You have your mother's eyes." I said, "You've never seen her," and he said, "Yes, I have: I peeked inside your ID."

I emerged from the dream and shook it off with a sense of relief. "You have your mother's eyes"—that was what Eli had written in the margins of a student exam when he tried to seduce me outside the law building. I remembered being surprised by that comment, because he'd known my mother, whose eyes were round and blue, while mine were like upside-down Vs and very dark. If anything, my eyes bore a slight resemblance to his.

Eli . . . why was I thinking about Eli, when I wanted only to sink back into the sweet memory of Khalid's kisses? His style, for example, was different from Matar's. He was less hesitant and cautious—though of course the encounter with Matar had taken place under very different circumstances.

I was thinking about Eli because of what Khalid had said. *Do you resemble any of your mother's friends?*

Maybe Eli made that comment about my eyes because he was trying to ward off an unconscious fear, to deny a buried suspicion. On the other hand, if in any remote corner of his being he thought I might be his daughter, surely he would not have tried to seduce me. Of course, his arm around my waist may have been nothing but a manifestation of the sort of compulsive flirting for which he was famous. Maybe he never meant for it to go further; maybe he knew I would not give in.

What if it was true—what if his fear was founded in fact? It seemed impossible: how could someone like Eli be related to me? Even if he was my mother's lover . . . well, the timing was about right; I was born shortly before his first marriage. My mother's periods were no longer regular, and she had not had one in several months when she conceived. Eli, who was in his early twenties at the time, could have easily been persuaded that she was too old to have a child. And maybe in those days he was not quite as careful as he became later, after his first wife's abortion. He had written about that abortion extensively in his books; it was a turning point in his thinking.

But surely my mother would have known if it was him, and she'd have told me: why wouldn't she? She would have told him, too, and asked for child support. It was more likely that my father was someone with a family, and she didn't want to ruin his marriage and career. Her experience with the Russian physicist may have decided her against a replay of that doomed situation. For I no longer believed her claim that there were too many potential candidates to choose from, as if she'd slept with dozens of anonymous men. She was quite picky, actually, and she often told us about the men she'd rejected. Teeth in bad shape. Dandruff. Cracked nails. The smallest things were reason enough to dismiss an offer. Instead, she would invite her unsuccessful suitors for supper. If they couldn't have her, at least they would be treated to a sample of my brother's cooking.

It was possible, though, that my mother knew my father was Eli but wanted to protect me from him. Given his views on parenthood, she may have felt that I would only be hurt by his inevitable rejection.

All the same, it seemed very unlikely. We were so dissimilar— though now that I thought of it, the way he organized his papers at the end of each class, with a determined defiance of lackadaisical tendencies, was nearly identical to my own brisk offensive on my briefcase. And maybe, if I really thought about it, if I really wanted to think about it, there were some other things, too: his sense of humor, his careful logic, his love of teaching. He was a patient teacher; he was informal and friendly in the classroom, and respectful of even the most annoying or rude students. He liked people; he was almost never seen alone. Though he slept with all and sundry, he needed one loyal, close person in his life at any given time. His spontaneity, his refusal to be intimidated, his quiet way of rebelling: these personality traits were familiar. Oh—he could be so cruel, though! But we are not created in our parents' image. I remembered a funny sticker I'd seen somewhere, showing a sloppy hippie kid and a conservative father in a suit glaring at each other. ANY GENETIC RESEMBLANCE IS UNINTENTIONAL, it said.

It would take some getting used to, if it was true. I remembered a film I had once seen about the grown daughter of a womanizer. *Daddy Nostalgia*, it was called. Scenes from the movie came forcefully back to me.

On the spot I decided to pay Eli a visit and question him. I was suddenly very impatient: it was imperative that I see him immediately. What if he died of a heart attack during the night and I never had another chance? Besides, if Eli was the person I'd been waiting for all these years, I had waited long enough.

I phoned Kostya and entered, *Going to Eli's to ask if he's my father, don't wait up.*

To my astonishment, Kostya replied, *I can tell you. Yes.*

I stared at the words on the little screen. *I can tell you. Yes.* Kostya knew. Kostya knew and he hadn't told me.

I turned to the window and looked out into the darkness. Beyond the darkness were the hills, beyond the hills houses, inside each house furniture, bodies, vases. The highway blocked out the walls and chasms. What I needed was a wall of light, a blinding light that would leave nothing out: nothing to find, nothing to search for. Inside it, every dead and living body would surface like a digit in a unique system that negates all the systems preceding it. I would float up to the wall, buoyed by the light, I would be the keeper of the wall.

I had trusted my family: my mother, my brother. I thought I knew them inside out, and in the end I had missed the most basic thing there was. In the end I was profoundly stupid. I had lived with three adults who were keeping a secret from me—for Iris must have known as well—and I'd never noticed.

But none of that mattered, really. The only thing that mattered was that I had found my father, after all these years. Thanks to Khalid, really.

And now I would go and tell him.

I brought my gaze back to the words on my phone screen. *I can tell you. Yes.* I was doomed to be surrounded by people who wanted to protect me. Kostya and my mother didn't understand that Eli's attitude to children or the sort of person he was were beside the point. All that mattered was knowing. You could deal with something you knew, find a place for it in your world, even if it was only a shed in the backyard. But if you didn't know, a ghostly absence accompanied you everywhere you went.

And really, how could Kostya and my mother have predicted his reaction, were he told that he had a cute little child? He might have been happy, he might have loved me.

Upon the surface of my love for Khalid and the euphoria of our time together, this new excitement of having a father came skimming like a dizzy dolphin. As for the creepy close call of seduction: my attitudes to dating must have convinced Kostya that I was safe from Eli. He was right. I *was* safe from him. But what a chance to take!

It was a little comical, really—the man who handed out free condoms to students, who wrote so brilliantly about the untenable ethical implications of having children, himself had a child. Maybe he would write a whole new book when he found out. *Parenthood, Purpose and Passion.*

Or *Parenthood, Panic and Predicament.*

⚜ NOAH'S DIARY, MAY 2, 1991.

In the news: poor Sonya.

I've been discharged one month early but I'm not at home, I've moved in with Marion and two other people, Dalia and Modi, downtown. Our apartment is on Henrietta Szold Street. I also applied to an art school in Berlin.

I have fantasies of killing those guys. I didn't think I'd ever want to kill someone, just kill another human being, just drive a knife deep, deep into another person's heart and watch with joy as he died, hopefully with a lot of suffering. Even with Mom I didn't have fantasies of killing the murderer, I just wanted him found, I wanted him to go to prison. But now I really want to kill those two. That's who I am, that's inside me. I imagine sneaking into the prison with a gun. I'd start with the kneecaps, I'd shoot them bit by bit, so they'd die with the greatest amount of pain possible. If I could do it, would I? I think I would. I really think I would, but I can't.

As for Sonya—I don't understand her at all. She's acting as if she just found out she won the Nobel Prize or something. She's in a great mood, cracking jokes, totally cheerful, she even ordered a cake with candles to celebrate her own recovery. Is she putting on a show so we won't feel bad, or is this a way of avoiding what happened? She says that's her way of winning. By not caring. She also says she's glad to be alive and that she appreciates life in a new way, like in eighteenth-century novels where the wayward hero reforms after a near-fatal illness. She says it was a non-event, because the past has no existence and no reality, as everyone knows: the only thing that gives the past form is memory. I think she needs a therapist and so does Dad, but she totally rejected the idea. Oh, God, she's so *weird*. Maybe that comes with a high IQ, I don't know.

Dad's holding on as usual but he looks like a wreck. He was furious that the police report went straight to the press, but there's no law against it. And Sonya didn't care, which is the main thing. She said those brothers made fools of themselves and now everyone knew what kind of perverts they were. If they'd had a brain they'd be embarrassed, she said, but most likely they lacked one. That's what she said in the hospital when I first came to see her. I was afraid that as soon as I saw her I'd feel sick again, the way I felt when Dad called me at the base. *I have something to tell you. It's about Sonya, she was attacked by two men.* That was it, that's all he said, I found out the rest from Dror, my commander, who had spoken to someone in the hospital. It was good that Dror told me. He was the right person for that job.

I thought that visit would be the hardest thing I'd have to do in my life but in the end it was easy because of Sonya's attitude. We'd been in a fight for three years and the first thing she said was, "So the break I had from your stubborn, annoying personality has come to an end. Oh, well, nothing that good can last." Then she gave me a long list of things she wanted me to get for her: Belgian chocolates, pomegranates, a mohair shawl, new earrings, a mug, thank-you cards, and a hardcover edition of *War and Peace*, which she would finally have time to read, because the doctors told her she had to take it easy for a few weeks.

What sort of family are we? It's as if we're marked or something.

Actually Oren's family is going through a lot, too. His parents are getting divorced—his father left for some girl he met, and his mother isn't taking it very well, she's threatening to kill herself. Also his sister dropped out of school and has gone wild. She's doing heavy drugs and living in some hole with all her addict friends. I was going to join him in Brazil and meet his girlfriend, but now I can't. I need to stay here, more for Dad than for Sonya.

We finally took Gran to a home. Dad just couldn't cope with her any longer, so I took the initiative. There was an opening for her at a private nursing home and Dad took her there just to see if she liked it. He made a list of other places for us to look at on the same day but Gran took to this one right away. The minute we got there she went up to the receptionist and said, "I'd like a single room with a view, please. There are seventeen oranges in the trench."

She didn't want to leave the residence so we left her there, and Dad went back in the evening to bring all her clothes and things and to decorate the walls. I think he's really relieved. He said Gran nearly set the house on fire last week.

It's sort of sad, but on the other hand she'll never be afraid of dying, the way most of us are when we get old and sick. That's a definite plus.

I just can't get the images out of my head. I feel totally haunted and I also feel so angry. Marion says I have to relive Sonya's experience a few hundred times in my mind before I'll be free of the images. She says she went though the same thing because her mother was an orphan who was sent to live with these senile ex-Nazis (they didn't know she was Jewish!) and their superstitious housekeeper (who was also the old man's mistress). Marion says that people we love are more vulnerable and defenseless in our imagination than they are in real life.

She's teaching me German. She learned it from her mother.

Dearest, such a very long time has passed since I've heard from you, it feels like at least a hundred years! Every time I walk on the beach at night I long for you to see the beauty of the sea, how it changes color with the light, how it brings out all the emotions inside you and carries them on its waves. I want you to feel the soft sand shifting under your feet as the two of us walk along the shore. I imagine you're with me and I carry on conversations with you in my thoughts. I know it may be a long time before we have the chance to be together again, but one day it will happen.

Two days ago in the middle of the night there was a desperate knock on the door. My heart froze because for one second I forgot I was in Israel and that here I don't have to be afraid. It was such a relief to remember where I was! I opened the door and there was Tanya, in terrible shape. Her boyfriend, or whoever he is, hit her again. There is unfortunately violence against women here, too— and without the excuse of drink. I suppose there is no avoiding these things, no matter where you go. I have heard that there are some African or Asian tribes in which women have never been mistreated. They must be descendants of another species that only looks like *Homo sapiens* from the outside.

Luckily Kostya is a sound sleeper and didn't stir from that little corner of his behind the bookcase.

Tanya has moved in for now. It's very crowded but she has nowhere to go. We found a foam mattress for her which we keep on my bed during the day. At night we move the table against the wall and there is just enough room for the mattress on the floor. She has told me a little about herself, it's a very sad story. But she's so lively and high spirited in spite of everything. She is really a good example to us all.

I don't think she will stay here long. She's very restless. She longs to have her own little place and says she "will do whatever it takes" to get it. I don't think she means robbing a bank . . . I hope she will change her mind. She looks up to me so much, it's very touching. She's only fifteen! Remember, I had a feeling that she wasn't telling us the truth about her age, and I was right.

My love, I await your letters and I pray you are getting mine. I want you to know how safe we are and how well we are doing here, despite the dreadful heat and the difficulties that crop up. But difficulties are an inevitable part of life. Above all, Kostya is thriving. He has really taken to this place, and you know, in many ways it's a children's paradise here. Some streets are not even paved and the boys and girls make bonfires on the sand and sing songs all night long. They bake potatoes and then they spread the charcoal on their faces and run around pretending to be *"kushi,"* which comes from the word Cushite and means a dark-skinned person from Africa. The children in this country are quite wild and talk back to their parents, but for all that they are sweet, on the whole. Do you know that on a crowded bus old people will almost always stand up for a young child, and a parent with a child will let the child sit while the parent stands? It's really quite something. Parents will also buy chicken (which is extremely expensive) for their children, while they themselves make do with sardines, chicken feet, *gorgels* (throat), *pupiks* (belly buttons) and tongue (and you know me—I would rather starve than eat those things!) or else they'll buy sour cream for the children and the cheapest factory cheese for themselves. Children are placed at the center of everything here, it's almost like a cult. They are the new hope, they are supposed to make all our dreams come true. Let's hope Kostya is wrong and there are no more wars.

Darling, I have read your last letter, the one that came in April, so often that I know every comma by heart. I keep it under my pillow along with your watch chain. It's so hot, darling! I've never known such heat in my life. But at night we go to the beach and it's quite wonderful swimming in the warm water and then coming out all wet. The beach is full of people and no one is shy about who they are here, so you get to see everyone in their true colors. There is quite a remarkable spectrum. Yet the heat seems to make us all very similar: hot!

I hope you too are enjoying milder weather and some sun, my darling, and that you have completely recovered your health. I await your next letter.

◈ SONYA

I knew where Eli lived, because I'd once ended up at a party at his place. He owned a beautiful split-level flat not far from the university. The flat was neat and clean and elegant; Eli was known for his personal library of rare books, carefully arranged by subject, and for his love of Japanese art. He also had the largest collection of classical CDs I'd ever seen in a private home.

Many of these were apparently gifts. According to Ma'ayan, there were two categories of women in Eli's life. The vast majority were women of all ages, backgrounds, shapes, and sizes with whom he had sex until they broke the rules, which was usually right away, sometimes even minutes after sex. For example, the woman might say, "Do you like Indian food?" or "When will you be in town again?" or "Are you coming to Dudu's party?" In the second category the women were also heterogeneous: Eli didn't care whether they were clever or stupid, sophisticated or infantile, beautiful or frumpy. In Eli's mind women seemed to be generic beings, endless replicas of Eve. Our distinguishing features weren't significant.

What the women in the second category had in common, however, was that they were astute enough to understand the rules, and masochistic enough to accept them. Women who didn't understand the rules vanished very quickly from Eli's life; Ma'ayan said he could be quite brutal in getting rid of them. Often he would say something sufficiently memorable to make the rounds on campus.

Within this second category, among his special coterie of three or four women (one of whom would be his wife), he inspired great devotion, and these women gave him wild, unaffordable gifts—all their savings, or a car, or a set of 100 classical CDs. Even the temporary women, while they were still in the running, gave him gifts. Something about Eli inspired gift giving in women.

The party I'd been to had ended dramatically, with Eli's fifth wife jumping out of the window. Luckily she landed on a bush and only broke one arm and cracked her hipbone. Eli began to cry; he'd had a lot to drink. "She never took anything for herself," he moaned, kneeling on the lawn as the police tried to keep the gathering crowd at bay. Eli made it sound as if his wife had had a choice in the matter, and though everyone knew this premise was faulty, people felt bad for him. The police suggested he get some sleep before coming to the hospital; what they meant was that he should wait until he was sober. He found consolation in the arms of a new student from Argentina, the star of the women's basketball team.

I didn't care about any of that. All I wanted was to stand in front of a flesh-and-blood person and know that I was his daughter, and for him to know it, too.

We pulled into Tel Aviv's new Central Station shortly before midnight. I took a taxi to Eli's: it was my eighth ride that day. I'd been in one vehicle or another with an odd assortment of people: my lover, Kostya, an ancient Yemenite, Lorelei, a lonely soldier, a Palestinian family, strangers on a bus, and now a garrulous taxi driver. The driver chatted the entire way, never once noticing that I couldn't hear a word he said. He seemed to be complaining about taxes, regulations, corruption . . . it was just as well I wasn't following.

I gave the driver the last of my cash and he drove off, leaving me alone on the dark street. The smell of cut grass and hyacinth swept through the night air and plunged me into a memory that was more an elision of time than a remembered set of images. In one of those rare flashes that seem to transport us bodily to a specific moment in the past, my old kindergarten room resurfaced, one afternoon during nap time. The same smell had drifted in through the open windows as I watched a ray of sunlight slant down on eight washed spoons lined up on a red checkered dish towel. For some reason I brought out everyone's solicitude back then: adults smiled at me, children gave me toys, dogs licked my chubby legs. Every detail of that afternoon came back to me: the eight spoons glinting in the sun, my excitement at the number eight and its multiples, the funny assortment of bare feet, white and brown and dark brown, on the blue mats.

I wanted this immersion into the past to stay with me, but it lasted only a second or two before retreating to the realm of mere memory, and there was no luring it back.

Eli's flat was on the first floor of a four-story building that was divided symmetrically into four split levels: two at the bottom and two on top. It occurred to me that he might not be alone—but maybe that was just as well: having a witness would add solidity to the encounter. I ran my hands along the sweet-smelling bushes that lined the pathway, as if confiding my hopes to the leaves.

For some reason, the door to the building was open and held in place by a doorstop. I walked in, climbed the stairs to Eli's flat and knocked on the door. *Here I am, your daughter*, I thought happily. *Hello, Father.* I had imagined this moment countless times, and though I'd pictured a somewhat different setting—a house rather than an apartment, an entire family rather than a solitary and difficult person, a stranger rather than someone I knew quite well—all the same, I felt like Aladdin coming across his genie. "Bring me to my father," I would have told the genie. And here I was.

There was no answer. I knocked several times without results. Most disappointing! I sat down on the hallway stairs, wondering whether I should wait for Eli to come home. As I was deliberating, the door opened.

Eli stared at me, then past me, with a bewildered look on his face. He said something I couldn't make out, something like *baba*. He was quite drunk.

There are people whose persona stays intact no matter what they do. Even when he drank, Eli came across as complicated, clever, and entirely self-assured: someone who could not be intimidated. He'd be at ease wherever he went, knowing exactly what to do or creating new standards of behavior if he didn't. Everything about him was just right: his casual jeans and black T-shirts and old running shoes, his battered leather briefcase, his cute sunglasses. And yet in spite of his informality and audacity, or the quick blow jobs in his parked car after class, there was a protective, impenetrable barrier around him, a message of *do not enter*. No one was afraid of him, but at the same time no one dared to cross him. *Trespassers will be prosecuted.*

And so even now, with his hair disheveled, his feet bare, his shirt half tucked into his jeans, and two of his toenails black with a fungal infection, he retained his infallibility, his handle on the situation— though when he turned back into his apartment he tripped on a chair and knocked it over. Eli's flat had been clean and tidy when I'd last seen it, at the party: despite the drinking and hashish and belly dancing, no one had dared displace so much as an ashtray. Eli's wife continually made the rounds, removing empty bottles, picking up pieces of tin foil, and straightening out the bathroom.

Now the place was in a dreadful state and smelled of decaying bananas. A hand-painted Japanese vase had tipped over and smashed into bits; the pieces lay scattered on the tiled stone floor amidst old newspapers and dirty dishes. I was afraid Eli would step on one of the shards. "Be careful," I said, maneuvering him toward the sofa. He flopped down against the fat blue sofa cushions and repeated what he'd said earlier, which I now understood was "Barbara." Barbara was expected, and she was late.

I went to the kitchen in search of a broom, located one in the adjacent laundry room, and swept up the shards, setting the larger ones aside for safekeeping; the delicate painted flowers on the white china were too pretty to throw out. Eli in the meantime was sliding his hands between the sofa cushions, apparently looking for his cigarettes.

He found the pack, finally, and tried to light a cigarette but he was having difficulty with the lighter. I took the cigarette from his mouth, lit it myself, and handed it back. I noticed an uncovered vial of Valium on the side table next to the sofa; it was half-empty.

I decided to call Raya. Had Eli been sober I could have managed on my own, but as it was I needed some backup.

At Eli's, can you come? I asked her.

Be right there, Raya answered. *Should I bring Lily?*

If she wants.

I put away my phone and went to the bathroom because I had to pee, but also because I wanted to feel that I was part of my father's house. I wanted to examine the rooms, become familiar with their distinguishing features. Here in the bathroom, for example, pale green guest towels had been carefully folded on the rack, and a little pink square of naphthalene deodorant—my favorite kind   had been placed discreetly behind the toilet. There was a substratum of order beneath the current mess.

When I returned to the living room Eli looked at me and said, "Sonya," pleased with himself not so much for locating my name within the fog, but for anchoring himself by means of the retrieval.

"Yes, I'm here."

"Come, Sonya." He clasped my wrist and tried to pull me toward him.

I freed myself from his grasp. "Eli, listen to me. I'm your daughter. Remember my mother, Anna? Remember you had an affair with her, when you were young? Before you were married? You thought she was too old to get pregnant, but she wasn't. Do you remember?"

"Turn on the radio, maybe there's been a bomb," he said, extending his arm in the direction of his elaborate sound system.

"The radio?"

"The news . . . maybe Barbara's . . . been killed in a bomb. Suicide bomb."

"There hasn't been any bomb, Eli. I'm sure Barbara's fine."

"Come, sit by me," he said, reaching out for me again.

"You can't start with me, Eli. I'm your daughter."

"Hey, aren't you supposed to be deaf or something?"

"Sometimes I can see the shape of sounds."

"The shape of sounds, I like that. The shape of sounds . . ." He mumbled something else, which I lost.

"Raya's coming over," I said. "Remember her—the belly dancer? She danced at your party. She's coming over with Lily, we're going to get you to bed."

"It won't work out. Barbara's coming . . ."

"I don't think Barbara's coming, and even if she does, you're too drunk for visitors."

"Never too drunk for a warm, wet cunt," he said, and began to cough. I was tempted to pound his back, but I held back. Kostya said pounding rarely did much good in any case.

Eli shut his eyes for a few minutes. Then he lifted the bottle of whiskey, which he'd set on the carpet by the sofa, and poured himself another drink. The glowing orange-gold liquid looked like a magic potion—something that could make you invisible, say, or fill you with love.

I strolled over to his bookshelves. Eli's own books took up nearly half a shelf; he'd published several poetry collections, two short-story anthologies (his least successful endeavor), and nearly twenty academic books on a wide range of topics. I took down his most recent book, a volume of collected poetry, and read the biography on the back flap, with its long list of awards and accomplishments. I felt a giddy pride. This was my father! I kissed the austere black-and-white photograph and held the book tightly against my chest. I wanted to waltz with it around the room. Instead, I opened the book and began to read one of the poems, an early one from 1973, the year I was born:

If only there had been a voice from the clouds
Or fiery letters moving across a wall—an *alef*, a *mem*;
But I was beguiled, half-senseless, and she
Braced herself for pain, panic—but just for herself.
She thought only of herself then.
This is the way of mammals:
Heedless, munching on apples,
Staring stupidly at the road while cars
Like flaming swords pounce and gorge on air
And we still can't add two and two.
Fate, which means chance, which means
The way things fall out,
A fat sacrificial well waiting for virgins,
Devours the placenta.
East of the garden the gate has been pried loose.
No matter what you do or pray
The gate has come loose.
Newborns stray.

In the news: talks, maybe. I'll believe it when I see it.

I was packing, getting ready for Berlin, and I was looking all over the place for my harmonica. I looked in Sonya's wardrobe and I came across a box marked *Anna*. Mostly it was letters in Russian on old blue airmail paper. Also, a whole bunch of dialogues. I guess Gran was working on a play or something, they're in her handwriting in these old school notebooks with pictures of Herzl on the back. The play is about a young guy and an older woman. The guy loves her and wants to marry her, but she refuses. They keep talking in circles and it's pretty good, actually—you can't tell whether she's refusing because she loves someone else (who died) or because she thinks he's too young or because she doesn't trust that he'll be loyal. The reader keeps thinking one thing, but then it goes in another direction, and then you start thinking there's a fourth reason that's a secret. But I guess Gran never managed to finish it.

I also found something else, a sealed envelope with the word PRIVATE written on it in Sonya's unmistakable handwriting. I steamed it open. It was a detailed description of what happened to her down in Beersheba, in the classroom. I forced myself to read it. Then I put it back in the envelope, resealed it, put the box back in the wardrobe and went for a long walk. I was supposed to meet Marion but I stood her up, I didn't feel like seeing anyone. I knew she'd understand, she's very good about stuff like that.

Though I walk through the valley of the shadow of death. I shall fear.

LETTER TO ANDREI, JULY 25, 1957

Dearest, can you imagine it, that teacher I told you about, who came to complain about Kostya, has sent me a letter proposing marriage! How ridiculous! Poor man. I am sorry to be hurting him, but how could he be so deluded, so out of touch? Even if he had the slightest chance, which he does not, imagine proposing to a complete stranger! That is hardly the way to go about these things. I am reminded of your arranged marriage and how badly that turned out. To think that love can be forced or created out of nothing . . . Love is the most uncontainable thing there is!

I have not had any other marriage proposals, but men here are very forward. And the women are cooperative, they like the attention. Everyone knows not to waste their time on me, though. There was one poet in particular, a shy young man, whom I finally had to shake off quite heartlessly. I have explained that I am married (for we are, even without the official stamp) and that I shall never be disloyal, ever. I am only yours, yours, yours. I know you told me I have to forget you and try to start life over, find a husband who will love me. That will never happen. But if I do not hear from you soon, I am sure I will die.

I must cheer you up now, and myself, with a marvelous story

about our Kostya. Last month I took him to a free outdoor chamber music concert and immediately he decided he must learn to play the violin. He went up to one of the violinists after the show, a pretty young woman, asked her a few questions, and told me of his decision. Of course we don't have a penny to spare for lessons, let alone an instrument! But Kostya told me not to worry.

You will hardly believe how resourceful he was—but of course you will, remembering what our son is like. He collected scraps of paper from here and there and he wrote on each one: *12-year-old boy will do cooking and small chores in return for violin lessons and violin practice time. Please contact Kostya at 8 / 12 Spinoza Street.* He put these notices up all over the neighborhood. Well, the following day at seven in the morning there was a knock on our door, and it was someone from the radio! They wanted to interview him! So we went down to the radio station in their car (Kostya was very excited to be in a private car) and Kostya explained his situation on the air.

When they asked, "What do your parents think of this?" he replied, dearest, "They are both very supportive." I was so moved. You see, you are on his mind.

Of course he had many offers! People responded from all over the country. It was really something to see. One person offered us a violin! A man from a nearby town whose daughter died of leukemia—he said we could have her violin. He had not wanted to sell it, but felt that this was the right thing to do, finally, with her instrument. We didn't feel it was right to take it for free, so we agreed that it would be a loan for now. We've become friendly, and this man comes over for Kostya's *lokshen* (noodle) kugels quite regularly now. He is divorced; the marriage broke up after his daughter's death.

So now Kostya has a violin and an excellent teacher—the pretty young woman (her name is Dafna) whom he approached after that concert. I wonder whether this entire endeavor was meant to snare her! Several other teachers contacted us, but Kostya seemed to be waiting for her. However, he has not taken up the violin merely in order to have lessons with Dafna, for he really is talented and spends all his free time playing. I wonder we never noticed his love of music before.

In some ways, living here in Israel is like living with a huge extended family—with all the advantages and disadvantages that come with families. I long for you. Come soon.

SONYA

People said that Eli was different when he was younger; they said he was once shy and introverted. Maybe when he knew my mother he was kinder. If only I could ask her! But my mother, like Eli, was another person now. She had been transformed into an alien being who spoke no known language.

My last visit to the nursing home had been almost implausibly surreal; I could have been on the set of some experimental horror film. It was night, and there had been a power outage in the building; under the emergency lights objects seemed to waver, as if trapped inside the eerie violet shadows. The receptionist on duty was a young immigrant I'd not seen before. He was red faced and puffy, and he was paging through a bodybuilding magazine, staring at photos of men who had molded their bodies into grotesque shapes—inspired, no doubt, by childhood fantasies of comic-book superheroes. It struck me that the young immigrant was looking at one anatomical disaster while surrounded by another, the kind brought on by age. I wondered whether one canceled out the other for him, and made the human median more tolerable.

I signed in and made my way down the long corridor. Bleak human odors half smothered by disinfectant clung to the airless gloom, and the small square windows on the doors peered at me like glazed eyes in a heart-of-darkness jungle. I reached my mother's room and peeked in. It was pitch black inside and smelled of urine. I left the door wide open so the weak light from the corridor could filter in. My mother was awake. Like a wrinkled human doll she watched me impassively.

The bars along the bed were not easily adjusted, and I had to struggle to bring them down. I led my mother to the carved wood chair by the side of the bed; I'd brought the chair here long ago, to replace the depressing institutional one that had come with the room. I did it for myself, of course; I wanted to cheer myself up when I came to visit. I lifted my mother's wet flowered nightgown over her head and replaced it with a freshly laundered one. Her small breasts were still beautiful, as smooth and round as they had been when I was little.

I changed the sheets, brought her back to the bed, and climbed in with her. We sat there, side by side, my mother propped up on pillows. I held her hand and told her about the bodybuilding magazine and the power outage, and her breathing fell into rhythm with my voice.

Eli came over and took his poetry book from my hands. He stared at his own image on the back cover and said something I didn't catch.

"What did you say?"

He seemed to be looking around for a pen. I handed him mine. He opened the book and wrote on the title page, *For Sonya, whose heart is pure, from Eli.* His handwriting was a little choppy and he had some trouble with the word *tahor*, pure. "Take it, please," he said, giving me the book.

"Thank you."

"How about some music?" he asked.

"What do you want?"

"You choose."

I pulled out a CD at random; it was the Vienna Boys' Choir singing Mozart. Like pools of crystal water, their voices would promise peace: *Ave verum corpus natum de Maria virgine* . . . Could an implant really restore hearing? Or would it just mean noise and distortion, a muddle of sounds you couldn't control, a robot feeling of being attached forever to a portable machine?

I felt a hand on my shoulder. Raya and Lily had entered the flat.

"I'm so happy to see you," I said.

"Yes," Raya said. "What's going on?"

"Oh, nothing. Eli's a little drunk, that's all, and I came to tell him something important."

"More mysteries! How was Jerusalem?"

"Very wonderful—I'll tell you later. Eli asked for some music." I handed her the CD, but she dropped it carelessly on the coffee table.

Eli was both baffled and pleased by the arrival of two more women. "The three muses," he said, looking at us. It was a relief having Raya there to translate. "Melpomene, muse of Tragedy," he said, staring at Lily with flattering interest. "And . . . Clio." He moved his glance to Raya but quickly looked away, for just as he knew intuitively which women he could seduce, he also knew which ones disapproved of him. "And you, Sonya, are of course Calliope. Three such lovely creatures . . . I never hurt anyone."

"You've hurt hundreds of women, Eli," Raya said. "We're going to make you coffee. And I'll bring you a glass of water."

"Come to think of it, I have a strong suspicion that I'm going to be sick," Eli said. He made his way to the bathroom but didn't shut the door. After a few minutes I went to check up on him. He was sitting on the edge of the bathtub and holding on to the shower curtain for balance. When he saw me he tried to get up, but made the mistake of pulling on the shower curtain for leverage. The entire apparatus came crashing down on his head, and the curtain, a large sheet of nylon covered with blue swans, enveloped his body. He began flailing his arms wildly from under it, as though battling some giant squid. I burst out laughing.

Lily and I untangled Eli while Raya made coffee. Eli wanted to stay in the bathroom in case he had another wave of nausea, so we left him there and began to clean up a little. I wiped a sticky patch on the floor and Lily collected dirty dishes. Then a sound caught her attention and she looked at me with a worried expression on her face.

But before I could react, Eli emerged from the bathroom. He looked much better. He'd tucked in his shirt and washed his face. *My daddy is a handsome devil,* I hummed to myself.

"Thank you," he said, as Raya handed him a glass of water. He sank back down on the sofa, pulled a cigarette out of the pack, and handed it to me. He wanted me to light it for him again.

"No," I said. "You're not going to smoke any longer. That's it, you're quitting!" I broke the cigarette in half. Eli was dumbfounded. "Raya, I have something amazing to tell you. I'm Eli's daughter. Eli, are you listening?"

Everyone looked at me. "My mother knew all along. So did my brother, but they never told me. Eli didn't know, of course. They never told him, either. Eli, do you remember being with my mother? With Anna?"

"Anna . . . yes, I remember her very well." He leaned his head sideways against his hand. It was a familiar gesture, one he was famous for: the long fingers supporting his skull as though to keep the thoughts inside from spilling out or misbehaving.

"It was before you were married. You thought she was too old to have children, but she wasn't. Look at me, I have your eyes, your hair."

Raya was very surprised, of course. "Poor Sonya! Yes, you look alike. I don't know how I never noticed it before."

He sat up with the abrupt anxiety of someone who suddenly re-members an important meeting or a pot left on the stove. "Where's Barbara? She was due hours ago, hours and hours ago."

"Barbara's not coming," Raya said with satisfaction, as if she'd kept Barbara away herself.

"Bitch. Bitch. I'll make her pay. . . . What a cunt though. A cunt from heaven . . . Well, she can go to hell, for all I care. It's this new generation. A generation of screwed-up feminists, don't know what they want."

Raya, who was still signing for me, looked thoroughly disgusted.

I came to his defense: "You always claim to be a feminist, too, Eli."

"Are the two of you lovers?" he asked Lily. He was hoping to discover a less personal reason for Raya's hostility.

"No such luck," Raya answered.

"What are you all doing here?" Eli asked, sinking back into confusion. "Pass me that bottle, please." There was only a small amount of whiskey left. Raya shrugged and handed him the bottle. Her careless, aggressive gesture made me realize just how much she disliked Eli, and I was hurt.

"I came here to tell you you're my father. And you were drunk, so I called Raya and Lily to help me."

"You're my daughter?" He took a swig from the bottle.

"Yes."

"Anna . . . She was beautiful, but neurotic. She had lots of lovers. That what's-his-name, the editor, you know. That schmuck . . . you know."

"She told my brother it was you. And look at me, Eli. We look alike and we put our papers in our briefcases exactly the same way."

He stared at me. "Yes, you're a beauty, all right."

"Eli, I love you. Because you're my father and people love their parents, no matter what."

"I don't have children. I've never had children."

"Well, it was an accident, Eli. Now you're stuck with me."

"Really? I have a daughter! And so stunning, though you could stand to lose two or three kilos. Smart, too. Aren't you some sort of genius? Finished university at twelve or something?"

"You have to love me now. You're my father."

"Yes, I love you, Sonya. I love you. . . . What time is it?"

Raya couldn't bear this conversation any longer. "Why don't you go to bed?" she suggested. "We'll help you."

"Okay, okay. I have a meeting tomorrow, I think. What day is it? I think I have a fucking meeting with those impotent morons. If you knew the contempt I had for the world of academe—I don't mean you, Sonya, my daughter. You're in . . . math. Yes. The sciences are fine. Everything else should be banished. Universities are meant to advance humankind, and that means science. The humanities cause *regression*, not progression. Are you really my daughter?"

"Yes."

"I'm glad. I'm glad," he said. "You sprang fully formed," he added in English.

"I'm going to tell everyone."

"Good, good. I'm very proud of you. We'll go see a movie."

We helped Eli up the stairs and into his bedroom. He lay down on his bed and smiled. "Barbara likes to be tied up," he said, shutting his eyes. "She asks for it. She begs. So much for feminism. She asks me to hit her with a belt. 'Harder, harder,' she says. I've given women what they asked for. I've given them all what they asked for. Isn't that right, Raya?"

"I'll answer when you're sober," Raya said.

"They ask for it," he repeated, opening his eyes and looking at Raya. He wasn't challenging her: he was truly curious to hear what she'd say, and he suddenly looked like a small child trying to understand a difficult adult concept.

"Women in love will do anything to get love back," Raya said. "If they think that's what it takes, if they think that's the only way to be intimate with you, then they'll try that. And tell me the truth, Eli. Isn't that the only way to get intimate with you? Isn't it?"

Raya was right: people in love were desperate creatures. We fell in love with different sorts of people, and our desperation took different forms, but love was as strong as death. I hadn't known that until today. Noah once told me how bothered he was when his high-school girlfriend said she would die for him. What does that mean? he asked me. What does it mean?

"Thank you," Eli said, and his eyes softened. He looked at us with gratitude. "Thank you very much. You've saved my life."

"You haven't taken anything else, have you?" Raya asked, looking at him with reluctant concern.

"No, no. Just a Valium or two. Help me get these off." He was struggling with his jeans.

"I'll do it," Lily said tactfully, for clearly neither Raya nor I were the best candidates for the task. "It's okay, I'll look after him, you can go."

Raya and I left the bedroom and returned downstairs.

"How did you find out?" Raya asked.

"I'm not sure. I had a dream, and I began to wonder, and then Kostya confirmed it. I don't know why I never thought of it before. I guess because Eli's so famous for not wanting children. Or maybe because when Narcissus looks at you he sees only himself reflected back, and you get sucked into that when you're with him; you also start believing that he must be a closed system."

"They shouldn't have kept it a secret from you."

"They thought he'd hurt me. But they were wrong, they couldn't be sure. We almost had sex! Imagine! I feel sick thinking about it."

"You and Eli?"

"He made a pass. I don't know, maybe it wasn't serious. Maybe he knew I'd say no."

"I guess Kostya wasn't worried about that, seeing as you refused even to sit at a café with a guy."

"He couldn't know. He took a horrible chance. He could have destroyed my life."

"By the way, your brother's totally smitten with Lily. She likes him, too. They already have a date for tomorrow."

"What's her story?"

"Another casualty . . . but she's trying to pull her life together. Lost her husband when she was pregnant, back in the late seventies."

"In the war?"

"No, some sort of accident—a hostage-taking incident, Ibrahim's son was involved. That's why his son went to prison, that incident. He paid for the army's mistake."

"Oh, yes, I remember that story. My mother knew him, they were in a play together once. . . . What a small world."

"I met him once, too, at a party at Ibrahim's. Lily remembers me, but I don't remember her. It was ages ago, I was just a kid. I hope she's okay up there with Eli."

On cue, Lily reappeared. "He's fast asleep and snoring away," she said. "I washed his feet with a towel, they were filthy."

She sat down on the sofa and said, "That nap I had earlier really refreshed me. I fell asleep at Raya's after you left," she explained. "So rude of me, but I didn't plan it, I just drifted off."

"The things people think are rude," Raya said, shaking her head.

"It's your cozy apartment, Raya," I said, switching to English for Lily's sake. "There's something irresistible about it. What a strange day I've had! I feel like Alice in Wonderland. I saw the wall today, by the way."

"The *wall*. The *wall* used to refer to the Wailing Wall!" Raya exclaimed.

"Well, I did wail! At least I felt like wailing when I saw it."

"How did you get through?"

"I just said 'open sesame' and the door magically opened. . . ."

"You're charmed, Sonya. Does anyone want the coffee, by the way?"

We shook our heads. "I hope Eli's okay," I said.

"He seems fine," Lily answered in Hebrew. "I used to have one of his books on my reading list, you know. He's such an original thinker."

Raya looked unconvinced as she translated for me.

"It's funny," Lily continued. "You read someone, and they seem so . . . together. They seem to have their act together, to be so sharp and clear. And you're sure that when you meet them, they'll have this wise, organized life."

"It's easier to see things than to do them," Raya said. "It's harder to do things, and it takes more damned courage—something Eli's never had!"

"Raya, please don't hate him."

"Sorry, sorry. It's just that he's so obnoxious!"

"He's very charming," Lily said. "Even drunk, it showed through."

"I guess we can go," I said. "I just want to leave a note."

I tore a sheet out of my notebook and wrote in big letters, *Eli, please contact me. I want to meet and talk. Your loving daughter, Sonya.* I placed it on the kitchen table.

Then we left.

Noah's diary, Christmas, 1992.

Berlin. Snow, Christmas lights everywhere. Marion's away and I'm feeling a bit lost without her. Not literally, the way I was at the start, because I have a handle on the city now. But in every other way. Especially because I'm not sure she's coming back.

At first everything was great. We saw a play every three days, went to a gallery every two days, walked around nonstop—I just felt I had to catch up, somehow. Marion's been here twice before so that helped a lot, plus her German's not bad. In the beginning it was hard admitting to myself how inferior and backwater I felt in this place. Then I stopped being defensive and started enjoying myself.

The school is great. I don't know how they accepted me, my portfolio wasn't that good, but they felt I had potential, I guess. In the beginning, the first week or two, I saw what the other students were doing and I got all depressed, my stuff was pretty pathetic in comparison. But I'm much better now. I feel really inspired, ideas come to me in the middle of the night or while I'm brushing my teeth or taking out the garbage. The hardest part is German, though everyone speaks some English, too. If only I had Sonya's brain! Luckily I picked up a bit of Yiddish over the years, God knows where. Maybe from Rabbi Spiro, our fourth- and fifth-grade math teacher.

"Yosseleh, gey shoyn aroys fun tsimer!" We used to laugh so hard at him, imitating his Yiddish all the time. Little did I think how handy it would come in one day. The only thing I still can't get used to is saying *"platz."*

I've stopped having Holocaust creep out moments. At first I had them a lot, which I never expected. Our second day here we were at this café, surrounded by all these bohemian arty types, very cool. It was so relaxed and nice, the coffee was fantastic, then suddenly I hear someone yelling *"Schnell, schnell!"* I almost had a heart attack. I never knew I had Holocaust phobia! Another time this guy on Roller Blades, who looked exactly like one of those Hitler Youth guys in the movies, ran into me and knocked me over. He felt terrible about it, he literally lifted me up from the sidewalk, brushed me off, couldn't stop apologizing. He was ready to put me in his will or offer me his kidney or something. But that second when he ran into me, I had this crazy panic—anyway, all that's passed now. I'm thrilled that no one knows anything about Israel here. The conflict isn't on anyone's mind and most people probably couldn't find Israel on a map. What a nice break. The janitor of our building asked me, when I said I was from Tel Aviv, *"Sind die Palästinenser jüdisch?"* I was so happy, I kept repeating this wonderful question to myself all day.

Oren was here for three days, he and his new wife did a detour on their honeymoon to visit me. She's not my type. She sat there the whole time talking about her pregnancy, morning sickness, ankle problems, and God knows what—I thought I would die of boredom before the evening was up. Finally, though, she went to sleep and Oren and I went out for a drink. Oren's back in Israel, setting up this high-tech company with some friends. He wants me to study computer graphics and come in with them eventually.

I said maybe, but I doubt I'll leave here anytime soon, or if I do it will be to see some other parts of Europe. It's the art, he doesn't understand that about me. I guess I never understood that myself. But now that I have it I don't think I could live without it. The art scene at home is okay but it's just too small—there's an entire world out here that I need to be connected to. Of course there are a million problems here—the economy, social problems, racism—the unification is still causing a lot of headaches and disagreements. There are definitely things here I'm not crazy about. The people I can't stand in Israel are bearable. I mean I hate them but they're familiar, I can cope with them. But the people I can't stand here I can't deal with at all, like this student who walks around with a rat on her shoulder. I actually know her schedule so I can avoid her. That's just one example, though. There are old people, too, very stiff and sort of fascist looking. . . . I'm more aware here of having to be selective about who I hang out with. Then there's the fact that everyone speaks German (or Turkish or whatever) and not Hebrew for some reason ha ha. Every now and then I suddenly hear Hebrew, some Israelis are talking in the lobby of the concert hall or on the bus, and I think I'm going to pass out with longing.

Now that I have some distance I can see a lot of things about Israel I didn't see before. War keeps you in a time warp, in my opinion. The rest of the world progresses and you're still stuck in some endless eternal fucking conflict about nothing which is never going to end, ever, it just goes on and on in circles like that poem, "The Kermess," that Gran used to read about dancers going round and around. That's what we're like. Or like those people at the end of that Bergman movie, all stuck to each other. And we can't get out of it because we're in that warp. We think that's what's important in life, hanging on to some settlement or transportation on Saturday or when to turn the fucking *clock* back. No one has the guts to just get up and say, "Enough, let's stop being idiots, for God's sake." But on the other hand, there's something missing here. I can't put my finger on it—some sort of sharpness. It's hard to explain. Some sort of crazy sense of humor that comes from living in a mad place like Israel. A kind of acceptance, like—what's the point of pretending, I know who you are, and you know who I am. Not taking yourself too seriously, I guess. I don't know. Maybe no matter which way you choose there's always a price to pay.

Anyway, the big problem in my life now isn't where to live, it's Marion. I love her and I don't want to lose her. She went to Sweden because her father was having heart surgery, but now every time she calls she changes the date of when she's coming back. She pretends it's because of her father, but we both know it isn't. I suggested that we marry. I really want children, three or four or even five, and so does she. We don't have a lot of money but we can manage. Marion suggested the exact opposite, that we break up.

It's true we've started fighting a lot and I don't want to end up like Mom and Dad, fighting every day of their lives practically. It started with Frederick but got on to other things. She didn't like Frederick coming over all the time, she was jealous. Even though there's nothing between us. Frederick is really only a friend and he's lonely, he's from Poland and doesn't know anyone. I'm loyal to her and I'd never lie to her. But she says she can't cope with the stress of living with a guy who's got all these male admirers constantly drooling over him, and she doesn't want to be the person to stand in my way. She says it's a humiliating role and that one day inevitably I'll resent her and I'll also give in and betray her. She's wrong. She's not in my way, I want things to stay as they are. But on the other hand I have to admit that at school I'm surrounded by temptation. Lots of gay students and they like me. Maybe she's right. Maybe she can see something I can't. But I'm ready to make the sacrifice.

That's what the fight is about: sacrifice. The fight is that she doesn't want it to be a sacrifice, and my side is that there's always a sacrifice—what does it matter if it's where you live or how you spend the evening or what to have for supper or not sleeping with other people? But she says being attracted to men is a whole different category, and you can't compare it to whether to have spaghetti for supper. I think she's wrong.

I talk to Dad on the phone around once a week, sometimes

more, sometimes I call him just to find out what's going on in our messed-up country. He and Sonya boss each other around, I think. I don't know how healthy it is for them to go on living in the same house. Dad told me she's still absolutely off guys, she refuses to date or have anything to do with them, and also refuses to go into therapy. I feel so sad about that—what if she never gets over what happened and she never knows what it's like to fall in love, to be with someone you love? I tried to talk to her about it before I left (which Dad was hinting I should do) but she doesn't think there's anything wrong with her or with the way she lives. She says when she meets a man she likes who also knows how to sign, she'll go out with him. She's very attractive and she has plenty of offers, that's not the problem. Though the truth is that most guys probably wouldn't want to get into a serious relationship with a deaf woman. Maybe she knows that and maybe Dad is the one who is in denial. Or maybe he does know and that's why he schleps her to all sorts of deaf events, but nothing has come of it, she's only going in order to please him, I can tell. Poor Sonya. Such bad luck. She seems okay, though. Had another article published last week, which made her very happy.

The really sad news is that King Kong died. Sonya called to tell me. We both cried our hearts out over the phone—you'd think we'd lost our entire family in a bomb. But really that dog was special. She said he died peacefully, in her arms.

I think I'm getting too old for a diary. I think this is my last time. Also, Frederick's coming over in an hour, I have to start getting supper ready. I promised I'd make him Dad's potato-and-cheese thing. We'll go out for beer after. There's so much to do in this place.

Dearest, I don't know whether I will mail this letter. I have betrayed you. The man who gave us the violin, whose daughter died, he invited me to his apartment, he's had such a sad life and I have been feeling so lonely, we talked, I told him about you and about my parents . . . I am filled with remorse but I am not sorry, can you understand? It was impossible to say no, not for either of us, you said I must find someone, that you would never escape they keep such a close eye on you with what you know they would kill you first but I don't want to find anyone else, I only want you and that's not the reason for unlike you I have never given up hope and it wasn't love or anything close just loneliness. . . . I will write when I can think more clearly I am adrift

Dearest Anna, I am so terribly sorry to be writing to you with tragic news, though perhaps you have already read about it in the papers. I am afraid that our dear and beloved Andrei has passed away. He died of pneumonia in his bed at home, at six P.M. on Friday, the second of August. I was with him, as were members of his family. It was a peaceful passing. When we were alone he told me to send you his love and he said you made him the happiest he has been in his life. My dear Anna, this is why your letters never reached me. I delayed my return to Vienna in the hope that I could be of some use, and knowing as well that this might be our last chance to be together in this world. There was a state funeral with many speeches singing Andrei's praises. He really was a special soul and a friend I shall never forget. Giselle and I both send you our deepest heartfelt condolences and I enclose your last letters, which unfortunately were waiting for me when I returned. However, I have sent the sweater on to little Olga. I am sure she will be delighted with it.

Yours very sadly,

Heinrich and Giselle

❧ Sonya

We left Eli's building and walked single-file down the garden path to the dark street. "The night is young," Raya announced. She rarely went to bed before two or three in the morning.

"I'm wiped out," I said. "I need to head home."

"How long will you keep me waiting to hear about today?"

"I'll call you tomorrow. I'll know more tomorrow, too. But one thing's certain: I'm moving out, Raya. I can't go on living with Kostya."

Raya nodded but didn't comment. She never interfered in other people's lives or passed judgment on the decisions they'd made; she was too modest, and she also believed that we were such complicated and stupid creatures, so helpless in the face of both our own impulses and those of the people around us, that none of us really knew what we were doing. It was all a pretense, she said, acting as if we had some sort of plan. She felt that people who went into math knew this, and were looking for escape into a world where everything was allowed, without consequences or danger. In math you didn't pay a price for promiscuity, lawlessness, the rejection of all you had been taught. Those things were expected.

On the dimly lit street her little green Honda looked like a patient turtle. Lily let herself in the back, even though I was getting off first. My ninth and last drive today, I thought, as Raya took me home. She hugged me hard before I left the car, and I saw that she was crying.

"What's wrong?" I asked.

"Oh, nothing. PMS, that's all. You know how emotional I get. This morning I cried because someone's dog tore up a few violets in the garden downstairs. . . ."

"I hope you're not sad for me! I've had the happiest day of my life. I don't care that Eli's such a weirdo. Who isn't?"

She sighed. "That's true enough."

I turned to the back of the car. "I'm glad we met, Lily. Are you living here now, or is this just a long visit?"

"I don't know." She smiled and placed her hand on my shoulder.

I climbed out and waved good-bye as Raya drove off, the way Khalid had waved at me a few hours before. Had it really been only a few hours? It seemed as if several light-years had passed since then. I felt a stab of pain so harsh it was almost physical. Parting was not sweet sorrow. It was sorrow, period.

Kostya opened the door as I came up the walk. He'd heard the car pull up; he must have been waiting impatiently all evening.

"The prodigal daughter is back," I said.

"So I see," he replied happily. He didn't ask any questions; he didn't want to pry.

I dropped my shoulder bag on the floor and headed for the kitchen. It occurred to me that I had not eaten since breakfast, apart from the little snack at Lorelei's store. I opened the fridge, took out a bowl of potato knishes.

"I can heat that up for you," Kostya offered.

"No need, thanks." He sat down at the table and watched me as I ate the cold knishes. He seemed very relaxed. I'd imagined him tense and worried, but he was neither. He was just happy that I was back.

"I had a good time in Jerusalem. I found Khalid, though I had to get past two walls. The first one was a temporary wall, I climbed over. Look." I showed him my scraped palm. "The second one was a thing from hell. Even in hell it would stand out. A million feet high, you can't even see the top. It's like the Tower of Babel, the success-ful version, the one that manages to reach God. But I was lucky, it's still not finished—the door inside the wall wasn't locked. It doesn't have a locking mechanism yet. Then a soldier drove me to Khalid's house. Everyone was nice to me. I love Khalid but I don't know whether I'll ever see him again. I don't know if he slept with me be-cause he felt sorry for me or whether he's attracted to me."

"I'm sure he's attracted to you, Sonya—who wouldn't be? But he may think it's too complicated to have a relationship with you."

"His mother had just died, but he hadn't done anything about it. I decided to leave because he didn't seem interested in me and he had to look after her. When I kissed him good-bye he jumped. Why? He says it was because he didn't want to hurt me."

"In some cultures kisses are taken more seriously than here."

"Oh, that's just ridiculous! Kisses are kisses the world over. It doesn't matter where you go. I hate all this anthropology. It's so distancing."

My brother laughed. "Okay," he said.

"I left, he came after me, he brought me back in. Maybe he felt bad for me. Why would he want to be with a woman he'd have to learn a whole new language for? A language that takes years to master? Or maybe I'm just not his type. Just because he's my type doesn't mean I'm his type, unfortunately. I figured out about Eli on the bus. I had a dream. . . . Anyway, I figured it out."

"How did he take it?"

"He was drunk, I'm not sure it really registered. But he was happy. He said he was proud of me. He told me I could stand to lose two or three kilos. He said I sprang fully formed."

My brother laughed again. He was in a very good mood, for some reason. "You don't need to lose any weight."

"I wouldn't mind being one of those thin, slinky women, but I don't think it would suit me. You should have told me, Kostya. I almost had sex with Eli! How would you have felt then?"

"Very bad."

"Why didn't you tell me? Why?"

"We were planning to tell you when you were twelve. We figured you'd be old enough then to deal with rejection, if that's what happened. But then you lost your hearing and we just didn't have the heart. I'm sorry. Maybe it was the wrong decision."

"It was. It was the wrong decision. And what about now? Why not tell me now?"

"I don't know, Sonya. You already had such complicated feelings about men because of what happened. At least, that's how it seemed to me. I thought knowing about Eli would just make it worse."

I had finished with the knishes, and I got up to pour myself a glass of grapefruit juice. "What happens when you mix Valium and whiskey?" I asked.

"Depends entirely on the amount," Kostya said.

I leaned against the counter with the glass in my hand and peered at him. "You should have told me. You were wrong not to tell me. And I want to know who killed Iris, too. Noah and I deserve to know."

"Kimror or one of his cronies killed her. But you'll never prove it, Sonya."

"Kimror! Well, I can't say I'm surprised. This whole country is being run by thugs. Do you still have the death threats?"

"One was on the phone. One was in writing and it's in a safe at the bank."

"She got death threats all the time, though. 'Thus shall all your enemies perish, O Israel'—remember that one?"

"Yes, but this was different. These two threats specifically warned her to drop that case if she knew what was good for her and her family. She would have sent that entire gang to prison. They'd have been finished in every way."

"What did they do?"

"Faked intelligence reports, endangered the state. Maybe out of misguided ideology, but more likely to save their arses. They were up to their necks in corruption. Drugs, weapon sales, bribery, forgery—it was a real party."

"How could you have kept quiet about it all these years!"

"I'm pessimistic, Sonya. I don't think there's any point."

"Do you still have the files?"

"Yes. They're in the safe along with the letter."

"I'm going to publicize this. I'm phoning Ella tomorrow."

"I'm not ready to lose you, too."

"Don't be ridiculous! It was a fluke with Iris—people here don't get killed for that sort of thing. Scandals are exposed every day—I don't see the corpses of journalists and lawyers lining the streets. Iris was just incredibly unlucky. She shouldn't have worked alone, for one thing. Is that why you didn't pursue it? Because you were intimidated?"

"It just didn't seem worth it. Nothing will change. You get a brief uproar, and then a year later no one remembers and everything goes on as before. The problems are just too deep by now, and too widespread."

"No wonder nothing changes, with everyone taking that attitude."

"It's true. We're tired out. You know, when I was twelve I wrote an article for *Ha'aretz*, and they published it. I pointed out all the things we were doing wrong and how we should change our approach. I gave this long detailed step-by-step plan for peace. And the amazing thing is that now, over forty-five years later, I wouldn't have to alter a single word. I've given up hoping that there will ever be sanity in this place."

I sat back down at the table. I was suddenly very tired. "I saw a demonstration today," I said. "A rabbi was being dragged away on the sidewalk. At least some Israelis are doing something!"

"Yes, and getting shot at in the process."

"That was only once or twice. Maybe I should get a bit involved. . . . Do you know the Palestinians think Iris died for them?"

"Yes."

"I have something else to tell you: I decided that I'm moving out, Kostya. I'm too old to live with my brother."

"No, no. I'll move out."

"This place is too big for me. I'd be lonely here."

"I suppose we can sell it. The market isn't great right now, but if we both buy flats it might even out."

"Have you ever thought of moving in with Tali?"

"Tali won't even let me see her when she wakes up. I'm only allowed to view her when she's fixed herself up—though I've told her a million times that it doesn't matter to me. But that's not the only reason. It wouldn't work out."

"I'm sorry. Will you be okay?"

"I'm not sure what I'll do when I have to tie my shoelaces."

I yawned. "I have to get to sleep. By the way, I hear you have a date with Lily." I smiled slyly at him.

"Not a date—I'm taking her to the Cinemathèque library, she wants to do some research."

"Will Tali mind?"

"I don't know, Sonya. I'm not a prophet. I don't know what's going to happen in the next five minutes, never mind the coming months. Oh, I almost forgot. Someone dropped by with a package for you. One of your students, Matar. I put it on your bed."

"Matar! He was here?"

"Yes, he showed up around suppertime. He was disappointed that you weren't here. He left a small box for you."

"He's the student I've been telling you about. With the eyes."

"I thought it might be him."

"Did you notice his eyes?"

"Yes. He reminds me of someone, but I can't for the life of me remember who."

"I can't believe he came here. He's the one who has a crush on me. They've become really strict at the university, I told him that."

"I wouldn't worry about it," my brother said, looking amused.

"What are you so happy about?"

"I'm just glad you're back."

"I'm going to bed. But first I have to send an e-mail."

I went into the computer room, opened my e-mail and wrote: "I came home safely. Please write only if you want to see me again. If you don't write, I'll understand. Love, Sonya."

I sent the message to Khalid. *Send*. The hopes and dreams and fears contained in that short, flat word printed inside a tiny rectangle on a computer screen.

Then I walked to my bedroom and shut the door. There was a small white cardboard box on the bed. I sat down on the crumpled sheets, the sweet sheets that had held me and Khalid this morning. Inside the box was a delicate hourglass filled with white sand and set in a beautiful blue ceramic holder. A gift from Matar.

He was waiting for me.

If Khalid didn't contact me, if Khalid didn't want to see me again, this would be my consolation prize: a few months with Matar. Matar would seduce me—with his charm and youth and beauty he would make me fall in love with him and then he'd tire of me and leave. If I couldn't have Khalid, I would have a baby, I would have Matar's baby, and I'd raise my child alone. Matar would take her to the park every now and then, swing her on swings while his wife or girlfriend sat on the bench and watched. The sky would be blue, it would be very sunny; he'd swing her up and down in the baby swing. She'd know who her father was.

I began getting ready for bed. I threw my clothes on the floor; I was too tired to hang them up. Then I pulled a clean pair of pajamas out of my dresser drawer. They were white with blue swans, like the blue swans on Eli's shower curtain. But suddenly I decided not to put them on. They didn't belong here in my room, they belonged in a convent, on the body of a woman who had given up entirely. I stuffed them back in the drawer and chose instead a long lace night-gown that had belonged to my mother. I turned off the light and stretched out sleepily in bed. Yes, at least on the surface of things, my future was set clearly before me: the options, the choices, the deci-sions I'd make. It was all very simple, really.

But underneath, in the tumult of my emotional life, nothing was clear at all.

About the author

2 Meet Edeet Ravel

3 A Conversation with Edeet Ravel

About the book

8 Edeet Ravel on *A Wall of Light:*
  Creating Loving Characters

Read on

12 Understanding Ravel's Trilogy

15 Have You Read?
  More by Edeet Ravel

Insights,
Interviews
& More ...

Meet Edeet Ravel

© Pam Comeau

EDEET RAVEL was born on an Israeli kibbutz and completed graduate studies in English at the Hebrew University of Jerusalem. She has been publishing stories and prose poems in English and Hebrew since the age of sixteen, and is the recipient of several writing awards, including the Norma Epstein Award for Poetry. She holds a PhD in Jewish studies from McGill University and has taught creative writing, English literature, Holocaust studies, and biblical exegesis. She has one daughter. ✑

A Conversation with Edeet Ravel

Why and when did you start writing?

When my father read stories to me on the kibbutz, I always identified with the writers and thought about how they wrote the story. I told my father I would be a writer, and that has been a part of my identity ever since. It's not something I ever decided or thought about—it was simply part of who I was.

I remember when I was five or six, I "edited" *Cinderella;* I felt the story should mention at the start that Cinderella had unusually small feet, to make it more realistic, since one shoe would ordinarily fit many feet. I wanted realism in a fairy tale! So I rewrote the story, dictating my revised version to my father.

The first full-length book my father read to me was *Alice in Wonderland.* I've noticed that echoes of *Alice in Wonderland* often appear in my writing, though this is not something I have ever planned. Another early literary experience was *The Little Match Girl.* I would beg my father to read it to me, and he would refuse, because I would burst into hysterical weeping each time. Finally he'd relent, and of course I would cry for about half an hour at the end of the story.

I identified with the match girl, because even though I was part of a close-knit community on the kibbutz, I was isolated from my parents at night and during most of the day, which was difficult for us. Our care-worker was unpleasant and sometimes sadistic, which did not help matters. As an adult I tried to read the story to my daughter in the library one day, and had to disappear ▶

> 66 'I remember when I was five or six, I "edited" *Cinderella;* I felt the story should mention at the start that Cinderella had unusually small feet, to make it more realistic.' 99

behind a shelf, as I was crying helplessly again. I was at the same time laughing at myself, and my daughter was also quite amused, but I couldn't stop.

I guess it was also empathy that made me cry when I was little. I could not bear that this match girl had so little, and that no one cared about her. As a good little Marxist, I already knew that this was not mere fiction. That made me very sad.

My first attempt at fiction, though, was far from compassionate! I wrote a short novel when I was twelve, which bears some slight resemblance to Stephen King's *Carrie*. An unpopular girl takes revenge . . . needless to say I was an outsider at school in Montreal. As a friend of mine once said, society rides on the accomplishments of all the people who were tormented when they were children.

You wrote for many years without trying to get published. Why is that, and how has being published changed your life?

I have never been ambitious in terms of publishing, though I am extremely ambitious when it comes to the quality of my writing. I've been writing for thirty years, but I didn't think about publishing, because each time I finished a story or novel, I thought: the next one will be better.

I was fifteen or sixteen when I saw Pasolini's *Decameron*—Pasolini, himself, plays an artist who is working on a fresco. At the end of the movie, the fresco comes to life, the angels begin to sing, and Pasolini says something like: What is the point of creating, when what you dream is always so much more beautiful?

66 'My first attempt at fiction . . . was far from compassionate.' 99

That struck me very powerfully as a motif that would follow me all my life. The vision and the creation drift apart in the process of creating, and that is a continual source of despair. But over the years, I've learnt to accept and even be amused by the phenomenon. When I completed *Ten Thousand Lovers,* I felt that the novel was close enough to my initial vision to be published. I was still hesitant, though, because I was afraid of some aspects of publishing.

My fears were justified, in fact, but the letters I receive from readers, and the freedom I now have to write fulltime, more than make up for the drawbacks. Really, there is only one drawback: permanence. The permanence of ridiculous misquotes in the press, the permanence of the published text—no more rewrites!—the permanence of recorded opinions that later change.

The misquotes ranged from major distortions to smaller tampering, such as editors changing my gender-neutral pronouns to masculine pronouns. I now understand why some writers don't want to give interviews, and why performing artists often make only the blandest statements. The Internet adds to the phenomenon of misrepresentation.

There was also an unexpected disappointment: the discovery that when reviewing a book, some reviewers read other reviews instead of reading the book. I suppose it doesn't seem worth it to them, to read an entire novel in order to write a short review for which they may not be getting paid all that much. At the same time, reviewers do influence potential readers, and it's a pity ▶

66 'The vision and the creation drift apart in the process of creating, and that is a continual source of despair. But over the years, I've learnt to accept and even be amused by the phenomenon.' 99

to see some of them copying other reviews instead of arriving at their own evaluations.

But on the whole I'm glad now that some of my books are in print, because the miracle of reaching readers through my writing is very inspiring.

The trilogy is set in politically hot territory; do you feel that it is somehow propagating a specific political view?

Inevitably, my political perceptions come through in my writing, as does my view of life in general. Writers expose themselves completely in their fiction: one is stripped naked. But my activist-self and my writer-self are separate. As an activist, I have a specific analysis, though it takes into account the complexity of the situation. But as a writer, I deal with ambiguity, unanswered questions, unknown territory.

As the South African writer Njabulo Ndebele has said, fiction frees you from the predetermined formula. A novel seeks to expand possibilities rather than narrow them. That is the great pleasure of writing: the freedom to delve as deeply as one wishes, look at things as closely as one wishes. I am always interested in the human story, in the way people experience their surroundings and how they are affected by them. Even when I do political work, such as Women's Checkpoint Watch, I feel I've been hurled into a human drama, and I want to know what everyone involved is feeling and thinking. I live with my characters before I start writing, and it's their story I want to tell; their story dictates what I write.

66 'My activist-self and my writer-self are separate. As an activist, I have a specific analysis, though it takes into account the complexity of the situation. But as a writer, I deal with ambiguity, unanswered questions, unknown territory.' 99

How does your Canadian identity help you write about Israel?

Like many Israelis who live outside Israel—about 750,000 according to some estimates—I have never lost my Israeli identity, even though English is now my primary language, and even though I have lived longer in Canada than in Israel. As soon as I step off the plane in Israel, I feel completely integrated. When I return to Canada, the adjustment takes much longer. My personality appears to be more Israeli than Canadian—especially in terms of the informality one finds in Israeli culture.

In this trilogy that dual perspective emerges in different ways. In *Ten Thousand Lovers*, Lily moves in and out of memory; she is both deeply immersed in the events that took place in Israel, and watching them from a distance. In *Look for Me*, Dana is the daughter of South Africans, and she's an activist, which means that she's taken a step back in order to protest against policies that others take for granted. She's grown up reading Miss Read! You can't get more of a contrast to Israeli life than the quiet English villages of Miss Read's books. In *A Wall of Light*, I move closer to the heart of Israel, but once again my main character, Sonya, is an outsider.

The result of all this is that the entry to the world of my novels is probably easier for non-Israelis than it would be if I were writing from an entirely Israeli perspective. When we write as insiders, we open the doors to our literary world, and our readers enter at their own risk. When we write as partial outsiders, we offer more guidance, a tourist booth with brochures. ❧

> " 'My personality appears to be more Israeli than Canadian—especially in terms of the informality one finds in Israeli culture.' "

Edeet Ravel on
A Wall of Light
Creating Loving Characters

I FELL IN LOVE with the characters of this novel, and I felt truly bereft when I'd finished. I wanted to meet them; I didn't want to accept that they didn't exist in the real world. When I was in my twenties, I wrote such dark stories and novels! That changed gradually after I had a child. This was not a conscious decision, but I think I was so focused on creating a gentle and friendly environment for my daughter, and she amused me so much, that I began creating more hopeful worlds. I didn't lose interest in the lunatics and dour pessimists, but I found myself writing more about gentler people who were trying to find their way in a difficult and often tragic world.

Where do characters come from? I really can't say. They arrive as if out of nowhere. I adore Noah; he's so honest and funny and straight-forward, and he's also quite strong. I think I was interested in his strength: how does he manage to remain so centered in the midst of crisis and tragedy? I was probably exploring this question as I wrote. I love his relationship with Kostya, and how he decides to ask Kostya for advice when he begins to wonder about his sexual orientation. I enjoyed writing about Noah at different ages, from ten to twenty-two. One sees how his basic personality never really changes, and the clues to his future are all there from the start. I am very drawn to diaries, and have several boxes of diaries myself, going back to age twelve. I like to think about the way we choose to narrate our stories, and the relationship between those stories and fiction—the way events are recreated and redefined the minute you find words for them—and of course the endless ways in which a single event can be recorded.

I encountered technical challenges related to having a deaf character; Sonya uses Sign, which is visual. But I discovered that people who lose their hearing when they are older continue to think in spoken language as well as Sign. I've always been interested in Sign, and I was glad to learn more about it—for example, I had no idea that there were so many signing systems (a different one for every country).

Kostya is also a character in *Look for Me*, and I knew from the minute I mentioned his sister that she would be the third woman whose love story I would try to tell. I also enjoyed further developing his character in *A Wall of Light*.

As I wrote, I began to sniff an allegorical undercurrent. I made every effort not to think about it, to ignore it, because thinking is anathema to writing, in my experience. Writing for me has to be almost entirely intuitive; when I decide a word or passage or plot element isn't right, it's because it feels wrong. But I have academic training, and I'm an analytic reader, so that side of me is also quite active. I simply push it away. I was half-way through the novel before I noticed that Sonya's name has allegorical resonance.

When I finished writing the novel, an Israeli read the manuscript and told me that Sonya is an old-fashioned name, and in 1973, when Sonya was born, that name would not be an obvious choice. So I had the nurse at ▶

> 66 Thinking is anathema to writing, in my experience. Writing for me has to be almost entirely intuitive; when I decide a word or passage or plot element isn't right, it's because it feels wrong. 99

the hospital write Tziyona on the birth certificate. My main characters almost always come with names, though I do use a name book for minor characters. Noah appeared with his name, as did Kostya. It never ceases to amaze me how much coherence emerges from the unconscious mind.

(In *Ten Thousand Lovers* I also had a nurse influencing name choice—this would not be unusual in Israel. I was almost called Ada instead of Edeet, but the kibbutz had already made the poster that said, "Welcome Edeet," and when my mother changed her mind, on the day I was born, she was told the poster was already in place, and it would be a pity to have to redo it.)

Eli is not based on anyone I've known, though I suppose the campus womanizer is a familiar figure in universities everywhere. I think the way I present certain aspects of Israeli culture may strike readers who are not familiar with that culture as unrealistic. A reviewer of *Ten Thousand Lovers* thought it was strange that the characters moved so easily from politics to personal topics—but that is typical of Israeli discourse. Directness, informality, easy conversation about subjects which might be considered taboo in other cultures, openness about sex, the acceptance of eccentricity, the personalization of politics—all these are quite characteristic. Within minutes, a taxi driver in Israel will start describing his hernia operation, his son's drug rehabilitation, his despair over the conflict. No two people are alike, of course, but there are cultural tendencies.

Israel is also a small country. One of my editors asked me how Kostya would know

> ❝ A reviewer of *Ten Thousand Lovers* thought it was strange that the characters moved so easily from politics to personal topics—but that is typical of Israeli discourse. ❞

about Eli's behavior. But in Israel everyone knows everything about everyone, it seems. The wonderful writer Etgar Keret signed one of his books for me, and added a few words in Hebrew, which I had trouble deciphering. When I told an Israeli friend about this, she said, "Yes, his handwriting is quite original." She didn't know Etgar Keret, and had never met him, but she had read an article about him that mentioned his handwriting!

For all three books in the trilogy, I gave my completed drafts to Israelis to read, including at least one army person, so they could find any mistakes I might have made, or offer suggestions. Though in Israel my views of the conflict are considered left wing, I make sure to give the manuscript to right-wing Israelis as well, as I want to hear all comments, from all sides. Everyone who read the manuscript had important contributions to make, and helped with accuracy of details and credibility of the characters. The six-year-old who wanted to turn Cinderella into *l'Assommoir* is the same hopeless perfectionist who examined maps of Tel Aviv to see how long it took to walk from one point to another.

> " Though in Israel my views of the conflict are considered left wing, I make sure to give the manuscript to right-wing Israelis as well, as I want to hear all comments, from all sides. "

Understanding Ravel's Trilogy

I HAD NOT SET OUT TO WRITE A TRILOGY, but halfway through *Ten Thousand Lovers* I realized it would take three novels for me to release all the feelings about Israel that I had stored inside me. I saw the novels as interconnected by theme, structure, and setting, as well as through the minor characters.

Writing the first novel, *Ten Thousand Lovers,* was an extremely emotional experience. I cried often, and I postponed writing the ending because I knew how hard it would be for me. I was looking at very painful issues in that novel, very painful events. The tragedies of war, the madness of the conflict, and the cruelties of torture. I was also looking back at the early days of the Occupation and at Lily's past. In *Ten Thousand Lovers,* I focused on language, meaning. The novel was influenced by *midrash,* which is a form of "free" textual interpretation, where layers of meaning are unraveled through association and imagination. I love Hebrew, its etymology and development, and I wanted to write about language because the way we use words is so closely tied to the way we understand and create our reality.

The original title of *Ten Thousand Lovers* was *The Things We Do,* and that is what the novel is about: the things we do with our bodies, for example: how the same body, the same few limbs and organs, can perform acts of intense love, as well as acts that cause unbearable pain. The image at the end of the novel, the body of the child on the altar, is an

> 66 Writing the first novel, *Ten Thousand Lovers,* was an extremely emotional experience. I cried often, and I postponed writing the ending because I knew how hard it would be for me. 99

image of purity and potential—of the choices we make, to bring down the sword or to let the child live. The first Israeli who used that image to condemn war created an uproar, and his sculpture was banished to the museum's basement. Today there is more acceptance of the view that fighting is not the only alternative, and that sending our beloved sons and daughters to be killed in war is not always as necessary as our leaders would have us believe.

Though I did a lot of research for *Ten Thousand Lovers,* it was small-time compared to what I had to do in order to write *Look for Me.* Research for that novel quickly merged with activism. Was I terrified the first time I boarded a bus to go into the Occupied Territories to see new outposts (unauthorized Jewish settlements)? Yes. It was the height of the second *intifada;* and I was entering a war zone. But the fear passed as I became involved and committed to working toward peace; in fact, it was replaced by a desire to be even more involved. It is uplifting to see Israelis and Palestinians meeting, seeing eye-to-eye, wanting the same things. It is also important to see the Palestinians as they are, and not in the distorted way the media often portrays them. Palestinian society is diverse and complex, as is Israeli or any other society. This seems obvious, but it needs to be said, because we always carry misconceptions about cultures we aren't familiar with— which is why communication and interaction are so crucial.

Dana, the character in *Look for Me,* is a resident of Tel Aviv, unlike Lily in *Ten Thousand Lovers.* Lily remembers her love affair with Ami, long ago, but Dana is waiting for a missing husband, who is alive but in ▶

66 Research for [*Look for Me*] quickly merged with activism. 99

hiding, following an army accident in which he was burnt. Dana is more practical than Lily, I think. She has a romantic streak but she is also quite down-to-earth; and this dichotomy is reflected in her profession—she writes formulaic romance novels. She doesn't take the novels seriously; she knows they're silly. She writes them to support herself. At the same time, like a romantic heroine, she can't forget her husband and refuses to become involved with other men. But as the first clues to her missing husband's whereabouts reach her, she falls in love with another man. Lily is a linguist; Dana is a photographer. In some ways *Ten Thousand Lovers* is about what we say (and don't say), and *Look for Me* is about what we see (and don't see).

There are links among the characters in the three novels. Alex, who was inspired by an Israeli pianist I was married to in my twenties, helps Ami with his play in *Ten Thousand Lovers,* reappears as one of Volvo's helpers in *Look for Me,* and is the baby Anna names in *A Wall of Light*. The prostitute Ami encounters reappears as the cleaning woman who comes to help Dana. Anna was in a play with Ami. Lily is only briefly mentioned in the last paragraph of *Look for Me,* but she shows up again in *A Wall of Light*. Kostya is Dana's friend, and Dr. Hillman, who treats Lily, is Dana's uncle.

I wrote these novels because they urged themselves upon me. The writing was personal, solitary. I was alone with my stories, and I tried to tell them as well as I could. If they now speak to others, and do some good, I am grateful. ✎

“ In some ways *Ten Thousand Lovers* is about what we say (and don't say), and *Look for Me* is about what we see (and don't see). ”

Have You Read?
More by Edeet Ravel

TEN THOUSAND LOVERS

Israel, 1970s. Lily, a young emigrant student exploring the wonders and terrors of her new land, finds the man of her dreams—Ami, a former actor. Handsome, intelligent, and exciting, but like his beautiful, disintegrating country, Ami has a terrible flaw—he is an army interrogator. As Ami and Lily's unexpected passion grows, so too does the shadow that hangs over them. They must face the unspeakable horrors of Ami's work and their uncertain future.

While set in the seventies, *Ten Thousand Lovers* is a brilliant and terrifyingly contemporary tale of passion, suffering, and the transcending power of love.

"This is a brave and beautiful book."
> —Nancy Richler, *The Globe and Mail*
> (Toronto)

"*Ten Thousand Lovers* is both a curse and a lament. It is immensely to Edeet Ravel's credit that this novel, far from being a rant, balances deep bitterness with an abiding tenderness for the country she once called home."
> —*New York Times*

LOOK FOR ME

Look for Me tells the story of Dana and her quest to find her husband who disappeared while serving in the Israeli army. Every year Dana places a newspaper ad that says, "I will never ever, ever stop waiting for you," the word "ever" repeated so that it fills the entire page. She gives interviews hoping her husband will contact her. She knows for a fact that he is alive. . . .

In the midst of curfews, demonstrations, and confrontations with the police, Dana falls in love with another man—just as she learns her husband's whereabouts. Will she forget the past and follow her heart with a new love, or face the dangers involved in setting out to find the man she has sought for eleven years?

"A love story that aches with the passion and politics of the Middle East, where lovers find sometimes improbable ways to share their lives against the backdrop of so much loss, confusion, and ambivalence."
—Thane Rosenbaum, author of *The Myth of Moral Justice* and *The Golems of Gotham*